Fran O'Brien and Arthur McGuinness
established McGuinness Books
to publish Fran's novels to raise funds
for LauraLynn Children's Hospice.

Fran's fourteen novels, *The Married Woman,*
The Liberated Woman, The Passionate Woman,
Odds on Love, Who is Faye? The Red Carpet,
Fairfields, The Pact, 1916, Love of her Life,
Rose Cottage Years, Ballystrand, Vorlane Hall,
The Big Red Velvet Couch, and *A Spanish Family*
have raised over €750,000.00 in sales
and donations for LauraLynn House.

Fran and Arthur hope that
A Sense of Place
will raise even more funds for LauraLynn.

www.franobrien.net

Also by Fran O'Brien

The Married Woman
The Liberated Woman
The Passionate Woman
Odds on Love
Who is Faye?
The Red Carpet
Fairfields
The Pact
1916
Love of her Life
Rose Cottage Years
Ballystrand
Vorlane Hall
The Big Red Velvet Couch
A Spanish Family

Buy now online www.franobrien.net

A SENSE OF PLACE

FRAN O'BRIEN

To Ann with many thanks,

Fran

McGuinness Books

McGuinness Books

A SENSE OF PLACE

Published by McGuinness Books,
15 Glenvara Park, Ballycullen Road,
Templeogue, Dublin 16 RR71.

A catalogue record for this book
is available from the British Library.

ISBN 978-0-9954698-9-1

Cover design
A painting by James Christopher O'Brien Copyright ©

Typeset by Martone Design & Print,
Celbridge Industrial Estate, Celbridge, Co. Kildare.

Printed and bound in Great Britain by
CPI Group (UK) Ltd, Croydon, CR04YY.

www.franobrien.net

THE STORY SO FAR

Alva's personal life disintegrated when she found her partner, Darren, in bed with another woman. Trust between them was gone. She threw him out. But after that, he stalked her relentlessly.

When her father died unexpectedly, she was faced with more problems, and discovered financial fraud in their company, Purtell Vintners. The culprits are forced to resign and include both her partner and her brother David. This mix of emotions threatened to destroy her until she met her birth mother, Julie, for the first time, and also Carlos, the son of Julie's partner.

Her mother had left home and gone to live in Spain when her children were very young. Their father never revealed the reason why. Alva and Cian were overjoyed to meet Julie at last. Her brother David was reluctant to meet his mother.

In Spain, Julie was thrown from her horse, and needed a kidney transplant. Alva and Cian both offered to be live donors, but they were not compatible, and unless a donor was found, Julie would die.

Alva and her brothers cleared out their father's house in Dublin before it was sold. In the safe they found letters written by Julie to him since she left Ireland. It is only then David realised his mother was not allowed to see her children by their father.

David offered to be a live donor and was compatible with his mother. He saved Julie's life.

Alva and Carlos fall in love and the two families are finally reunited in Spain on the happy occasion of their wedding.

Chapter One

In Andalucia, Spain, at a tiny village church, Alva and Carlos walked down the aisle after their wedding to the music of *Pachelbel's Canon* played by a quartet of musicians, smiling at the guests who were now all standing and applauding. Outside the church they were showered with rice and pink flower petals from a crowd gathered there and by the guests who followed them out of the church. Photographers flashed their cameras from every angle, and it was only then that Alva realised what had actually happened. At last she was married to the man she loved most in the world. As if he could read her thoughts, Carlos turned and held her close, his lips soft on hers. Again, there was applause from everyone, and it made this day the most wonderful in her life. Her mother, Julie and her partner, Pedro, Carlos's father, both walked towards them, arms reaching out to embrace. They were followed by her two brothers, David, Cian, and their families. Carlos's Spanish family crowded around as well, kissing and hugging. Alva and Carlos climbed into the carriage which was drawn by four pale grey Andalusian horses, and waved to everyone as they were driven back to the stud, *Caballos Rodrigues*, Carlos's family home, and they were there in the reception marquee erected on the lawns of the big white house waiting for the guests to arrive. Waiters served cava and canapés, while musicians played soft Spanish music in the background.

After the drinks reception the chauffeur, José, drove Carlos and Alva to another part of the estate with the photographers. It was a special place which Carlos had always loved. 'This is Casa Valentina.' He pointed to the old sprawling group of sun blushed buildings where the car had stopped. His great-grandparents had lived here when they first built their horse farm, and although no one lived here now, there was an old world feeling about the straggling group of houses which she could see. 'My great-grandmother was Valentina and it's strange but I always feel my ancestors' spirits here,' Carlos murmured. 'They are looking down on us,' he smiled.

Her eyes moistened with tears of happiness. So emotional she found it hard to control herself on this, her wedding day.

He dried her tears with his finger.

'Hope I look ok for the cameras.'

'All you have to do is smile,' he said.

The photographer indicated where they should take various poses. Walking towards him hand in hand. Standing together under the trees, or in front of the old façade of the house which was reflected in the water which meandered along the pathway left behind by a heavy shower the previous day. They enjoyed this short time to themselves.

'Are you looking forward to the reception?' Carlos asked, with a grin.

'I'd prefer to stay here together.'

'So would I.' He took her hand as they finished the video and photographs but then they had to head back.

The dining-room was in another large marquee, decorated lavishly with white flower arrangements and tiny fairy lights. There was a round of applause when they walked in and took their places at the top table with their two families. Cava was served and Pedro stood up to raise a toast to the bride and groom. Then dinner. The catering done by the restaurant where Carlos took Alva when she first arrived in Seville. There were various courses, and as before, it was delicious. When they had organised the evening, they decided to include the speeches between the courses as there were a lot of people who wanted to say a few words.

After the meal, Carlos and Alva stood up to cut the wedding cake which consisted of three narrow tiers of an almond nougat and custard cream cake decorated with white and red roses matching Alva's bouquet. There was just enough for the people at the top table for dessert. All the other guests received small mini versions of the cake. When coffee was served and the final toasts over, Carlos and Alva went around all the tables and chatted to the guests which took quite a while, and filled in the time before the band began to play for the dancing. In the meantime, Alva went back to the house with her main bridesmaid, Naomi, to freshen up, and then she took off the veil and the long train on her wedding dress.

'You'll be able to dance to your heart's content,' laughed Naomi.

'The detachable train is lovely but I couldn't have danced wearing it.'

'It's been a wonderful day, I love weddings,' Naomi giggled. 'And the marquee was amazing. So many flowers and ribbons everywhere and with the lights looped around, it's really pretty.'

'One of these days you'll be next,' Alva assured.

'Yeah?'

'Why not?'

'I'll be lucky to find a man, never mind getting married, that doesn't matter anymore.'

'You never know, there are some very interesting guys here. I thought one of those friends of Carlos from Beaumont Hospital looked pretty cool, and he doesn't have a partner apparently. I'll introduce you.'

'Thanks. Was he the guy who said a few words about Carlos?'

'No, not him, it was the man sitting beside him.'

'This could be interesting,' Naomi raised her eyebrows and grinned.

'I've never met any friends of Carlos, we keep such a low profile at home because of Darren, we hardly ever go out and admittedly both of us work long hours.'

'That's a terrible way to live, I hope Darren will get a stiff sentence when his case eventually comes up.'

'If it ever comes up. Why does it take so long?'

'It has to go to the Director of Public Prosecutions firstly, and then you have the Domestic Violence Act which only became law in 2019, and add to that the attempted rape, it makes it all very complicated.'

Alva refreshed her lipstick.

Naomi stood beside her, and did the same.

'How do we look?' Alva glanced at her friend in the mirror with a smile.

'You look a million dollars,' Naomi admired.

'Thanks, so do you. Let's go down.'

'Or your new husband will be banging on the door looking for you.'

When they arrived back, Carlos met them at the entrance to the reception. 'Where have you been? I'd thought you'd left me already,' he grinned, and hugged her.

'I persuaded her to hang around a bit longer,' Naomi smiled.

'Thank you. Now it's time for us to start the dancing.'

'Oh, romantic. I'll have to grab myself a man,' Naomi laughed.

'We begin the dancing and I've chosen a very special song for our first dance.' Carlos took Alva's hand and led her on to the dance floor, as the band started to play.

'It's a song called *Te Amo,* although you may not know it,' he said, as he took her in his arms and they started to dance to the slow love song.

'It's beautiful,' she murmured.

'Especially for you,' he smiled as they swirled around the floor.

'May I ask the bride to dance?' Alva's brother, David, came over and Alva took his hand.

Carlos walked across to where Julie sat, and he escorted her on to the dance floor and they began to dance too, and all the other guests joined in as well.

Alva enjoyed herself particularly when there was a break in the dancing and a flamenco group came on to give a superb display. Now she watched the dancers, sitting beside her Mum and Carlos's grandmother, Abuela.   Julie took her hand. 'I've never seen you look so beautiful. I'm so glad you married Carlos, you'll make him a very happy man.'

'I'm lucky,' Alva smiled.

'You've no idea how happy I am that I've finally found my three children again. All those years I longed for you, so angry with Frank for preventing me from seeing you and my boys.'

Alva squeezed her Mum's hand sympathetically. She could see how lonely her mother must have been when she had to leave home and her young children because Alva's father didn't want her and she was forced to leave their home in Dublin and go to live in Spain. Carlos came over and sat beside them. For Alva to have met her mother only a year or two ago meant everything to her, and to fall in love with her Mum's adopted son, Carlos, who happened to be a neurosurgeon working in Dublin, was the icing on the cake.

'Will you excuse me, Mum, while I take my wife out to dance?' Carlos took Alva's hand and they moved on to the dance floor. It was an amazing night and they partied until late. Carlos and Alva stayed on until the party wound up just after seven o'clock in the morning, and they saw their guests off as the sun crept over the horizon.

'What a marvellous day, Alva, it's been the happiest in my life,' Carlos said, and kissed her. 'You are mine now,' he said softly.

Alva hugged close to him. 'Me too. It's been amazing. Our wedding day.'

'Every day in the future will be just as happy.'

They walked up the stairs to the balcony and into their bedroom.

'My love,' Carlos embraced her, and kissed her.

'I don't want to take off my dress,' Alva smiled at him. 'It's probably the last time I'll wear it.'

'You could have it remade,' he suggested.

'Then it isn't a wedding dress any longer.'

'All day I've been thinking about taking it off,' he smiled at her. 'Can I?'

She laughed. 'You sound like a little boy - can I?' she laughingly imitated him.

'I do want you very much,' he murmured.

She turned around so that he could open the side zip and she stepped out of the white lace dress. He held it up, and gently placed it on the armchair. Then quickly he removed his tuxedo, and within minutes they were undressed and they lay on the wide bed, their arms around each other, his lips on hers softly gripping. Their need was aroused and they caressed each other until that exquisite moment of orgasm swept through and their desire knew no bounds and took them to intense heights of elation.

They slept, as the heavy shutters had been folded over the windows and kept the piercing sunshine at bay and it was after one o'clock when they eventually awoke. Alva felt refreshed and all she wanted was to make love again with Carlos. He was still asleep, contentment etched on his features. She turned to him in the bed and pressed her lips against his, anxious for him to respond to her. His dark brown eyes opened then and he kissed her, their bodies hugging close, craving their need. This time it was a slow discovery, unhurried, a gentle yearning for love to satisfy their passion.

'Querida, my love, my wife, how wonderful that sounds,' he murmured. 'To have you to myself is astonishing. I never expected I would meet someone as beautiful as you. A person who would love me and put up with me.'

'And you have to put up with me as well,' Alva giggled.

'When we get back home to Dublin, we'll have to make decisions about our lives, we both work too hard and need to compromise. Otherwise there will be too many problems between us and I do not want that to happen. As you know already, the life of a surgeon is very demanding, but our marriage is too precious to me and I refuse to put us in danger of losing each other,' Carlos said.

'I never want to take that chance.' She kissed him.

There was another gathering the following day with just the immediate family present, and it was as enjoyable as their wedding day for both Alva and Carlos. She had bought a new outfit for the evening, a full-length silk skirt and jacket with a scattering of gemstones through the fabric which was in those creamy tones she loved to wear. David and his wife Sarah and the children, Cian and his partner Natalie, were all still there, and it was only now that she really had time to chat to everyone.

They dined at ten and sat out in the open air, as it was a particularly warm evening. She had taken a siesta with Carlos and felt now she was becoming as Spanish as the Rodrigues family. She needed those couple of hours of rest in the afternoon to be able to survive another evening of entertainment. Spaniards all partied long into the small hours. There was much chat and laughter this evening, and she did enjoy herself, but was looking forward to getting away with Carlos on their own in a couple of days.

'Are you happy, my love.' Carlos took her hand as they sat together after dinner.

She smiled at him, and squeezed his hand. 'Utterly, Carlos.'

'I can't wait until we go away for a glorious two weeks, and doing whatever we please, whenever we please.'

'It's going to be wonderful,' she agreed.

Chapter Two

Darren pushed the remains of a pizza away, opened a can of beer and slurped. Then he went to the window and pushed back the curtain. Where was Alva? He wondered. He hadn't seen her for ages. He shuddered. Hating the thought of that. Anger surged and he wanted to make her pay for avoiding him. She had no idea what was in his mind.

He would have to find out what was going on with her. He had seen the engagement ring she was wearing that last time, a great rock of a diamond thing, and he was determined to prevent her getting married. How dare she do that on him. But then the possibility that she might have married that foreign guy already crept into his mind. Pierced into his brain like a knife, and twisted, making itself felt so deeply inside, he almost couldn't bear it.

He stood up, pushed back the curtain and stared along the street. It was a miserable evening. Surfaces shone with the sudden rain which had fallen recently, and cars sprayed accumulations of water near the kerb as they drove past. Regardless of the weather, he put on his anorak, pulled up the hood, went downstairs and out the front door. This was a regular routine each night. He persuaded himself that he was keeping himself fit. That was all. He wasn't living very near her office. He had been lucky to get a small apartment in a house a couple of miles away. A studio in one of those old Victorian houses, with a pull-down bed and kitchen in the living-room, and a bathroom. He hated it here. Hated the smallness of the place. Hated the fact that there was nowhere to put anything. Every time he opened the door and came in, a feeling of claustrophobia came over him and he had to make a supreme effort to shake it off. He blamed Alva for all of it. And for the fact that she had accused him of fraud, along with her brother, David, and Hugh, the accountant, in Purtell Vintners, the family firm.

All three were forced to resign from the company by Alva. It was her company. She was CEO. The only good thing about her decision was that she decided not to take a legal case against the fraudsters once they returned the money they had embezzled. And saved their reputations. That was why he found himself living here in this cubby-hole instead of the luxurious apartment he had shared with her.

If only Alva had not found those bank statements which revealed that they had lodged the monies in accounts in a bank in the British Virgin Islands when she was throwing him out of her apartment because she had caught him with another woman. That gave them away immediately. And how stupid of them to keep that money until they had enough to invest in the hotel they planned to build. If only. He swore silently.

He padded along the street. A loose running stride. His arms bent at the elbows and working in time with his feet. He knew the way now. And didn't have to think about the route. When he arrived opposite the offices he stopped and stood in a doorway. It was almost ten o'clock now and as Alva and himself had lived together for almost four years he was well aware how late she often worked on at night. If she was still there then this would be a good time to talk to her. She wouldn't be expecting him. He stayed where he was, head down, only looking up every now and then, until eventually he gave up at about twelve o'clock as there was no sign of her coming out. He was, by now, frustrated and

12

angry.

He was a changed man by the following morning, when he dressed in a suit, shirt and tie, ready to go into the office of the company he worked for now. He was a salesman and sold a wide range of hardware products and was good at his job. He had managed to get the position by falsifying a reference, having access to the company notepaper of Purtell Vintners, and the new company seemed to be very pleased with his work so far, paying him a generous salary, commission on sales, and giving him a company car. But he was always very nervous. Dreading the day when he would receive word from his solicitor that his case for the attempted rape of Alva was coming up in court and he knew that if he couldn't keep his past a secret from his employers then he was out of a job.

He hadn't meant to attack Alva. He just wanted to make love to her. To persuade her to come back to him. But when her fucking boyfriend burst into their apartment, followed by the Gardai, he realised how bad it looked for him.

During the day he organised his calls so that occasionally he would pass through the area where Purtell Vintners were situated. His eyes watching people who happened to be walking along the street and sometimes recognising them.

He couldn't understand how he never saw Alva. Where was she? How could she disappear? He would ask himself. It wasn't possible to hide from him all the time. Sometimes, he would park his car across the road. He had sold the previous car he drove, and now had a comfortable Toyota in a shade of dark blue in which he would slump down in the front seat appearing to be on the phone. He knew that Alva would never recognise the car and hopefully wouldn't be aware of his presence.

Darren wasn't going to go into the office and ask to see her. The last time he had done that he had been arrested for breaking the barring order, and his solicitor had said that having done that might add further time to any sentence he might receive when he appeared in court. And that he could be accused of stalking if he wasn't careful.

In his own mind, all he wanted was to get Alva to himself. He had every intention of persuading her to tell the police that she had no evidence against him. He had told her that the last time they met, but she said the police were taking the case and not her. Anyway, he was certain they couldn't take a case against him if she didn't agree to be a witness. Alva could say nothing. It was easy. She had always loved him. She couldn't have just switched off him just because she found him at their apartment with that woman a couple of times. She had got it all wrong. He was certain that she still felt something for him. He just had to talk to her. Make sure she understood. And then maybe he could persuade her not to get married to that guy. If he could just have that chance, one chance, that's all he wanted.

Chapter three

Carlos and Alva left Seville early, before the heat of the day descended. Although there was air conditioning in the jeep Carlos was driving, staring out through the windows to see the landscape against the sunshine was blinding and she had to put on her sunglasses.

'There are the mountains of the Sierra de Castellar,' Carlos pointed. 'And we'll drive along this plain.'

'It's so dramatic,' she said, enthralled.

'This is the region of Extremadura and we're driving along the route which was in Roman times called the Via de la Plata. In English it is known as The Silver Route, and the Romans built a settlement here.'

She looked at the map which she had opened up on her phone, to get a better idea of where they were going.

'Have you decided which place will be our first stop?' she asked Carlos curiously. Rather than go somewhere exotic for their honeymoon, Alva had asked Carlos to take her through parts of Spain where she had never been before. He had been delighted and they agreed that they would wander north of Seville, making no bookings, but just stopping for a night or two in any place they particularly liked.

'There's a beautiful town nearby called Zafra, often called Little Seville, and we'll come to it soon.'

She searched for it on the map. 'I see it.'

'We can have a look at the town and decide if we want to stay, otherwise we can go on ahead.' He turned off the road.

'This place is amazing,' she breathed, captivated, as they entered the town. 'Look at the fortress,' she pointed.

Carlos drove through the main gate ahead, into the Alcazar Fortress.

'There is a parador here, let's see if they have a room,' he suggested.

'It doesn't look like an hotel.' Alva couldn't believe it.

'We'll go in.' He parked the jeep, and they went through the main entrance, into a courtyard which was surrounded by beautiful archways.

'The fortress was originally built by the Moors, and inside it's a palace,' he explained as they walked into the foyer, went across to the desk and enquired if they could book a room. The girl smiled, and looked at her computer. 'I have only one room but it is the bridal suite.' She looked at them, her expression uncertain.

Alva and Carlos looked at each other and burst out laughing. 'That would be perfect,' she said.

It was an amazing place. They climbed up the stone steps, in preference to taking the lift, which felt far too modern in this ancient palace. Carlos carried their bags, and Alva was astounded by their bridal suite. A large room, with patio doors which led out on to a balcony overlooking the rooftops of the town. There was a huge four poster bed with rich red hangings, and white bedlinen. At the other end of the room, there was a couch, two armchairs and a coffee table.

'They must have known we were coming,' Carlos laughed.

'I wouldn't be surprised if you booked this parador,' Alva smiled. 'Go on, admit it.'

'No, I didn't, I wasn't sure where we would stop. Anyway, I like the surprise of not knowing what's going to happen next, or where we'll find ourselves. There's not a lot of people who would like a holiday like that, most people want everything to be booked in advance. So I love that wandering side of you, Alva Purtell, and the fact that you and I share the same ideas,' he smiled, put his arms around her and held her close to him. 'I have such a predictable organised life as a surgeon so this rather uncertain way of travelling around really appeals to me.'

They had coffee in the courtyard and then set out to explore the medieval quarter of Zafra, walking through the network of narrow cobblestoned streets, surrounded by whitewashed buildings inside wrought-iron railings. They wandered into the Plaza Grande, a square lined with shops and restaurants, and followed through to the Plaza Chico, a smaller square which was connected through the Arquillo del Pan.

'That means the Arch of Bread,' laughed Carlos.

'It's so quaint.' Alva was captivated.

They spent the next couple of hours exploring. Stopping to have lunch at a restaurant in the Plaza Chico. They ordered a bottle of red wine, and ate a platter of cured meats, before deciding to return to the hotel for a siesta.

'I'm turning into a Spaniard,' Alva laughed as they rested on the huge bed. 'I almost feel sleepy, would you believe?'

'Don't sleep yet,' Carlos put his arms around her. 'This is the bridal suite.' He pressed his lips softly on hers and curled his body close. 'You are the most wonderful woman I have ever known. I love you so much it is difficult to stay away from you.' Their lovemaking was slow and sensual, a gentle reminder of how much they felt for each other. Their need dominated, until orgasm exploded through them and they were fulfilled and satiated with love.

They rose later, and wandered again through the town, having dinner in a tiny restaurant in the shadow of the walls of the fortress. A guitarist played Spanish music in the background and it was utterly romantic.

'I love you,' Alva whispered to Carlos.

'And I love you.' He covered her hand with his.

'For ever?' she asked.

'For ever,' he smiled.

The next day they drove towards Mérida.

'I suppose you've been here before?' Alva asked, staring at her phone.

'Years ago, it was a school trip.'

'It sounds like an amazing place.'

'The ruins are the best preserved in Spain.'

'Let's start exploring.' Alva was full of enthusiasm. 'There's so much to see.'

Carlos pulled in and parked the jeep.

Alva climbed out, and put a small haversack on her back. Both of them wore shorts and tee shirts which were all they needed in the warmth of the day.

'Have you got a bottle of water?' asked Carlos.

'Yeah, two, we'll need it.'

'The different sites are all over the city, so we'll have to walk a fair bit.'

'There's a sign for the Teatro Romano.' Alva pointed, and they walked in. She read a sign. 'It was built around 15 BC and could seat six thousand spectators. Imagine.' Hand in hand, they climbed up the tiers of seats and sat above taking photos. There were some other tourists there as well, but not too many to take away from their enjoyment of this ancient place.

Later, they wandered through into the amphitheatre, and second and third century mansions which had beautiful frescoes on the walls and floors.

'They're astonishing, look at the colours, the houses must have been owned by the very rich families in town.' Alva was fascinated.

'The city is amazing, around every corner there is something different,' Carlos said, as they stood admiring the enormous Temple de Diana.

They wandered down to the river, to cross one of the longest bridges built by the Romans in Spain. 'Look at all those arches, how many of them are there?' Alva asked.

'I think it's sixty.'

Alva started to count, and then gave up, laughing.

They wandered on and she suggested they might visit the museum.

'Anything for you, querida,' he kissed her.

'Maybe you're not quite as interested in all this as I am?' she asked, suddenly worried. How well did she know Carlos? She asked herself. If she added up all the time they had spent together then it didn't amount to very much. Not the usual few years other couples had known each other. And now this was the first time they had been together really. Long days and nights. Would the inevitable differences between them become even more pronounced and might she find it impossible to live with him? How long does it take to know someone? While she would have loved to wander around the city for much longer, she felt obliged to suggest that they take a break and see the museum later. 'Have you had enough, my love.' She turned to him.

'What do you mean? Of you?' He looked shocked.

'Of all this,' she indicated the aqueduct.

He shook his head. 'I'm enjoying every minute of our time together. Every moment you look at something with delight, I enjoy it twice as much. That's why.'

'That's a relief, then, I thought you might be bored.'

'Never, querida.' He swept her into his arms and held her close for a moment.

She was unable to understand this sudden feeling of

uncertainty about Carlos.

They had lunch in a café sitting under a blue umbrella. Drank cool white wine, and ate gambas al ajillo. Big juicy prawns, swimming in tasty olive oil and garlic. When they had finished, she put her hand on his and held it gently.

'I'm sorry, Carlos, for giving you the impression that I thought you were bored. I didn't mean it. It's just for me it's the first time I've been here, and for you it's not, so maybe you mightn't enjoy it as much as I do.'

'Just know that I like whatever you like.' He squeezed her hand, and leaned to press his lips on hers.

She looked into his eyes, but still felt she didn't know him, and was afraid that she wouldn't come up to his expectations of her.

Chapter Four

Unexpectedly, Darren met Hugh in town. He had been the accountant in Purtell Vintners, and the leader in the embezzlement of the money they had stashed away in the British Virgin Islands. It had been all his idea from the start.

'Long time no see,' Hugh said, stopping.

'Yeah.' Darren wasn't sure what to say. He hadn't seen him since that day both of them had resigned from the company, cleared their offices, and left.

'What are you doing these days?' Hugh asked.

'I've a sales job at a hardware company.'

'That's good, I'm glad for you.' Hugh nodded.

'What about you?'

'I've set up my own accountancy firm.'

'Going well?'

'Happy enough.'

'How's the family.'

'They're all well.'

Darren ran out of conversation. He felt awkward.

'Did you and Alva get back together?' Hugh asked.

Darren shook his head. 'I'm still hoping.'

'Do you see her?'

'No.'

'You should make contact, you never know how that may go.'

'I try to but she doesn't want to see me.'

'Is there someone else?'

'She's engaged.' Darren felt foolish even admitting that.

'I'm sorry, that's tough on you.

Darren shrugged. 'I'm not sure if she's married yet. Do you think you could find that out for me from one of her brothers?' he asked.

'I don't have any contact with them. Even David has never returned any of my texts, or calls, and neither has Cian. I felt I just got out in time before Alva took legal action against me. I was never sure whether she would do that, even though she said she wouldn't, but you can never tell when the legal people are involved.'

'You know she threw me out of the apartment?'

'Threw you out?' Hugh looked surprised. 'I knew you had broken up but I didn't know it had been that ugly.'

'Very ugly. You wouldn't believe. Do you ever see any of the staff in the company?' he asked.

'One or two in my department. They actually made contact with me, as none of them knew exactly why I had left.'

'Maybe you could ask about Alva when you see them? I'm sure they would all know if she's getting married.'

'I could ask.'

'Then if you find out you might text me. It's just to know if she is married then I can forget about her, and know that I have no chance of persuading her to give us another chance.'

'If she's married, then you'd be better off making a new start. I'm sure you'll have no problem meeting someone else,' Hugh said with a grin.

Darren was glad to have met Hugh, and to know that he would let him know about Alva. She had promised to give him a financial settlement originally but now he wasn't so sure about that anymore because of the court case coming up. He didn't know why he had attacked Alva, he had been crazy that night. He wanted her so much, he couldn't bear to think that she was with that other guy, as every time he saw her, he was there too. Anyone could understand that, he rationalised to himself. And he would tell the judge if it ever got that far. But he felt sure that she would change her mind about testifying against him and then the whole thing would collapse.

Hugh texted him a few days later and his heart dropped when he read that Alva had already got married in Spain. He was furious. He was the man she should have married. They had talked about marriage many times but now he didn't know why they had never actually taken that step. He had always wanted to, but it was Alva who didn't want to. Maybe she was the one who was playing around all the time. He grew very suspicious. How long was she with that guy? Had it been a year, or even two years or more? They had made a fool of him. He was insanely jealous. That man had no right to Alva. He and Alva had always been together, and for that man to come along and persuade her to marry him was treacherous. He wouldn't let her continue to live with him. He would take her back, and she would love him like she always did. Now he was so certain that when she saw him again it would be like those days when they had first met. It had been a magical time. And it would be again.

Darren worked hard in his new job. He needed to be a success. Just as successful as Alva herself was in her family business, Purtell Vintners. He had always been on the sales side, and resented that he hadn't been promoted higher up the scale in the company since he had met Alva. Maybe she didn't want him to be as powerful as she was herself as CEO. Now he was determined that he would be every bit as powerful, so that he would never find himself in the position he had been in when she was able to force him to resign from the company, destroy his prospects, and put him in jeopardy of having to face a prison term. And it had been that man she had married who brought the police to their apartment when he had just been about to make love to her. He had had a few run-ins with him before. And when Hugh told him that she had got married in Spain it all made sense. That guy was Spanish no doubt. He knew he was foreign but hadn't been able to pinpoint his accent. He should have given him a better thumping that time he caught him at Alva's old home. How dare he assume that he could marry his Alva. Anger surged as he remembered seeing them that night. I'll get him again, whoever he is, he thought, and he won't know what hit him. Then he'll know all about it.

Chapter Five

The next stop for Alva and Carlos was a town called Cáceres. They loved the place and decided on the spur of the moment to stay a second night in a charming old-fashioned hotel, seemingly the only hotel which had a room in the town as crowds of people were there for the Fiesta de San Jorge, the patron saint of Cáceres.

'Should be fun, there's a parade on tonight.' Alva was feeling better today. Somehow that mood which attacked her yesterday had disappeared, and she felt her normal confident self again.

This place was a mixture of a modern town and another amazing old-world walled city from the fifteenth century which was completely intact, and hand and hand they wandered through its winding narrow streets. Visiting ancient palaces which were now museums, and old churches. An unexpected pleasure they encountered was when they heard the sound of a piano being played. The music was a classical Spanish piece, the delicate melody drifting from an open window. They sat on an old stone wall and listened for a while, very surprised when the music ended and a young boy put his head out of the window, looked at them for a moment, and then disappeared inside again and closed it, and left them wondering if he had been the pianist who had entertained them.

'That was beautiful,' Carlos murmured.

They had both been captivated by the music, but continued on with their tour, the streets silent once again.

'The atmosphere is amazing. There's so much history here, I love it,' Alva said.

'And many of the buildings are still owned by ancient families. See the heraldic shields,' Carlos said and pointed to one on a house they had just walked past. 'Look, the lion rampant, the castle, and a flag on either side.'

'I'd love to know who that family were?' Alva peered closer to the shield which was sculpted in the same colour used in some of the bricks of the wall.

'Most of the mansions have them.'

'We'll have to get our two heraldic shields for home,' Carlos said.

'Mine is gold with a black *x*, and the words are, *Aut Vincam Aut Periam,* which means something like *Either I win or I lose.* I always think it means I'm going to do it anyway regardless of the outcome,' Alva said, laughing.

'That's interesting, it's the way you are,' he smiled.

'Do you know yours?'

'I'll have to look it up,' he took his phone out of his pocket and searched. '*In domino spes mea* is the motto.'

'What does that mean?'

'It's something like *On Holy ground* maybe, I'm not too sure. But you can see a photo there.' He showed her.

'A castle and a knight, and an eagle above,' she stared at it, fascinated. 'Scroll down, there's a lot of info about the Rodrigues name which originated in Germany.'

He looked over her shoulder. 'Our family name now,' he laughed, and put his arm around her.

'This is like a history lesson,' she laughed as well. 'The Spanish really preserve their old buildings, we in Ireland should take a leaf out of your book,' Alva said. 'I'm always reminded of the old Viking remains on Wood Quay which were not preserved because the Council was planning to build its new offices there

26

and only some of the artefacts were eventually held in the museum. It was an enormous site and here in Spain I'm sure they would have left it intact and covered with glass so that we could see it at least. In Seville, there are Roman ruins preserved under glass below that big structure called *The Metropol Parasol*, although it's awful looking,' Alva laughed. 'And what's going to happen to the amazing finds under a new motorway in Cork, they're 6,000 years old.'

'There was a lot of controversy about the building of the Parasol, and it cost the city an awful lot of money too,' Carlos said.

'What do your family think of it?'

'Nobody I know likes it,' he said, laughing.

'It's completely out of place, so modern in such an ancient city. At least they've created nothing like that here. I love Cáceres,' she looked around enjoying the ambiance. In the evening they watched the parade which was a re-enactment of the conquest of the city by the Christians over the Moors. The streets of the city were decked out with flags and decorations and events included the burning of a huge paper dragon. Many people were dressed up in colourful costumes as Christians and Moors and even their horses wore medieval coverings with insignia on them. Carlos and Alva joined the crowds of people on the street. The evening was really enjoyable, and afterwards they had dinner at a small roadside bar and raised a glass of wine to San Jorge.

Once again, they were on their way, driving through the country. Taking short detours here and there to explore a castle they could see on a distant hilltop. Or a village clinging to a cliffside, gleaming white houses, and red roofs. In the mountains, Guadaloupe was a stunning town huddled around the massive stone hulk of a monastery. They walked through narrow cobbled streets, sat by sparkling fountains and explored the monastery.

Afterwards, Carlos surprised Alva.

'I've arranged an appointment for us to meet the owners of a bodega, and we'll be taken on a tour of the winery,' he announced.

'What's the name?'

'Bodega Lopez.'

'I've heard of them but they are not one of our suppliers in Dublin.'

'I know their wines and they are very special. The family have been producing wine since the early 1900s.'

'Thank you for doing that, I'm really looking forward to seeing the winery.'

She was very grateful. It was just like Carlos to surprise her.

'I knew you'd enjoy it.'

The bodega was surrounded by gardens and fountains, and on the land surrounding grew acres of vines, which were the basis of Lopez wines. They walked across the main courtyard and went through the high doors which stood open. Alva rang the bell. A young woman came out to meet them, and Alva introduced herself and Carlos, handing her a company business card.

After a few minutes, a man appeared, his hand outstretched. 'Senorita Purtell?'

'How are you?' she asked, still shy of using the minimal amount of Spanish she possessed.

'I'm Mario Lopez.'

'It's good to meet you, Senor Lopez,' Alva said. 'This is my husband Carlos Rodriguez.'

They shook hands also. It was all very friendly.

The underground wine cellars were cool, kept at a constant twelve degrees centigrade by the thick walls. The curved brick ceilings and arches seemed to go on and on into the shadowy distance, where thousands of stacked wooden casks were stored.

'This is an amazing place,' said Alva.

Mario then suggested they taste some wines and they went

back upstairs into a warmer atmosphere and he poured some of the different types of wine that Bodega Lopez produced.

'These are really mellow, and very rich,' Alva responded. 'I'm glad to have an opportunity to taste them. I'll make a note of the different ones and when I'm back in the office we will consider ordering some.'

'I'm sorry, Mario, I can't drink as I'm doing the driving. Anyway, Alva is the expert here,' Carlos apologised.

'Thank you, I am glad that you like them. I will send you some sample bottles to try when you are home in Ireland. Just let me know when you would like them. Send me an email.' He handed her a card.

'Thank you, Mario, that would be good.'

Afterwards, a waiter brought tapas, and they enjoyed the different flavours.

'The tapas are delicious, particularly the meats,' Alva said.

'They are a local speciality,' explained Mario.

'And this wine is so rich.' She tasted another wine.

'That is a Tempranillo and Cabernet Sauvignon blend.'

'I particularly like it.'

'It is very popular, maybe you might order it for some of your clients?'

'I shall certainly consider it. We have a wide range of different clients internationally, and also many outlets in Ireland.'

'I'll include it with the samples,' Mario promised.

'I have to say Mario was very nice,' commented Alva when they had left Bodega Lopez. 'And to send some of the wines for us to sample is generous, it would have been hard to remember the flavours by the time we get home.'

'It was an interesting visit,' agreed Carlos.

'Thanks for arranging it, you're a pet,' she smiled at him.

'Have a look at your map, where shall we go next?'

'I don't want you to have to drive too far, we're in the

29

mountains now and it's very slow.' Alva checked her phone. 'We're heading for Madrid so that's north-east.'

'What's on the way?' Carlos asked, keeping an eye on the road ahead as some of the turns curved sharply downhill.

'Talavera de la Reina. I'll find out what it's like.' She googled. 'It doesn't sound exciting, but then it says there is a charming village called Oropesa and that's a better stop apparently.'

'Never heard of it. Has it got hotels?'

'It has La Hosteleria and a parador in the castle.'

'Which do you prefer?'

'I don't mind.'

'We'll have a look when we arrive.'

'We weren't in a fancy place last night and it was fine, clean, adequate.'

'La Hosteleria is just below the castle so we can see both.'

'Oh my God, be careful.' She looked down the mountain side from the window to see a very sharp drop into a steep chasm. She hated driving on narrow roads dreading some other vehicle would come up in the other direction.

'I'm not looking down there,' he said, with a wide grin. 'My eyes are straight ahead on the road.'

She twisted her hands together.

'Don't worry, querida,' he said softly.

'I'm a terrible passenger,' she had to admit. But Carlos was careful and she had his confidence.

'Would you prefer to drive?' he grinned.

'No thanks, not along here. I'll drive later or tomorrow. Give you a rest, I'm sure you get tired driving.'

'I don't get tired, and there's no need for you to drive, I enjoy it.'

'Take care along here please, that's all I ask.'

The castle in Oropesa was built hundreds of years before, and huge red bricked medieval towers overlooked the village below. The parador was part of the castle, and when they walked through the entrance and saw the pool, they immediately decided to see if there was a room available.

'I'd give anything to dive in, it looks so cool and inviting.' Alva was full of enthusiasm.

There was a room available, and within a short time they were swimming in the deliciously cool water of the pool, delighted that they had the place to themselves.

'I haven't had you close to me all day,' Carlos embraced her in the deep end of the pool, and kissed her wetly. 'We've been so busy.'

'Let's relax tomorrow,' suggested Alva. 'Do nothing.'

'I'd like that. You will be mine all day.' He kissed her.

'And I yours.'

They stayed in Oropesa for three days. The weather was warm, with cloudless blue skies and bright sunshine, and they explored the ancient castle leisurely, looking across the plains to the Sierra de Gredos mountains from its topmost point. They wandered through the village, and took long walks into the countryside. And on one day hired bicycles and cycled out across the plain, going through wooded areas with gentle inclines, and stopping at smaller villages. In one particular one, Lagartera, they visited the museum of embroidery, which also had ceramics and paintings as well.

'This is an amazing part of Spain,' Alva was most enthusiastic. 'And there are hardly any other tourists here which is surprising.'

'I picked up a leaflet about the ceramic museum in Talavera de la Reina, and thought we might go there too.' Carlos pulled it out of his pocket and handed it to her.

'A town which has churches decorated with ceramics sounds amazing.'

'We can have a look as we go through.'

'Where is our next stop?' Alva asked. Enjoying the feeling of a gentle breeze through her hair as they climbed up on their bikes and rode along together.

'We'll have a look at the map this evening and decide.'

Before they ordered dinner, they chatted about the possibilities.

'We're heading towards Madrid, would you like to visit?' Carlos asked.

'No, I've already spent a few days there a couple of years ago, so I think I'd prefer to explore smaller places, like we've been to.'

Carlos opened his phone. 'We can just drive through.'

'Yeah.'

'So, where's next then.'

'How about Toledo?'

'I haven't ever been there.'

'Right, we're heading that way.'

'I can't believe how much we've seen, it's incredible.'

'And when you come to Toledo you'll be blown away. It's an amazing place with so much character and if we just wander around the twisting lanes, and get a feel for the place, it will mean much more,' Carlos suggested.

'We're probably churched out at this stage, just to wander appeals to me now. I enjoyed Oropesa so much, I'd like to visit somewhere else like that.'

'There are plenty of small places.'

'We'll spend the morning in Toledo to get a feel of it, and then drive south,' he smiled and covered her hand with his, a warm comforting gesture.

There was a beep from a phone.

'Someone looking for one of us?' Alva asked, hoping that wasn't the case. So far there had only been texts from their families wishing them all the best.

'Probably Mum,' he said, taking his phone from his pocket.

'She texted me this morning,' she said.

He looked at the screen, and his smiling expression changed suddenly to one of concern.

'What is it?' Alva asked.

'It's one of my team at the hospital, do you mind if I take it outside? It's a bit noisy in here.' He stood up and left the restaurant.

She shook her head. But was suddenly worried. So far there had been no calls from work for either of them, and that had meant that they had enjoyed every moment of their honeymoon without any interruption. She took a sip of her wine, twisting the stem of the glass between her fingers as she watched the door, and waited for Carlos to return. He didn't take very long, but she could see immediately that he was still very concerned as he sat down.

'I'm sorry, querida, but I must go back.' He held her hand tightly.

Her heart sank. 'Why?'

'I operated on a young man before I left but he has taken a bad turn and I may have to operate on him again. There is another procedure on the brain which could sort out the problem, but I will have to check feasibility when I arrive.'

'I'm so sorry about that.' She was very sympathetic.

'I feel so bad, as it has spoiled our honeymoon, but ...' He kissed her.

'But that man's life is more important, we'll both go home.'

'Unfortunately, as it is so urgent, I will have to drive to Madrid which is the nearest airport, and catch a flight as early as I can tomorrow. I hope you don't mind that. And luckily I've only taken a sip of wine, so I'll be able to drive.'

'No, of course not, let's go back, pack our things and leave immediately,' she said, and stood up.

'Thank you, my love, for being so understanding.' Quickly,

he paid the bill, and they left the restaurant.

'I'll fly back with you too.'

'You could always go to Seville and spend the rest of the time there with your Mum and the family?'

'I'd prefer to keep you company,' she insisted.

He held her close as they went up in the lift to their bedroom, and kissed her. 'Are you sure?'

'Absolutely.'

'We've been away how long?' he asked as he pulled out one of their bags, and began to pack.

'About ten nights,' she counted it up in her head. 'It's all been a lovely dream, one wonderful day drifting into another wonderful day.'

'We'll take another break later, and continue our honeymoon.'

'We only have a few more days. Anyway, I want to be there for you.'

'Thank you, my love, if that is what you would like, although could you book flights on your phone for us as we drive?'

Quickly, she began to pack as well, and within a short time were checking out.

They were on the motorway quickly, and headed to Madrid. The distance was only one and a half hours and as they travelled, Alva booked their flights for the following morning, the earliest to Dublin being just before eight o'clock in the morning. There was very little traffic at that time and they made good progress.

'Are you tired? Would you like me to drive for a bit?' she asked Carlos after an hour.

'I'm fine, thank you, it won't be that much longer.' Without taking his eyes off the road, he put out his hand and clasped hers briefly. 'Only about half an hour.'

'I'm going to miss being away together over the next few days,' she said.

'We'll have another honeymoon as soon as we can,' he promised.

'Every day is a honeymoon with you,' she murmured.

'And with you,' he smiled broadly.

'What is the word for honeymoon in Spanish?' she giggled. 'I can't remember exactly.'

'Luna de miel.'

'So luna is moon and miel is honey. Moon of honey,' she laughed.

'Your Spanish is improving,' he nodded.

'I learned some from Mum when I was with her in the hospital in Barcelona when she had her transplant from David. I think I can understand more than I can speak.'

'I'd better be careful what I say then,' he laughed.

'You'll have to speak more Spanish to me, otherwise I'll forget all I've learned,' she said.

'Let's have a day when we speak only Spanish?' he suggested.

'I should probably take some lessons.'

'Good idea.'

'I'll look into that when I get back home to Dublin. You're lucky you speak perfect English, and with hardly any accent either.'

'Mum spoke English to us when she came to look after us after leaving your father, Frank, as she didn't have very much Spanish, so that's why we all speak English. And my father was keen for us to learn, so the whole household including the staff spoke English.'

They chatted on, and Alva was surprised that she didn't actually doze off at any point, and when they arrived at Madrid they booked into a hotel near the airport.

Looking at his watch, Carlos put his arm around her. 'Try and get some sleep.'

'Everyone in the family are going to be very surprised when

we tell them where we are in the morning,' said Alva.

They lay in bed, arms around each other, and before long were fast asleep, managing to sleep for about two hours, which refreshed them. Carlos had put on the alarm on his phone so they didn't sleep any longer, and when Alva woke up, he was already speaking on the phone to the hospital.

'How is your patient?' she asked when he finished the call.

'Thank God, he hasn't deteriorated any further overnight.'

'I'm so glad,' she hugged him.

Chapter Six

In Seville, Julie, Alva's mother, felt sad when she heard that Alva and Carlos had gone back to Dublin from Madrid as she had been looking forward to spending a couple of days with the newly married couple when they had returned from their honeymoon. But now that wasn't going to happen, and she would have to wait until she had an opportunity to visit Dublin to see them again.

Living on a stud farm, Caballos Rodrigues, with her partner, Pedro, the father of Carlos, Nuria and Pacqui, she was surrounded by horses, and loved to ride. But since she had her kidney transplant because of her fall from a horse, and subsequent transplant from her eldest son, David, she had had to give up riding for at least a year, but now she was looking forward to a gentle ride today. The doctors had warned that she should be careful, as had Carlos, and she had obeyed. It was something she missed. Loving that feeling of mounting her stallion, Fuego, the horse racing away and taking her with him.

One of the stable hands saddled the horse and brought him out from the stable. He held the horse quiet while she mounted, and it was only then she saw her partner, Pedro, walk up and run his hand along the flank of the horse, that she got slightly worried.

'I hope he's calm today,' he said.

'He seems fine,' she said, taking hold of the reins.

'Are you sure you are able to ride?'

'Of course, the doctors told me I could.' She wanted to be more firm with Pedro but was aware that perhaps she wasn't firm enough. If he had his way, he would never let her ride again.

'Be careful.'

'I will.'

'Don't be too long, I'll be worried.'

'I won't,' she said gently. Since her accident, he was always concerned for her. He fussed. Although he didn't have to. She was able to look after herself. She rode out. Pressing her calves against the side of the horse to encourage him to move on into a decent trot.

She wished she could get Fuego to gallop, the way he had done when they were riding on the beach that day in Cadiz. Now if he could only gallop without losing his head altogether, it would be marvellous. But then Fuego had got the bit between his teeth and taken control away from her, and there was nothing to be done about it. Was she going to take a chance and let him do that again, she wondered? Or would that be too dangerous? She remembered that time when she had been thrown, Pedro had wanted to put Fuego down, but because she had been so ill, he had held off making that decision thinking that having to tell her that her favourite horse was dead at that time would have been heart-breaking for her, and in the end had been persuaded by the family that her health was more important.

She was so glad now that he hadn't put Fuego down. Although it meant that every time she rode out Pedro was afraid for her. She was very cautious and held the horse gently as she took her usual route up to the copse of trees on the top of the hill overlooking the stable block. Dismounting and leading him through the trees. He was quiet now, and seemed glad to be walking with her. She whispered to Fuego. And stroked him. And he responded by putting his head up and down with a fluttering exhalation through his nostrils. 'Quiet boy, quiet,' she said softly. 'I'm here with you.' She mounted again, and rode him around the meadow a few times, enjoying the soft gallop, before seeing Pedro ride out towards her.

'He's behaving himself, I think,' he smiled.

'Yes.' She leaned forward and patted the horse's neck.

'Have you had enough?' he asked.

'You know I never have enough,' she laughed.

'Let's go back in,' he suggested.

She agreed, knowing he only had her own safety in mind.

When they arrived back into the stables, one of the men immediately came to help her dismount and took Fuego away to unsaddle him.

'I want to brush him,' she said, following him.

She used a curry comb to loosen any dirt in his coat, and then enjoyed brushing him in wide circles across his shining black coat. Fuego enjoyed it as well and she had an opportunity to check that he hadn't sustained any injury and re-plaited his long tail. She found spending time with him in the stables very relaxing and hated to leave and go back home for lunch.

Pedro's daughter Pacqui was the only one at home these days and worked with Pedro at the stud. His second daughter, Nuria, was lecturing in the University in Madrid and only came home occasionally at weekends. Of course, Carlos worked in Dublin and didn't get back to Seville very often other than once or twice a year. As they sat down to lunch, her phone rang. She took it out of her pocket and saw immediately that it was from David, her eldest son in Dublin, and was delighted to hear from him.

'Excuse me, it's David,' she said.

'Call him back,' Pedro said sharply.

'David, how are you?' she said warmly and listened.

'And I'm wonderful too. I'm sorry, would you mind if I call you back, we're just starting lunch. I won't be long.' She turned off the phone and began to eat again without saying any more.

Glancing up at Pedro she could see that he had a very cross expression on his face. He never liked anyone using their phones during meals, and as her Irish family never realised what time Spaniards eat, they seemed to call at the most awkward moments.

'Did Carlos and Alva get off in time?' Pedro asked.

'I think so. He was very anxious to get back to the hospital.'

'It's such a pity that they had to go back, I'm sure they were having a ball,' Pacqui said.

'Carlos hasn't had a break in a long time,' Pedro added.

'His career demands a lot.' Julie felt she had better say something. She didn't want to be silent. If she was then it would seem Pedro's reaction to David's phone call meant more to her than she wanted to admit. As it was, if he did lose his cool, then generally she would ignore it, particularly as he would always apologise afterwards.

They rose from the table and went upstairs for siesta. It was tradition in the family, but gave Julie no opportunity to call David back. The shutters had been drawn and as they lay on the bed, Pedro fell asleep almost immediately. But Julie stayed awake. She had become quite used to siesta over the years in Spain, but sometimes her Irish nature prevented her from sleeping, particularly if there was something on her mind. Now she was worried about not returning David's call. She had only made contact with her own children in recent years, and every time one of them called, either David, Cian or Alva, her heart did a double take and it meant a great deal to her. And David had saved her life. When she had that fall off her horse, David had been the son who offered to give her one of his kidneys so that she could live. While both her daughter Alva also offered to be a living donor, as did Cian, neither of them were compatible, so as David was the only one who was a match, he had made that supreme sacrifice. She couldn't thank him enough. She loved all of her children very much, having lost them when they were young, forced to leave her home in Dublin without them.

But she had been very lucky to meet Pedro, who was a widower and lived in Seville in Spain. He had needed a nanny to look after his own three children. It seemed to be the perfect fit for her. While she had tried to contact her husband over the early years about seeing her children, he never responded to her, and she became a mother to Pedro's children and grew to love them. It was only when her husband died and she went to Dublin to see his solicitor, that she actually met her children for the first time.

She wasn't sure of Pedro's reaction to this news, and held back initially. While he wasn't very enthused by the idea of her finding her Irish family, he did eventually come around. But even now, there could be odd moments when he might react negatively, like today when David had called. She couldn't say anything to her children, and had to hope that Pedro wouldn't be too annoyed by little things like timing. As they were all living in Dublin, the phone was the best way to communicate, so she thought of dropping a hint occasionally so that they might choose a better time to call or text. But of course, if they happened to take offence then she didn't know what she would do.

She slipped out of the bed and went downstairs, taking this opportunity to call David.

'How are you, love, sorry to have taken so long to come back to you, but we were in the middle of lunch.'

'No problem, Mum, how are you?' he asked.

'I'm fine, and you?' Every time she asked him that question, she half expected him to tell her that he wasn't feeling well, and that the loss of one of his kidneys was now affecting him.

But so far, to her great relief, that hadn't happened.

'Is your business going well?'

'Yeah, fine, I have plenty of clients and some good suppliers, in France mostly.'

'How are Sarah and my grandchildren, I wish I could see

them soon. Maybe you'd come over to see us?' she asked.

'I'm very busy, but maybe some time in the summer?' he promised.

'That would be wonderful, I'm looking forward to it already.'

'Don't keep me to it, we're very busy, but I'll try.'

'And something else, unfortunately Carlos had to go back to Dublin today, one of his patients was taken ill.'

'That was a pity, so they had to curtail their honeymoon?'

'Yes, and Alva went home with him.'

'I must give them a call.'

'It was very disappointing for them,' Julie said. 'And us, we had been hoping to have a celebration before they went home. But I hope that I might be able to come over if I can, so I could see you all soon,' Julie told him.

'That will be wonderful, we'll be really looking forward to seeing you.'

Julie left a message for Alva so that she would know she had been thinking of her and hoping that Carlos and herself had made a safe journey home. Later she talked with Pedro about her plans.

'I'm thinking of going to Dublin in a week or two to see Carlos and Alva. Do you think you might be able to come as well? The weather should be quite pleasant now.'

'For how long?' he asked, and a very surprised look flashed across his face.

'A few days. You never take holidays, and you've only been to Dublin on one occasion before.'

'Where would I get the time, and what would we do when we get there?'

'See the family,' she said.

'I can't imagine that Carlos would be able to get time off, he's only just gone back and didn't even take his full vacation,' he grunted.

'We can meet them all at different times, and travel to see various parts of Ireland. It's a beautiful place.'

'That would be impossible for me, Julie, I don't know what you're thinking,' he said bluntly. 'And leave Pacqui here to run things on her own? You're crazy.'

'You have the manager and other staff,' pointed out Julie, hoping to find some excuses.

'It's just not something I want to do, Julie.'

She was silenced.

'But if you want to go to Dublin, then do. But I'm not going.'

'Maybe you might change your mind?'

She felt she was almost begging and it was unusual to be in this position. She had hardly ever gone away on her own except to see Carlos and Nuria when they were students in Dublin, and it was never more than a couple of days. Admittedly, she had gone to Dublin a few times when she met her children, but Pedro had never come with her.

She loved to go back to Dublin. Then she had a chance to walk in the footsteps of her early life. The place where she had grown up, married, and had her three children. Before she had met her children, those Irish visits gave her an opportunity to watch the faces of young people who passed by. Trying to recognise something in them which would remind her that they were of her. But that never happened, until she walked into the offices of the family solicitor in Dublin and by chance a young woman came up to her and murmured her name, it was only then she knew she had come home at last.

Pedro always needed her in Seville. And she was happy to be needed. So grateful to him for the life he had given her. They were very wealthy, and she had everything she ever wanted. The stud run by the family was extremely successful, their horses and offspring always obtaining the highest of prices, and for one of

43

their stallions to cover your mare would ensure the line would continue. Win races. And ensure success in the horse breeding business, and perhaps earn untold riches. When Pedro Rodriguez and Julie fell in love and he invited her to share his life, she was unable to refuse, enthralled by his magnetism. They never married. Pedro, a widower, and Julie, a nanny, blended into a partnership seamlessly.

Chapter Seven

Alva lifted their bags from the baggage carousel, and put them on the trolley. Carlos had left for the hospital as soon as they landed, and now she made her way out of the airport to where the taxis waited. She waited in the queue and eventually was next in line. The man lifted the bags in for her and as he drove her home, she was worried about Carlos's patient. A young man. It seemed he was seriously ill, and she hoped that Carlos would be able to save him.

Alva arrived back at their apartment, and let herself in. She felt depressed. It was such a sudden ending to their honeymoon. So different to what she had expected. Here she was, all alone, and it almost seemed as if they had broken up. She went into the kitchen, put on the kettle, made herself a cup of tea, and sat down at the table. She blessed herself. Saying a prayer that the young man would recover. In her mind, she could see Carlos bent over an operating table with a group of other surgeons and nursing staff. Bright lights illuminated his gloved hands as he worked with delicate precision on a magnified area. She had never seen him at work, and could only imagine what it must be like. He was an artist. For Carlos, all he wanted to do was to save a life. It was his vocation.

She went shopping later, and walked the aisles deciding what she might cook over the next couple of days. And when she arrived back, she was surprised at herself for being able to go out shopping without even looking over her shoulder once. It was the first time she had done that in such a relaxed frame of mind without thinking about her ex-partner, Darren. He hadn't stalked her by sending letters and texts since last year, and she was very glad about that. But she reminded herself that letters could still have built up in the office as she had sold the apartment she shared with Darren. There had been hundreds of texts from him. Hundreds of letters. All because she had put him out of her life. But she had promised to give him some money when she would inherit from her father's will. He had died the previous year and they had to wait for probate to be granted before his estate could be divided between the beneficiaries. The main reason she had split up with Darren was because she found him sleeping with another woman in their own bed. And on a couple of other occasions as well, in spite of his protestations of innocence.

She had met Carlos then, and Darren had become insanely jealous when he saw them together. So much so, she had had to move to her father's house before it was sold, and when Darren found out she was living there, she moved into Carlos's apartment and to her relief he never discovered where he lived. Her solicitor took out a barring order against him, and he seemed to accept it. At the time, she needed some things from her apartment, and took a chance to go back and get them. But he found her there, and now she waited on his case to come up in court for attempting to rape her. She dreaded that, although as he had eventually admitted his guilt she wouldn't be forced to be interrogated and give evidence. The news coming through on her wedding day to Carlos. Still the thought of seeing him in the court room would be very hard, yet she didn't want to let him off having to face her there and accept that what he had done had been absolutely appalling.

She cooked a meal when she got back. A traditional Spanish stew, a tasty dish which used chorizo, lentils, onion, garlic, carrots, red and yellow peppers. She wanted to cook something Carlos would like, a dish he often enjoyed when he was at home in Seville. Now Alva had a quick sandwich herself, as she didn't expect Carlos to be home early, if at all. She listened to the radio to catch up on the news in Ireland and find out what was happening while they had been away in Spain.

She deliberately avoided even making contact with her brother Cian while she had been on honeymoon, as he had assured her that he had everything under control and would only call her if a problem arose which would need her attention. And she had been so glad that hadn't happened. But now she called him and they had a long chat about what was happening in the company since she had been away. Thankfully, there was nothing particular, and he assured her that there was no need for her to come in. She spent the time checking emails and replying to them, all the time waiting anxiously for a call from Carlos, or hearing his key turn in the lock. Eventually, as twelve o'clock passed and then one, she decided to go to bed. Although she just lay there in the big wide bed on her usual side and dozed a little on and off, she was very conscious of how much space there was on the other side accentuating the fact that Carlos wasn't close by her. Since they had been together, his loving presence had always reassured her that she was safe from the aggressive person that was Darren. Even though she was sure that her ex-partner had no idea of where she lived now, when she was alone, a creeping sense of worry would often overcome her and made her wonder if this was something which she would have to deal with in the future whatever happened to Darren. She got up at five o'clock in the morning, and waited in hope for Carlos, eventually going into the office.

She was waiting for her brother, Cian, when he came in after eight o'clock and was glad to see him. He was very sympathetic that their honeymoon was curtailed.

'We'll get away again soon I hope,' Alva said confidently.

'It's difficult for Carlos, but he seems to be very committed to his patients. They come first. And that might be difficult for you. It could mean that you'll have a very lonely life.'

'I've thought about that and hope that it won't be a problem. I do love him very much.'

'I'm sure you will always be very happy.' Cian hugged her.

'Now, give me the detail of what's been happening while I've been away.' She sat at her desk.

'Sales are going well.' He pulled up the figures on the laptop and they both examined them.

'Big difference to where we were this time last year, practically bankrupt.'

'And the fact that Julie is going to invest her inheritance in the company is going to make a major change. Has she mentioned how she will do that?

'No, we haven't discussed it. She'll be coming over soon when the final amounts are disposed of, and that's my job of course, although I hate the thought of it.'

'I know how you feel,' Cian said. 'If you want me to help, I will.'

'Not at all, our solicitor, John, will make sure everything is right. I'm the executor and I must divide up the estate.'

'Could be a lot of administration involved,' he commented.

'Probably.'

Her phone rang, and she picked it up immediately. 'Excuse me, Cian.'

He stood up. 'I'll be back later.'

'Carlos?' her voice wavered.

'I'm so sorry I didn't come home, but it took a long time.' He sounded very tired.

'How is the patient?' she asked.

'He is stable.'

'I'm so glad,' she sighed.

'It is good, I feared the worst.'

'When will I see you?' she asked excitedly.

'I'm not sure, I want to stay here so that I can see his progress during the day.'

'You must be exhausted, my love.'

'I dozed in a chair for a few minutes early this morning when my team had arrived, querida, so don't worry about me,' he laughed softly.

'I can't help it. I just want to put my arms around you.'

'I'll be home this evening, shouldn't be too late. I must go now.' He cut off the phone abruptly, obviously, someone was looking for him.

Alva was relieved.

Cian knocked on the door.

She opened it. 'Sorry about that, Carlos was held up at the hospital, a patient was very ill and he had to stay there last night and make sure he remained stable.'

'Sounds tough, when will he be home?'

'He hopes to be back later tonight. It's just part of the job which is very demanding.'

'I couldn't do that, I must admit. All that blood.' He shuddered.

'It's like a vocation for him.'

'Something else.'

'Thanks for looking after things while I was away. It made a huge difference to being able to relax, and no one bothered Carlos either.'

'When is Julie coming over?'

'I'm not quite sure, I've to let her know about the Will etc. and she must come over for that.'

'I'm looking forward to seeing her, both of us are.' Cian was very enthusiastic.

'How is David?'

'Seems fine, and his new business is doing well. I think he's delighted that he isn't involved with us anymore.'

'I'm sorry about that, I don't know what got into him and forced him to join with Darren and Hugh in that fraud on the company.'

'Greed.' Cian twisted his lips.

'Idiots, they were so stupid, particularly Darren who left his bank statements among his files at our apartment and I happened to spot them as I put all his stuff in bags when I turfed him out,' she laughed.

'You were right to do that. You've a new life now, and a husband. Carlos is a much better choice, and beats Darren hands down, particularly as he's going to do time hopefully.'

She stared out the window pensively, thinking that Darren's court case would be coming up soon and hating the thought of it. Normally, she managed to put it to the back of her mind, particularly since Carlos and herself had got married. She never mentioned Darren to Carlos at home as she didn't want to involve him in the situation. Although sometimes she would catch him looking at her with concerned eyes and know instantly that he was thinking of what might happen to her.

'We'll have a meeting after lunch when I've had a chance to absorb everything.' She indicated the paperwork on her desk. Minutes of meetings. Departmental reports. Accounts. And, to her relief, no letters from Darren.

'Will I get you a cup of coffee?' Cian asked.

'Thanks, would you?'

'Sure.'

Sipping her coffee, she went through the paperwork. She met Cian after lunch as arranged, but didn't hear anything from Carlos. Eventually, she left the office at about eight, and went home, delighted to find that Carlos drove into the carpark almost on her heels. They both parked, and she ran towards him when he climbed out of his jeep, and threw herself into his arms.

'Querida,' he murmured, holding her closely.

'I'm so glad to see you, come in, we'll have something to eat, you must be starving.' She kissed him.

She heated up the meal she had cooked the evening before, and they sat on the couch together to eat.

'I'm so happy to see you,' she smiled.

'I'm sorry I didn't even call you last night, but I was reluctant to wake you as I'm sure you were tired after the plane journey home.' He stretched out his hand and clasped hers.

'I don't know how you can work for so long without a break. You don't even look tired.'

'When you get to know a patient as well as I know this young man, it's like having another family who are all depending on me. So vulnerable. Waiting for me to come out of the theatre and tell them how their son is progressing. And if I show any anxiety on my face then they are all desperately worried immediately. And if I can help them come to terms with what might possibly happen then I must do that. It's my responsibility and I have to put them first in everything.'

'I never thought of it like that,' Alva admitted.

'And if the news is bad then I have to prepare them for that, and put myself into the background. It's very tough if I have to tell them that someone may have a very short time to live …' he leaned back on the cushions, obviously unable to finish the sentence. 'Or even that they will die in a matter of days.' He closed his eyes, his arm around her shoulder and fingers twisting through her dark shoulder-length hair.

She was silent, and couldn't think of what to say. So just leaned against him and hugged close. Wanting him to know that she understood. 'Is this patient going to …?' She couldn't say

51

the word "die". She hadn't realised the level of emotion which must fill Carlos every day he went to work. She hated herself for her ignorance. He hadn't ever spoken much about his day to day experience. And she didn't want to interfere. But this evening she felt she was meeting a new Carlos. A man with hidden depths.

'I'm sorry I don't know what to say,' she murmured, tears in her eyes.

'I'm just letting my emotions run away with me. Sorry.' He leaned down and kissed her.

'I'm worried about you.' She responded to his kiss.

'You don't have to be concerned about me, querida,' he smiled. 'Always remember that.'

'It's just that I really want to know everything about you, and not be a person who is completely involved in herself.'

'I feel we know everything about each other, and as each day passes, we become closer and closer, and that's the way I want to live with you. For always.' He kissed her again. 'Maybe you might find out that there are some things about me you don't like?' he smiled.

'To me you're perfect.' She hugged him.

'Then I had better be on my best behaviour from now on, I don't want to disappoint you.' He drew her close to him.

'I'll never be disappointed in you, but let's go to bed now, you've to be up early in the morning again.'

'I'll just make a quick call to the hospital,' he said and went to pick up his phone from the counter.

Alva finished clearing away the dishes, and went into the bedroom, already lying in bed when he arrived in. They lay together for a few minutes, arms around each other, and in spite of their exhaustion, they made love slowly, tenderly, and Alva remembered no more until she awoke the following morning when Carlos touched her face with his hand and pressed his lips on hers.

'I'm going, querida, I'll phone you later.'

'Have you had breakfast?'

'Just a coffee, I'll pick up something at the hospital.'

'What time is it?'

'Just after four.'

'So early.'

'I need to get in.'

'How is your patient.'

'They sent a text, he's holding his own.'

'Thank God,' she whispered.

'See you later.' He kissed her again before he left.

Chapter Eight

Julie had been very disappointed Pedro had not wanted to visit Dublin with her. Since she had found her Irish family again, she had such dreams about their joint families continuing to live together. Visiting each other in Seville and Dublin, sharing celebrations such as Christmas and Easter and of course the summer holidays in Cadiz. Now it seemed that Pedro was becoming disinterested. She couldn't understand that. When they had met last summer in Cadiz, and on the occasion of Carlos and Alva's wedding recently, Pedro had seemed to be really enthusiastic about meeting everyone in Julie's Irish family. But now to see that change in his disposition was worrying, even last night after dinner.

'You are sure you don't mind if I go to Dublin?' she had asked him.

'No, it is all right with me.' He shrugged.

'Will you miss me?' She went towards him, and sat on the arm of his leather armchair.

'I'm sure I will,' he said casually, and then pushed himself out of the chair. Poured a glass of sherry, wandered out on to the patio and sat down. Julie felt dismissed.

Things hadn't worked out quite the way she had hoped, and she prayed that they wouldn't worsen in any way. It would break her heart if that happened. But then she reminded herself that she shouldn't expect Pedro to embrace her Irish family. It would be too much to ask. And maybe he was worried that she might leave him and return to Ireland altogether. She was very involved with her three children now. Loving them so much. Especially David. Strangely, she felt part of him now. As if he was growing in her womb again and his vital organs were hers too. Suddenly she wanted to see him. To be with him. She opened up her phone, anxious to book a flight to Dublin as soon as possible. It didn't matter exactly what day. But perhaps it might be nice to spend the weekend in Dublin. She was always glad to come home to Pedro, reluctant to spend any longer than a couple of days away from him. He was the man who loved her more than anyone and she felt the same way about him. She hoped he wouldn't feel put out about the length of time she would be away.

She went out on to the patio and sat opposite him. 'I've booked a flight on Wednesday.'

'And when will you be back?'

'Monday.'

'Surely all you need is a couple of days?' he asked, surprised. 'What will you be doing while they are at work for that length of time?'

'Wander around the city. And they'll be free at the weekend.'

'You don't usually wander around?'

'I just felt I wanted to this time.'

'Go ahead, don't bother about us here,' he snapped. 'I have some meetings with clients set up, but if you're not too interested in being here, then …'

'It's not that I'm disinterested in meeting with clients, it's just I want to see my children.'

'But you saw them all at the wedding,' he pointed out.

'I know, but it was all rather rushed, I need to talk to them.'

'About what?'

'Nothing in particular, although there is the matter of what I might do with the money I inherited from Frank's will. There will be a meeting with the solicitor and decisions have to be made.'

'I don't know why you decided to re-invest the shares.'

'I want to put my inheritance back into the family company.'

He sighed. 'And have it squandered perhaps?'

'I hope not,' she said vaguely.

'Did I hear someone in the family mention there was a fraud committed in the firm?'

She looked at him, puzzled. 'No one told me that.' She was certain none of her children would deliberately do such a thing or conceal it.

'Apparently there were problems in the firm.'

'If it did happen then I'm not aware of it.'

'Then perhaps you shouldn't invest the money.'

'I'm willing to take a chance on it.'

'More fool you.'

She felt put down by Pedro for the first time, surprised at his rather scathing attitude towards her.

'Maybe you should talk to our accountants,' he suggested. 'They might give you some advice.'

She resented that. Did he think that she couldn't make a decision herself about what to do with her inheritance? 'I'll think about it.'

Pedro was still distant with her by the time she left Seville, and she felt somewhat guilty for going at all. As an unmarried couple, they had been so close since they met all those years ago, and it was a very strange thing for Julie to have to deal with such a change in their relationship. But something was pulling her towards Ireland and her children, and she couldn't resist. She tried to explain it to herself. Find out exactly why. But couldn't quite figure it out.

She made a decision not to tell her Irish children, Alva, David and Cian, that she was coming to Dublin, and hoped by doing that they would be happily surprised by her arrival. But at the same time, she didn't want them making plans. Arranging lunches and dinners and outings to make her trip more exciting, as she and Pedro had done when they came to visit them in Spain. Now she just wanted to be their mother. An ordinary person. Who would always be there in the background of their lives, and on whom they could depend totally. And who loved them more than she loved anyone else.

She called Alva first when she was in the taxi coming from the airport, having chosen a late flight so that her daughter would be finished work by then.

'How are you, Alva?'

'Lovely to hear from you, Mum.'

'Are you home yet?'

'I'll be there in about half an hour.'

'Could you come back a little earlier?'

'I could, why?'

'I'm on the way in from Dublin airport.'

'You are?' Alva sounded astonished.

'I decided to surprise you.'

'You've certainly done that,' she laughed out loud, sounding delighted.

'I'll finish off immediately. I hope you won't be at the apartment before me.'

'I'll wait in the taxi.' She didn't want to mention to Alva that Carlos had given her a key to the apartment so that she could open it and let herself in should he happen to be held up at the hospital. This was Alva's home now and it would be up to her to give Julie a key if she so wished.

Alva embraced Julie and they hugged tight. 'It's wonderful to see you, Mum. Let me take your case.'

'I was so sorry not to have seen you and Carlos after your honeymoon. It was such a pity you had to go back home so quickly. How is Carlos?' Julie asked, as they walked into the foyer of the apartment, and took the lift up.

'He was held up at the hospital in those first few days and was very worried about one of his patients who is stable now I'm glad to say.'

'Carlos worries too much about his patients. Always did,' Julie added.

'He doesn't show it,' Alva said. 'He always seems to be on top of everything.'

'I know him since he was a five-year-old child.'

'Of course you do, and I want to understand him, to know every last thing about him,' Alva said softly.

'But in many relationships that can take a long time,' Julie said.

'What was he like as a little boy,' Alva asked, with a smile. 'Come on, tell me, let me into his life.' Longing somehow to know more about her new-found mother, Julie, as well as the children she took care of in Spain.

'Serious, always reading books. Drawing. Doing scientific experiments with those sets we used to buy him.'

Alva laughed. 'I can see him trying to succeed, all enthusiastic, and then disappointed when it doesn't work.'

'With lots of explosions and sparks flying,' Julie laughed.

'You seem to have spent a lot of time with the children when you went to Seville at first?'

'I was so glad when Pedro offered me the job to look after his children. His wife had died and it was like I had been given another family. Although I had lost you, David and Cian, when I got to know Carlos, Nuria and Pacqui it was like I had a chance at another life.'

'It must have been very difficult for you. Pedro's family were strangers. And did they take to you? Children can be so strange in many ways. They either like you or don't, and there's not a lot you can do about it.'

'It was slow to start. They treated me like a maid at first, like any of the other staff around the house. But I spent so much time with them, taking them to school and picking them up, the girls went to flamenco classes, and Carlos studied guitar, and played football, so it was a busy household.'

'He studied guitar?'

'When he was young, but he didn't keep it up once he went to secondary school.'

'I know that he'll have no time now for playing guitar unfortunately.'

'I can understand that, he's a workaholic. I hope it won't be difficult for you to live with him ... I'm sorry, I shouldn't have suggested such a thing.' She looked at Alva with guilt in her eyes.

'I'm sure it won't be difficult, 'I'm just as bad really, I throw myself into my work. Anyway, I love him to bits.'

'And he tells me he feels the same,' Julie said.

'I was surprised when he told me you were so close,' Alva admitted.

'He was my eldest in my new family, and I loved him.'

'He was lucky to have you.'

'I was glad to be there for the family, they had lost their mother, and I was only a minor replacement.'

'I'm sure they appreciated you.'

'They certainly did, and Carlos was the first to show that connection.'

'He's a very loving person and I'm going to make him happy,' Alva said.

'I'm certain you will. When I saw how the two of you looked at each other on your wedding day I was convinced.'

'It was a wonderful day,' Alva remembered.

Just at that moment, her phone rang and she picked it up. 'It's Carlos,' she said. 'How are you, love?'

'I'm fine, querida.'

'When will I see you?'

'It shouldn't be too late, in about an hour I hope.'

'Great,' she was excited. 'And I've a nice surprise for you. Don't delay.'

'He'll be here in an hour.' She told her Mum.

'Lovely, I'll be so glad to see him,' Julie was delighted.

'I'll just get dinner.' Alva stood up and went into the kitchen to prepare it.

'I'll set the table.'

'Would you like a glass of wine?' offered Alva.

'No, thank you, water will be fine.'

She cooked fish, and made a salad, and was just ready when she heard Carlos turn his key in the front door.

Julie immediately stood up as Alva went towards the door, and hugged Carlos. But as he looked over her shoulder, his smile widened as he saw Julie standing there.

'Mum?'

She rushed over immediately and embraced him.

'This is certainly a surprise,' Carlos laughed, 'You've taken my breath away. Come and sit down, I want to talk.' He shepherded Julie over to the couch.

Alva went into the kitchen, to give mother and son a chance to chat on their own, and in about fifteen minutes she plated up and took a tray out to the table.

There was much chat between them. Julie bringing them up to date about what was happening in Seville and Carlos and Alva talking about their honeymoon.

'Are you going to go away again?' Julie asked. 'Take up where you left off?'

'We'd love to,' Alva said. 'Wouldn't we?' she smiled at Carlos.

'Somewhere altogether different perhaps or continuing your trip in Spain?'

'I'd love to go back to where we were. It was a beautiful place.' Alva was enthusiastic.

'I don't think I ever travelled that much in Spain, it's been mostly in the south,' said Julie.

'Dad isn't a holiday person, other than Cadiz in the summer. He can't be persuaded to leave his horses,' Carlos commented.

'They're his life.'

'The horses are all our lives.'

'How long are you staying, Mum?' asked Alva. Hoping it would be a few days.

'I want to catch up with you all, maybe we'll have a nice meal together,' Julie explained. 'Although I don't think your father is keen for me to be away for too long.'

'He hates to be left alone,' Carlos laughed.

'It's a little more than that,' Julie murmured softly.

'What do you mean?'

'It's as if he has suddenly become jealous of you,' she said, addressing Alva.

'Of me?'

'Of David and Cian too.'

'I'm surprised at that,' Carlos said. 'I didn't get that impression when we were at home for our wedding. In fact, he seemed very friendly towards all the Irish family.'

'It's just something between us,' Julie said slowly.

'Maybe you should be careful, it's foolish to allow jealousy to creep into a relationship. It can destroy the love that you have, Alva was about to say that to her mother, as she thought about her ex-partner Darren. Although she knew that seeing him with that woman on more than one occasion meant that she couldn't

61

possibly tolerate his behaviour as he seemed to expect. But she didn't think that Julie and Pedro's relationship was anything like Darren and herself, but still, any suggestion of jealousy was dangerous.

When she thought about her relationship with Carlos, she had wondered in the early days if she would be more pre-disposed to jealousy because of Darren's behaviour. She prayed that would never happen.

Chapter Nine

Julie called to see her son, David, and his wife, Sarah, and the children. It was especially important to her, although she didn't want him to realise exactly how much it meant. To see her grandchildren again was always special to her.

David put his arms around her, and held close. She hugged tight. Feeling again that mood which told her that he was part of her. A feeling that she was still carrying him, as she waited for her child to arrive.

'How are you, David?' she whispered.

'I'm fine, Mum.'

'I worry about you and always want to know how you are. So afraid that you might be ill. That the one kidney you have left will let you down. The one you've given to me is perfect but I don't want you to lose your life.'

She didn't want Sarah to overhear what she said, but was anxious for David to know how she felt. But could immediately sense that Sarah had overheard when she looked towards her and saw the fear in her eyes. She caught her glance and shook her head.

At that moment the door burst open and her two grandchildren, Sisi and Jon, ran in. Julie had presents for them, and the children were all excited as they pulled open the parcels and discovered what she had brought. After that, the kitchen was a mess with wrapping paper, and the toys. A new doll for Sisi and Lego for

Jon. But they weren't allowed to spend too much time playing at this time of night, and David took them off to bed while Julie helped Sarah in the kitchen.

'I'm sorry you overheard what I said to David,' Julie said to Sarah as she set the table.

'Don't worry.'

'Can you understand how I feel?'

Sarah nodded. 'It's the same way for me, worrying all the time that he won't live with one kidney.'

'I feel guilty,' Julie admitted.

'There's no need to feel that way, it's something he wanted to do himself, we did discuss it together at length of course,' Sarah said.

'I'm glad about that.'

'He wanted to give you what you gave him. His life.'

'Do you think he understands how much I appreciate his generosity to someone he really didn't know, Sarah?'

'I don't think you could say that. Even though you weren't around for most of his life he still knew he had a mother, and I know he longed to know you.'

'Did he?' Julie was surprised. 'I thought he hated me, particularly when he didn't come to meet me with Alva and Cian. I was disappointed. And there was never any explanation, just that he was busy. It seemed very strange.'

'He couldn't get the thought that you had left your children out of his head.'

'And he told you that?'

'Yes, and I wasn't able to persuade him to overcome those feelings when you met Alva.'

'He couldn't forgive me?' Julie was very upset.

'No.' Sarah checked the oven.

A wave of heat blasted out into the kitchen.

'This seems to be done,' Sarah said with a smile. Picked up

oven gloves, put them on, and took the roasting tin out.

'Looks delicious.'

'Just a simple roast chicken, with potatoes and veg.'

'Irish home cooking,' Julie said with a smile. 'It's a novelty for me, I've got so used to our spicy Spanish dishes, I'm looking forward to sharing this meal with you.'

'All asleep, and stories read,' announced David with a smile as he came in. 'What can I do?'

'Everything's ready, just sit down.' Sarah put the plates of food in front of them.

'I was just saying to Sarah that I love the Irish home cooking,' said Julie.

'And we all love the Spanish dishes, with plenty of garlic and chilli,' he smiled at her. 'And it's only because I spent all that time with you in Spain after our transplants that I fell in love with the cuisine.'

'That's wonderful,' replied Julie. Really pleased that he had said that.

His trip to Barcelona so that their kidney transplant could be performed had taken a large part out of his life and he had given that up voluntarily without a thought. She was so grateful to him and couldn't explain exactly how much she appreciated his generosity.

That evening was particularly pleasant, with just the three of them there, David and Sarah talking about their lives and the children. And her chance to play with Jon and Sisi before they went to bed was something she really enjoyed. Her grandchildren were very loving towards her and she wanted to take them home to Spain with her, the darlings. But as she lived so far away it wouldn't be possible to do that, until perhaps they were older and wanted to come to see their Nana themselves. They called Sarah's mother Gran, and they decided themselves that they would like to call Julie Nana.

The next day, she spent time with Alva, having lunch and shopping in town. Then home to relax. As the evening drew to a close, Julie mentioned one of the reasons why she had come over.

'I just want to ask if we could get together with your solicitor, John, to discuss what way I should invest my inheritance from Frank's estate in the family company?'

'Yes, I'm sure we could, I'll call John in the morning. He was on to me the other day as the probate is complete now and our inheritance is coming through at last,' she smiled. She knew how important it was to David as he had borrowed a sizeable sum from the bank to set up his new company.

Luckily, John was able to fit them into his schedule the following day and Alva, David and Cian managed to go in to meet him with Julie. She explained what she was thinking of doing and as she talked, he made notes.

'There are various approaches you could make to invest in the company, and I'll have a look at the possibilities for you. Now that probate is concluded Alva will supervise that and let you all know the amounts you each will receive from the estate.'

Before Julie left, they all got together for dinner. It was a jolly gathering, and she would have given anything to stay on in Dublin for longer. But she had been aware of Pedro's feelings about the length of time she intended to stay here and glad she was going back on Monday. And also, there was another reason for not overstaying her welcome. Now that Carlos and Alva were married, she couldn't just turn up unannounced whenever she felt like it the way she might have done when Carlos had lived alone. So now it made her feel hesitant about that, even though Carlos had always insisted that his spare bedroom was hers, and she should keep anything she needed there whenever she came over to see him. Also, she couldn't expect to stay with David or

Cian either. She could have booked a hotel, but the family would probably be insulted if she did that. She was in a quandary and didn't know quite what to do.

That evening, as Alva and Julie chatted after dinner, Julie was reminded of the remark Pedro had made about the company before she came over and decided that she should bring up the subject of fraud.

'I feel very awkward about this, but Pedro has told me that someone mentioned to him that there was fraud in the company. I wasn't aware of this, but I would be grateful if you could tell me,' she asked hesitantly.

'There was a group of people who tried to defraud the company, but when we discovered what had happened, rather than go to the Gardai, we asked them to resign, and we froze the funds which were in the British Virgin Islands and managed to eventually re-lodge it back into the company.'

'Who were the culprits?'

'Middle management, three of them.'

'Three?'

'Yes. And one of them was my ex-partner, and the company accountant was also involved.' Alva omitted to mention David was involved as well, it was just too sensitive since he had such a loving relationship with Julie now.

'It's amazing how they got away with it. How much money was involved?' Julie asked.

'Half a million euro.'

'That much?' Julie was astonished.

'Eventually it was my ex-partner who exposed them, he had done something really stupid.'

Alva took Julie to the airport the following afternoon. She was very emotional as they said goodbye.

'Take care, I'm going to miss you,' Alva said as she kissed her. 'Come over again soon, will you?'

'I will. I want to get to know all of you much better.'

As she said that, Julie thought how she wanted to know the deeper side of all of them. What way they thought when they were young children. And how they felt when they were growing into their teens and matured.

'I think I can see that you need to explore those empty spaces in your life which match the empty spaces in our lives, it's strange, but it's only us who understand that. No one else possibly can,' Alva said. 'It's like inserting pieces into a jigsaw and seeing the final picture emerge out of a mess of cardboard cut-outs.'

'You put it very well,' Julie smiled.

They hugged each other and said goodbye. Both in tears.

'It's been wonderful to see you, and I know Carlos feels the same. Come again soon.'

'Maybe you'd take a break with us?' Julie asked.

'As soon as we can.'

'I look forward to it.'

'Call me when you arrive back in Seville.'

'I promise.'

Julie waved goodbye to Alva, and found it hard to hide the emotion which swept through her. She was disappointed to leave at all, having wanted to stay longer on this trip. But she was glad to have had that meeting with her children and the solicitor, and also to have found out about the fraud which had happened, and was shocked that Alva's ex-partner was involved.

Pedro's attitude had put her off and now she was worried about his feelings towards her. But he had called her before she left, and seemed happy that she was coming home and had sent the limousine to pick her up. José was driving and she enjoyed chatting to him as they drove home from the airport.

As he swung through the high gates, and drove up the tree-lined avenue, she could see the house up ahead, brightly lit. Pedro stood on the patio waiting for her. When she stepped out of the car, he immediately came towards her and kissed her affectionately. She hugged him and returned his kiss. A sense of relief swept through her. He was his normal self, the man she loved, and who told her frequently that he loved her.

'Querida, how are you? The journey was not too tiring for you?' His hand curled over her hair gently.

'No, I'm fine, thanks. And you?'

'I am in good form, although are you in the mood for the visit of one of our clients. He couldn't make it at any other time.'

'Who is it?'

'Mateo.'

'I like him. But I'd better get ready quickly, I haven't much time.' She kissed him again, just wanting to indicate how much she loved him, and that she really didn't want to spend most of her time in Dublin as he had suspected.

'There's enough time, my love, no need to rush. I will be here to welcome him and we will be going down to the stables first.'

She took the lift up to their rooms, and quickly showered and dressed in a full-length black dress, with a side slash. She wore her diamond pendant, bracelet and matching earrings. Pedro always wanted to make an impression on his clients, and now she was only conscious of keeping him happy.

Dinner was served at ten o'clock, and their talk was all about horses. Mateo had a large number of pedigree horses and he was considering transferring them to Pedro's operation. He had very good reputation as a breeder and trainer and all the family were into horses. Now he wanted Mateo's business. It was a very pleasant evening. And Julie was glad to be home. Pedro never mentioned the length of her trips back to Dublin again.

Chapter Ten

Naomi's phone rang. She looked at the readout and was excited to see Darren's name there.

'How are you, Naomi?' Darren asked softly. His voice full of the promise of their first couple of nights together.

'I'm fine, Darren.'

'Are you home yet?'

'Just in.'

'I could call over if you like, I'll bring a bottle of wine.'

'I'm on a late shift tonight, I'll be leaving shortly.'

'That's a pity, I was hoping we could get together.'

'I'm sorry.' She was very disappointed.

'Tomorrow night?'

'Sorry, I'm on duty until Saturday.'

'What a job,' he burst out.

'I enjoy my work, although it's a bit unsociable.'

'You can say that again. When will I see you?'

'We could do something on Sunday if you like.'

'Let's do that. What time will I pick you up?'

'Afternoon.'

'About three?'

'Yeah. I will be well rested by then.'

'I'm looking forward to seeing you, I can't wait.'

She felt flattered by him. A way she hadn't felt in a long time. Although they only had two dates up to this. Dinner and a few drinks.

In her mind at first it had been just a simple catching up of friends who knew each other in the past. But his recent phone call had somehow taken her to a place of sensual desire. Suddenly she wanted to know more of him now. Beyond that of friendship. To discover another side to this man. She forgot about Alva. Forgot that Darren had been her partner. And that their lives had gone so badly wrong. And that he would pay for his violence towards her. She put all that out of her mind. She would find her own way into him. Get to know his inner depths. Was he as bad as Alva had painted him. Would he respond differently to her?

He called on Sunday as arranged. To her astonishment, he immediately embraced her in the doorway not even giving her a chance to say anything. She couldn't believe this was happening at last. His lips were gentle, pressing hers open, as he pushed closed the half open door behind him with one hand. But still pulling her towards him with the other. Their bodies clinging together sensuously.

He moved with her into the living room. She held on to him and they lay down on the couch. Now he seemed to infuse her with his being. Sweeping through her with a passion she couldn't resist, or understand. She wanted to discover him. To know him intimately. Everything about him. She persuaded herself that there had to be more to him. No one was inherently bad. There was good and bad in everyone. And she wanted to find the good in him.

His kisses became more ardent. His hands explored her. Her hands responded and within minutes their clothes had been discarded and lay around them. She was bewitched. She answered his advance with a soaring of her soul and gave herself to him with everything she possessed. She lapsed into this dream and didn't know herself any longer. Held in his arms she couldn't tell where she was. Simply absorbed in his promise. She didn't want this to end. Wanted it to last. For ever.

In her mind Alva didn't exist. This man had nothing to do with her. He was someone else. And Naomi had never met him before either. He was like someone from an alien world and she wanted him madly. To grab him and hold him tight. And get to know him so deeply she would probe the most intimate layers of him. Longing for him to be there for her whenever she wanted him. He whispered words of love. Something she could barely believe. He loved her. Saying over and over how much he felt for her, and how much he wanted her. Their lovemaking was so intense she was carried to a place of utter satisfaction in its passion.

'I love you,' Darren murmured softly again.

In reply she wound her arms around him, her lips touching his, and held him to her. Needing to persuade him that she felt as strong as he did about her.

He looked at her, his large blue grey eyes persuading her that his feelings were genuine. She couldn't believe it. So sudden was this unexpected love, she was almost moved to tears.

'Naomi, I want you,' he murmured. 'Be mine.'

She didn't reply, suddenly reluctant to commit herself. She couldn't do that. It was too risky. Alva's face flashed into her mind. Smiling. And that image caused her to stiffen. To freeze. And know that she was hurting her friend. She felt guilty and questioned herself. Why are you doing this? Looking into the eyes of the man Alva had loved so much and had given her very self to him.

In the days following, Naomi's life completely changed. She went into her job. Kept to her shifts. And tried to concentrate on what she had to do. She was on a team who were investigating a murder case and it demanded her complete attention. She split herself in two very glad to be able to switch off and spend time with Darren. There wasn't anyone in her life who had time to spend with her either. Alva was her only friend but she was as busy as she was herself, and now that she was married Naomi couldn't expect her to be available whenever it suited. Carlos worked very long hours as well although she spent a lot of time waiting for him to come home. That knowledge made Naomi think that if she ever had a partner, she might even give up her work, and choose a job which would give her more regular hours. Relationships couldn't be expected to survive under the conditions she currently worked. That thought caused a flutter of excitement in her heart as she wondered if Darren might continue to figure in her life.

Her phone rang and she picked it up. It was Alva.

'Hi there?' she managed to sound normal, at least she thought she was, although that was becoming more and more difficult.

'Are you home yet?'

'Yes, I'm here.' Naomi admitted that fact before she even thought about it.

'I'll finish up here about eight, and I thought I'd call around to you.'

Naomi was caught out. What if Darren decided to call around unexpectedly, or even telephone. How would she explain that to Alva?

'Sorry, I'm in the middle of a report which I have to finish for the morning.' She found an excuse immediately. But it was a lie.

'Oh …'

Naomi could hear disappointment in Alva's voice.

'Sorry about that.'

'Not to worry. Maybe I'll see you next week,' she suggested.

'Yeah, sure, give me a call,' Naomi said. Immediately aware that this could prove to be very awkward.

'Look forward to seeing you then.'

Naomi stared down at the photo of Alva on her What's App page. Guilt again sweeping through her. If Alva ever found out that she was with Darren then their friendship was over. Could she deal with that situation? Lose Alva to gain Darren. She wasn't sure. While she had known Alva since she was five years old, Darren might love her for much longer. It was a hell of a choice. Love over friendship.

Her doorbell rang later, and while her first thought was that Alva had decided to call in for a few minutes only, she was shocked to hear Darren's voice on the intercom.

'Thought I'd take a chance that you'd be home,' he said, a laughing undertone in his voice.

For a minute she didn't know what to say. Should she invite him in, and take the chance that Alva wouldn't decide to call in as well? But she couldn't resist his allure. 'Come on up,' she said. A wide smile on her face. Immediately she rushed into the bathroom and quickly applied lipstick, and combed her hair. Then she went to open the front door and saw him standing outside.

'Darren?' She stretched out her hands towards him, drew him inside and closed the door.

He moved closer. His arms encircled her and he kissed her softly. 'It's so good to see you, I've missed you. I felt if I rang you then you might say no, and I'd be devastated,' he smiled. 'It's hard to judge a different relationship with someone.'

'It can be, but I'd like to think that you knew me for a long time.'

'Loved you for a long time. Looking at you across the room. Various rooms over the years. Always wanting you. Trying to persuade myself that I had to hold back and just look. You were the prize in the window.'

'And I had you in my sights as well. And you were Alva's. That was the worst part of it.'

74

'Come here to me.' He held her even closer, his lips explored hers, and he drew her down on the couch and they began to make love. It was slow at first. Naomi encouraged him to explore her and search for those delicate little places which would send her into paroxysms of delight and she was then able to let him know how much he meant to her.

'I want you so much,' he whispered. 'I want to shout it out loud so everyone will know.'

'Maybe not yet,' she cautioned him.

'You're right, that would be risky,' he smiled.

'We'll keep it to ourselves for now,' she suggested. 'It will be our secret.' Immediately thinking of Alva and Carlos and that family, both the Irish side and also the Spanish side. And how they might react to hearing that she was now with Darren. 'No, it could explode and demolish what we have.'

'Let's be careful. I want you to myself anyway, I don't want to share you with anyone else. Do you mind?' He caressed her face with his hands.

'All right, it's what I want as well,' she said gently. Anxious to let him know.

'It could cause a problem with my court case coming up, although I don't know when that will be.'

'I'd forgotten that,' she admitted. 'Are you very worried about it?'

'Of course I am, it's weighing me down like a huge stone. I'll probably be turfed out of my job if I get a prison sentence.'

'You may get off. I've seen many a case dismissed because of insufficient evidence,' she said, adamant.

'Would you be able to look into it for me? Check what they have on me?'

'That could be difficult, it's not in my department and I'm not even sure who is handling it. Why don't you talk to your solicitor? He'll have all the detail.'

'He's useless. As I had no job at the time they gave me free legal aid, but I always think those solicitors are a waste of space.'

'But you've a job now, you could employ someone better, it would make all the difference. And you'd need a barrister as well.'

'I don't have that sort of money.'

'Have you admitted guilt.'

'The solicitor thought I should as the Gardai found me in the apartment and I suppose there was no point saying I wasn't guilty.'

'That's good, it will help. I'll do as much as I can for you, I promise.' She kissed him.

'Thank you.'

Naomi met Alva the following week. As ever, both of them were committed to their work and there was very little chance these days to get together. They loved the opportunity to sit down and catch up with what was happening in their lives.

'You're looking good. Married life is obviously agreeing with you,' she laughed. Envious of Alva.

'I have to admit we are very happy, but I don't see that much of Carlos. His work is so challenging. But still, I work long hours too. And we don't make any demands on each other.'

'It's an unusual way to live,' Naomi observed.

'Perhaps, but it's the way it is now, but hopefully it will improve as time goes by. I know Carlos had every intention of achieving some sort of a compromise when we first decided we were going to live together.'

'It can take time to adjust to a new life.'

'We're in no hurry, life is wonderful,' Alva said.

'It could be tough.'

'Was there any contact from Carlos's friend you met at our wedding?' asked Alva.

'No,' Naomi said.

'And?'

'Well …'

'You're being very coy,' Alva giggled. 'Come on, you have to tell me.'

'He never even asked me for a date.'

'He seemed so keen.'

'You're imagining that.'

'He even mentioned it to Carlos. If he asks you out, just go along with it. Give the man a chance,' encouraged Alva.

'It will never go any further, there's actually someone else.'

'What?'

'Someone I've known for a while.'

'Who is it?' Alva was very curious.

'I don't want to say …yet.'

'Hey Naomi, what's going on with you?'

'Nothing.'

'Is it someone in the job? Someone you work with closely?'

Naomi nodded.

'I thought you said you wouldn't consider getting involved with anyone in work again?'

'This was unexpected.'

'Is he free?'

'Yes. Is that vital, do you think?'

'I don't suppose it is. Although it could make life much more difficult if he happened to have a wife and family.'

'You can relax, he doesn't.'

'You seem …' Alva stared at Naomi.

'What?'

'I don't know, you're different somehow tonight.'

'In what way?'

'I don't mean to criticise you.' Alva didn't know what more to say.

'I hope not.' Naomi had an edge in her voice.

'This relationship will work out, I know it,' reassured Alva. 'I only want the best for you.'

'Thanks.'

'When will you see him again?'

'Not sure, both of us are very busy.'

'It's the same for everyone,' Alva laughed. 'Just life. And it must be awkward when you meet in the corridor, or at meetings. Taking a glance at each other and hoping no one appears out through a door and notices. Is it the same guy you fell in love with before?'

'No, it's not him.'

'Possibly better then, a new broom.'

'I'm hoping,' Naomi tried to give the impression of happiness.

'I'm delighted for you. Do you think it's a runner?' Alva grinned.

'Don't know. By now I'm inured to feeling positive about relationships with anyone. Do you think that's crazy?'

'You shouldn't feel like that. If it's for you, it won't pass you by. Isn't that the old motto. My father always said that,' Alva laughed.

'As did mine.'

'Then it will happen,' Alva persuaded. 'Never fear. There's always someone out there for you. You've met some very nice guys so far, maybe this one will prove to be the man.'

'Maybe,' Naomi said slowly. She felt very confused.

'You'll have to tell me who he is, I'm eaten up with curiosity. Go on, just a whisper,' Alva giggled.

'I will as soon as I can, I promise.'

Keeping the identity of this new person in her life from Alva was something she had never done before. They had always shared everything in their lives up to this. From their early days at school, where they had gone every day, hand in hand, sharing everything which happened between them. Sitting together at their desks in the front row of the class, answering the questions set by the teachers, and trying always to answer as well as they could. They wanted to be the best in the class when the teachers set the weekly tests and to their delight often achieved top marks. Their friendship was strong and lasted all these years, and now to keep this secret from her best friend cut through Naomi. But what to do? She asked herself. That was the question. She loved Alva and hated what she was doing to her. Always wondering if Alva would object to the fact that she had now chosen a man who would not be an agreeable choice to her friend.

Chapter Eleven

Alva went through the accounts paying a great deal of attention to every figure. Since the fraud was committed on the company, she was even more careful to ensure that such a thing would never happen again. It had been a terrible experience and it took her right back to that time her father had died, and the loss of the company he had built had possibly been the cause of his death. To think that three people in management had actually stolen money out of the company and when she had discovered what had happened, had insisted that they resign, and return the money. Her decision was taken for financial reasons, as she felt that the amount of money needed to take the fraudsters to court would use up all of the funds in the Caribbean bank account. Purtell Vintners was almost about to collapse and there had to be many changes made so that the business would continue to stay afloat.

Now she was happy. They were able to continue running their wine company once again. And it was viable. Also, her mother Julie wanted to invest money she had inherited from Alva's father's estate and she knew that would help. She was very grateful to her Mum and loved to see her when she had an opportunity to visit from Spain. Alva would have given anything to see her more often, but she didn't come over very much now. Alva was lonely too. Carlos was working as hard as ever and while she didn't want to complain, she missed him terribly. Her hours weren't much better but she could have reduced them if he happened to be home more often, but not seeing him until quite late at night was very difficult for her. Particularly when he had to work overnight on urgent cases.

Tonight wasn't much different to other nights. It was about ten thirty and she was on her laptop, catching up on the day's work, praying that she would hear Carlos's key in the lock any moment. But another hour passed before that happened and when she heard him open the door, she rushed to meet him.

'My love, how are you?' she put her arms around him. 'You look exhausted.' She kissed him.

'I am all right,' he put down his briefcase in the hall, and returned her embrace.

'Come in and have something to eat, you must be starving.'

'I had a snack earlier.'

'I've cooked some paella, just have a little,' she coaxed.

'Let me just shower first and I'll eat then.'

'I'll warm it up and we'll have it together.'

'Thank you, querida,' he smiled.

Quickly, she prepared the meal.

'This is delicious, pet.' He put his arm around her shoulders. 'Better than anything we'd get in Spain.'

Alva giggled, and helped herself to a forkful.

'It's so good to see you home earlier than usual tonight, I really miss you, it's very hard.'

'I'm sorry, but my patients need a lot of care. I know I promised you that I'd change and take more time off, but it's proving very difficult to keep my word.'

'It's hard for you, I know that, but we don't spend enough time together.' Tears filled her eyes. 'I love you so much, but you're not here for me. I'm lonely.'

'I am a hopeless husband.' He took her hand. His eyes meeting hers. 'I've tried, but the health service doesn't allow. Even trying to get a theatre when I need it is difficult sometimes. Taking time off is almost impossible.'

'I understand how it is with you. We did go out to dinner last Saturday night, but it's been three weeks before that since we went anywhere, even a walk or to see a film. I shouldn't complain but when night after night passes without even seeing you until the small hours, I find it terribly difficult.'

'You have every right to complain. I haven't done what I promised when we were married. I feel guilty.'

'Don't blame yourself. I love you so much, I want to be with you all the time. I can cut back on my own work just to be home early if you're here.'

'It's very hard for me to choose. I can't decide to finish at seven or eight when a patient needs care.'

'I understand, my love. Truly I do.'

'Maybe I shouldn't have asked you to marry me.' He took her hand. 'It is too much of a sacrifice for you. For me, I was so sure that I would be able to change my life. Spend less time in the hospital. Take weekends off so that we can be together from Friday to Monday. But it seems I'm not able to do it. I feel so ashamed.' He leaned closer and embraced her. 'Querida, I don't know what to do.' He sighed deeply and seemed very concerned.

'We love each other, there's no doubt about that,' she said, reluctant to even mention that there might be another course of action. She couldn't even countenance anything else. It would have broken her heart completely.

'I love you so much you don't even realise how deep my feelings are for you,' he said.

'I do, Carlos, and I feel the same as you.'

'I am afraid I will lose you,' he murmured.

'That will never happen, my love.' She tried to persuade him to avoid that way of thinking.

'I have a dread of it. It's always there in the back of my mind. Always. pounding on my brain. I can't escape it.' He thumped his forehead with a fist. Hard. 'I see you walk away. Just turning and going. Without even a bag. Just you. Not even saying goodbye.' He looked up at her. His dark brown eyes so loving.

She put her arms around him and pulled him to her. They hugged together. His head leaning on her shoulder. 'We'll make it through, Carlos, don't worry.'

They made love there on the couch. Threw off their clothes and took hold of each other as if they had already parted. Holding tight to prevent the other slipping out of their arms. A feeling of loss suddenly permeated the room which was keenly sensed by Alva. Their lovemaking was emotional and she had never wanted Carlos so much as she did tonight.

'Come to bed, querida,' he whispered, and together they went into the bedroom, lay on the bed and held tight, bodies clinging to each other.

'I love you,' Alva said.

'Te amo,' Carlos murmured softly. Caressing her face with his lean dark fingers. 'Let me love you forever, Alva, please? Never leave me?'

'I will love you forever, Carlos, and I promise I will not leave you.'

'I will try to improve myself,' he smiled.

'That sounds like there's something wrong with you,' she laughed out loud.

'There is. I am a very bad husband.'

'No, you're not,' she smiled. 'Never say such a thing. You're my husband and a perfect one. I am very lucky.'

As Alva parted from Carlos the following morning, each going to their day's work, she felt guilty that she had mentioned that she was lonely for him the night before. She hadn't intended to do that, but the words just suddenly burst out of their own accord. There was something inside her that needed to be said. To tell Carlos how she was feeling. So that he would understand her deepest thoughts. And know how she longed for him.

But she didn't know whether she could live with him. She loved him deeply but was she the right person for him. That question echoed in her heart. Could she force him to live the way she wanted. That wouldn't make him happy, she was certain. His heart was with his patients, and his greatest wish to make them well again. All he wanted was to save lives.

She had a busy morning, and because the sales manager for France was ill, she had to arrange to travel to see some new clients there a couple of days later. She couldn't cancel all the appointments which had already been arranged and felt that Carlos might think she had deliberately decided to go away just so he would feel that she had wanted to leave him. Let him know how it might be to lose her. 'I have to go to France for a few days next week, my love, but I'd rather not.'

'When will you be home?'

'Saturday.'

If you have to go, then I'm going to miss you.'

'Sorry.' She felt guilty all over again.

'I'll be waiting,' he smiled. 'I will organise something when you come back, I'll surprise you,' he kissed her.

She enjoyed being away for those few days. Flying to the south of France where the sun shone warmly on the vineyards from morning to evening. Meeting with the owners and deciding on which wines she would choose to purchase for next season. Tasting the different flavours they presented to her and hoping that her choices would prove to be popular with her clients.

Most of the vineyards were in the countryside, and she

enjoyed driving out into the famous wine region. Bordeaux was home to a number of wonderful vineyards and fantastic chateaux. The land was grown with acres of vines and north of Bordeaux was best known for red wines, and south for white. Their company, Purtell Vintners, already bought wines from a number of vineyards and she enjoyed meeting new owners on this trip and she placed a number of orders for their next season, particularly interested in their organic wines.

Each evening she was entertained by the individual vineyard owners, which was very pleasant and it was only when she arrived back at her hotel that she managed to get a chance to call Carlos. Although she actually only spoke to him on one evening. So far away she couldn't bear their separation. Back in Dublin at last, she brought some wine with her, and picked up an Indian takeaway on the way, hoping that he would be home.

She had phoned when she landed but there was no response from him. Suddenly she felt that perhaps he had some other reason for spending so much time away from her. Her heart thumped with dread and she had to force herself from going down the road of negative thinking once again. She couldn't do that. Although she knew that she was predisposed to that possibility because of her experience with Darren. God forbid Carlos wasn't involved with some other woman. It could happen to anyone she knew. And she was certain that there were a lot of very attractive women at the hospital. He did spend an inordinate amount of time working late. She set the table. And tried to prevent the wave of suspicion from taking her somewhere she didn't want to go.

She was only in a short time when she heard his key in the door.

'Querida, it's good to see you,' he murmured, holding her so tight she could barely breathe. 'I have spent this last week rolling around that big bed on my own. Every time I moved, I could feel cold draughts. Before I met you, I never noticed how big it was, now it seems like it's as big as a football field. I don't think I can bear to sleep there on my own.'

'It was the same for me,' she laughed.

'That's so good.' He kissed her.

As she returned his kiss those suspicions which had spring into her mind were all forced out again. She couldn't countenance such things about Carlos. He didn't deserve it.

'Let's have dinner.'

'Si, I'll help you.'

'I brought some wine.'

'I'll have to raise a glass of water to you.'

'Sounds exciting.'

'We'll get away somewhere soon and there will be no patients waiting for treatment.'

'I'm looking forward to it.'

They walked into the lounge, and together they plated up their meal and sat down to eat. She poured a glass of wine for herself, and afterwards, she made coffee for them both.

'I have to be honest, Carlos,' Alva said.

'About what?' he asked, looking surprised.

'Since I haven't seen very much of you, I began to think that you might have been seeing someone else.'

He stared at her. There was silence for a moment. 'How could you think such a thing of me?' he asked slowly. A look of horror in his dark eyes.

'I have to admit I'm very unsure of myself since I was living with Darren, somehow I can't help it. Before that I was very different, I was confident, I knew what I was about, but now I'm not that person any longer, and suspicions can come into my head without warning and I can't get rid of them.' Tears flooded her eyes.

'Querida,' he put his arms around her and pulled her close to him. 'There is no one else in the world I love more than you. It would be impossible for me to even look at another woman and feel anything for her. And it is not in my nature to do that. You are the only one I have ever met since I came to Dublin to study in whom I had any interest. I did have friends of course, and teenage romances too which were physical as well as emotional, but that is all about growing up. During my working years as a doctor there was no one special until you came along. Maybe you find that hard to believe but I am telling you the truth.' He kissed her. 'And I would never deceive you, living with such lies is not me and I could not do it. I can remember how Darren treated you, and I would certainly never disrespect you or put you through such trauma ever again.'

'I'm sorry to have accused you.' Alva regretted her words now. 'I shouldn't have said such a thing or even thought about it. It's not as if I had any proof, it's just all in my mind. My imagination. Carlos, can you ever forgive me?' she begged.

'You do not have to apologise, my love, I will never expect it. I should be the one to apologise.'

'Not you. It's my fault.' She embraced him. 'I don't deserve you.'

'I don't want you to worry about our marriage, Alva. I take all the blame.'

'I have exaggerated everything,' she said.

'I must examine how much I have contributed to your upset. To the way you feel.'

'But I understand that you have to work long hours, it just got to me. You explained it all to me before and I obviously didn't realise what it would do to me. When I was with you before we got married, somehow I never noticed how you lived.'

'You had a lot going on then, all those problems in the company because of the fraud. I don't know how you could even think of anything else and that included me. But now I must make an effort to change, I promise I will do that, I love you so much.' He kissed her.

Alva was grateful that Carlos seemed to understand how she felt. But at the same time, she knew that if he couldn't manage to change his working hours then she might not be able to control the anxiety which she suffered from now. And however hard she might try would that ever be enough to persuade Carlos to make some change to his working schedule and would she be able to accept it however insignificant? Seeing so little of him, would the man she married be the person she had always hoped to be her husband. And would their relationship improve as he had promised. Was that ever going to be possible?

Chapter Twelve

Darren waited. He had parked his car close to Alva's office again. Any time he was in the area he could be found there. And he enjoyed it. So much. The fact that she hadn't a clue he was nearby made it all the more gratifying and he found himself laughing inside every time he thought of it. He wanted to boast to everyone he met that he would get her back, especially Hugh. They had met a couple of times recently, and he always enjoyed his company. But didn't dare open his mouth about what he did in the shadows of his life.

'How is Alva these days?' he had asked on that last occasion. Very anxious to find out how she was.

'I haven't heard. I didn't meet anyone from the company lately.'

Darren was disappointed. 'How is your own business?'

'Still going well. It was unfortunate we lost the money we had stashed away in the Virgin Islands. Our plans to build a hotel would have been up and running by now only for …' he hesitated.

Darren felt he was referring to his own mistake of keeping the bank statements at home, and which Alva had found.

'And even if we hadn't decided to go down that route, I could certainly do with the money now.'

'You're not the only one,' Darren quipped.

'Although the accountancy business is successful enough, I

may need to invest more into it before long. To keep up with all the clients, I must employ more staff.'

'I could work with you. Would you have a position for me?' Darren asked enthusiastically.

'I don't think you'd suit us, Darren. You've always been in sales. That's your forte.'

'But I could work around that. Surely you can find something?' He was trying too hard, he realised that, but he would have given anything to work with Hugh. In spite of the fact that he had resigned from Purtell Vintners as well as he had himself, he had managed to establish himself without any problem and now was obviously on the way up. David, Alva's own brother, had also been involved in the fraud, and he had already set up his own wine company, and was doing very well too.

He was the only one of the three of them who wasn't in a position to set himself up. He was even suspicious of both David and Hugh. Where did they get the money to invest in new companies? Had they been stealing money from Purtell Vintners before they even admitted it to him. Of course, he had overheard them talking about their plans one evening when they were having a few drinks, and after one too many, suddenly he was part of the group.

Of course, Darren didn't appreciate that it was purely through Alva's generosity that they had been allowed to resign from the company, hadn't been arrested or had to face the rigour of the law.

His own job in the hardware company was going quite well, and he hoped to climb the ladder. The MD, who was also the owner, kept a tight rein on everyone, and it didn't seem like there was much opportunity for promotion. And when his court case happened in the future, it would probably quash any chance of success at all, that's if the boss heard anything about it. His one hope was that as he had admitted his guilt the judge would look kindly on him and maybe give him a suspended sentence. After all, he had never been in court before for any incursion of the law and he had heard many reports of other people who didn't serve any time at all for their various crimes. Anyway, he didn't consider what he did to be a crime. After all, Alva had been his partner, and she had thrown him out of their apartment just because he had strayed a little. Every man strayed, he said to himself, looking for excuses. And that woman he had met had pushed her way into his life, and he hadn't been able to resist her. Alva had been away, and what else was he to do? This woman wanted him. She had made that very clear. He didn't love her, it was just sex. And he told her so. But she wouldn't back off when he wanted her to get out of his life.

He had told her he had a partner and that there was no future for them. There were times he thought that he could manage to play around with her, and continue living with Alva, but when he was caught by her with the woman a third time, it seemed very unlikely, yet he was more than surprised when Alva gathered his stuff in the hall, and told him to get out. It was her apartment after all, he had to admit to himself. His idea of looking for a position in Hugh's company suddenly seemed to be rather juvenile, he would never give him a job. Bastard. Hugh probably thought he was at the bottom of the barrel in Purtell Vintners as both David and himself were much higher up the scale in the company than he had been. His confidence had been dealt a heavy blow after that whole episode, particularly when he was out of a job altogether.

It was after eight. Alva didn't know the car he was driving now so wouldn't notice that he was there. He waited for the lights to go out in the offices. That was the signal. Alva was always last to leave. He straightened up in the seat. His heart began to thump. He ran his fingers through his short hair. Ready to meet her if the opportunity presented itself. But something stopped him. He would be in trouble with the Gardai if he did that. Alva had taken a barring order out against him and his solicitor had warned him about breaking it. He had listened to what the man had said, but didn't really take it on board. If she didn't know he was there, what harm was there in it. He climbed out of the car. Hugging the shelter of other buildings, dodging in and out of doorways where he could find shadow. He reached the exit to the underground carpark and went inside. It was dimly lit, and he was glad of that as his eyes searched for Alva's red BMW in her usual parking space. But he couldn't see it as he darted from pillar to pillar so that if she suddenly appeared out of the lift, he could remain hidden. At this time of the evening there weren't many cars here, and he stood there waiting. His chest expanded and his breath was short. He tried to calm himself but didn't succeed. With the possibility of seeing Alva at any moment, his hands sweated profusely. He dried them on the sides of his jacket reluctant to meet her in that condition, she wouldn't appreciate his sticky palms touching her.

He heard the sound of the lift as it arrived into the basement. His heart thumped and he smiled, anticipating the moment he would reveal himself. There was a musty aroma in the place and fumes of diesel and petrol and it took him back to when he worked there too. He stayed hidden behind a pillar and prayed it was Alva who would appear. The door slid back. She stepped out carrying her briefcase in one hand and the laptop in the other. He bit his lip. It was painful. He could taste blood. He wiped it and stared down at the streak which appeared on his hand. Fuck. A car alarm flashed across the carpark. It was a dark red Mercedes. He was puzzled and only after a few seconds he realised that she had changed her car and parking space.

She opened the boot and put the laptop and briefcase in. He stepped forward anxious to get to the car before she drove off.

But she slid into the driver's seat and banged the door closed. The idea of rushing across and climbing into the back occurred to him. If he ran quickly she would be unaware of his presence. But he didn't make it in time, as with a screech of tyres she put the boot down and drove quickly up the ramp. He was left there staring after the car. A flood of joy swept through him. To have actually been that close to her after all this time was so satisfying he could imagine the scent of her perfume. She always used that same one and it brought him back to when they had lived together and she had loved him and he had loved her, bound together like a pair of swans who would never mate with any other swan for the rest of their lives. But she had turned against him and married that Spanish guy when he had wanted to marry her. That was his plan. He could see children playing in a sunlit garden and felt a dreadful feeling of loss. He couldn't imagine how he would live without Alva.

He ran out of the carpark on to the street, disappointed that he couldn't see Alva's car, it had disappeared. He should have been sitting in his own car when she drove out and followed her. But then, it would have been the wrong car. He was glad that he knew that. He took out his phone and called Naomi. But all he could hear was the rather impersonal voice asking him to leave a message. He didn't bother.

Chapter Thirteen

Alva waited for Naomi to return home. She had texted that she had been delayed and Alva found the waiting intolerable. Somehow, it reflected her own life. The only part of which she could control was her work. These days, herself and Cian were very much on top of the business. She was particularly happy with the Sales Manager for France who seemed to know the market incredibly well by now. Alva knew that her father would have been delighted with the achievements they had made. She thought of him now. Remembering how he kept the company on an even keel for all the years. A man who loved the wine business and certainly would never have wanted to retire but would have worked his butt off until he eventually was forced to give up if perhaps his health had failed. Still she often felt that his sudden death was a blessing in disguise. She would not have wanted him to endure a long illness like some other family members. That unexpected parting had been the best thing for him, although for herself and all the family it had been a terrible shock.

The carpark was lit up suddenly by headlights as Naomi drove up to the gates. Alva flashed her own car headlights, followed her in and parked. She climbed out, and picked up a bouquet of flowers which she had bought at the florist.

'Sorry to be so late.' Naomi called out.

'A few flowers,' Alva handed her the bouquet.

'Thank you so much, these are beautiful.' She breathed in the scent of the blooms.

They took the lift up.

'How is Carlos?' asked Naomi.

'He's all right, when I see him,' Alva said, with a rather grim look on her face.

'Is he still working late every night?' Naomi asked.

'I can never be sure what time he'll be home.' Alva hadn't wanted to complain, but it was very hard not to. It was something very close to her heart and always spurted out whenever she was with Naomi. She could really confide in her friend which was something she couldn't do at all with the family. To have to admit she had made a mistake in deciding to marry Carlos was not anyone else's business and she felt ashamed. How could she ever tell them that the wonderful wedding which had taken place only a couple of months ago had been a complete sham?

The two girls chatted on for a while, although again Alva felt there was something strained about their conversation.

'Naomi, how is your new man?'

She smiled. 'It's all going really well.'

'That's great.' Alva was particularly pleased for her. 'Can you divulge his identity yet?'

'No, unfortunately.'

'That's such a pity, I'd love to meet him. I'll have to give him the once over, to be sure that he's going to make you happy,' Alva said.

Naomi shook her head.

'There's something about him then, maybe a lot of baggage?'

'Perhaps.'

Alva was quiet for a moment, unsure what to say. 'It looks like we both have problems,' she said.

Naomi looked at her sympathetically. 'Yes.'

An unusual awkwardness crept between them. 'To be honest, I'm beginning to wonder whether Carlos wants to be with me at all,' Alva said. 'I can't get that out of my head however much he tries to persuade me that he loves me and only me. Maybe he doesn't even have any interest in changing his working life. I really wonder if that will ever happen.'

'But you love him, don't you? I remember how you described your feelings when you first met. Love of your life you said.'

'He was …he is.' Alva hesitated.

'Why not book a weekend away, surprise him,' Naomi suggested.

'He said he was going to do that but I had to go to France on business so it didn't happen. Maybe I'll arrange it instead, thanks for suggesting it.' Alva was suddenly filled with enthusiasm.

'Where will you go? Paris maybe? Very romantic?'

'If I arrange all of that and then he has an urgent case he mightn't be too pleased, and feel guilty that he can't get away.'

'But I thought you'd continue your honeymoon in Spain, has he made any suggestions about that?'

Alva shook her head. She had waited for Carlos to do that, but so far there had hardly been time to even discuss the possibility. Even when Julie had come over from Spain and asked when they would be over to Seville, he hadn't given her a straight answer.

'Just mention it, but don't go into detail. If you have to cancel then you can do that without him knowing.'

'I'd love that, a few days in Paris sounds heavenly.'

'It was a wonder he arranged time off to get married. And I don't think you're happy, in fact I know it.' Naomi peered at her quizzically.

'And you could do the same,' added Alva. 'Surprise your new man and maybe we could make up a foursome. You would be completely incognito and no one would be aware that you were a couple. How about that?'

'No, we couldn't take that chance.'

'But we'd give our word not to mention you were a couple, I promise,' Alva said. Although she knew in her heart of hearts

that she wanted to be away with Carlos on their own. She needed
to get to know him all over again. He had drifted away from her
and she felt his loss keenly. Where are you, Carlos, she asked
from somewhere deep inside. But there was no answer. And she
didn't know whether he still loved her or not.

'Thanks, but that wouldn't be possible,' Naomi said slowly.

'I think we're both in a quandary somehow,' Alva said.

'Not for the first time in our lives,' Naomi agreed wryly.

'And we'll have to sort it out together.'

'We always have. And I'll never forget your wedding day.
There is no way you can turn away from Carlos. He's a lovely
guy.'

'I love him, but I don't know if I can live with him.' Her eyes
moistened.

'What about Saturday and Sunday?'

'He could be called in then as well. He has a lot of patients. I
can't ask him to turn away from them and not be available. It's
their lives.'

'But you're important in his life too.'

'I know that.'

'He shouldn't have married you if he couldn't offer you a
decent life.'

'He did promise to change.'

'That's all very well, but he has to seriously consider how he
might do that.'

'It's hard for me to say it to him.'

'Maybe you're being too easy. Why should you sacrifice
yourself to his work? You should get back to working out in
the gym, like you used to do. And don't forget about yoga and
Pilates, you always enjoyed both of them.'

'Since Covid they've been on hold.'

'Well, fill your evenings with other things.'

'I must do that. Carlos has gone back to the gym at six in the morning.'

'Why don't you go too?'

'Maybe I will, I'm awake at that time anyway as he is up.'

'At least you'll be doing something together.'

'Yes, that's a good idea. I might.' Alva was grateful to Naomi for her interest. She could always talk to her about anything and knew the advice she would give was always down to earth and reliable. 'You're so wise.'

'That sounds like I'm an old witch,' Naomi giggled.

'The three witches in Macbeth, stirring the cauldron and chanting spells.'

'I wish I could cast some spells, be able to make some wishes come true.' Naomi pulled a face.

'What would you wish for? Top of your bucket list?'

'I suppose I'd love this new relationship to become a reality.'

'Why not? Does he seem to be really keen?'

'He does, but you know how things can disintegrate without warning. I'm afraid of that.'

'That's you being negative. There's no point thinking that way. Look to the future, and be positive,' Alva urged.

'I find it difficult.'

'Naomi, you've met someone now, so that's the first step.'

'I know, but I can't see around the baggage. It could destroy other things in my life that are very important to me.'

'Maybe you'll have to compensate, like Carlos.'

'It could be difficult for me to make choices.'

'It's always hard to do that, but you'll have to choose what's best for you, and your life. That's all that matters,' Alva assured her. 'You can't put that aside.'

'I suppose.' Naomi seemed glum.

'Come on, you've found someone at last so grab hold of him and make the most,' Alva grinned. 'And all I want to know is who this mysterious lover is?'

'You know I can't tell you that.'

'It's not someone I know, is it?' Alva asked curiously.

'No, of course not, it's just, the circumstances.'

'Ok, I know I'm trying to drag his name out of you, and I shouldn't be doing that.' Alva felt guilty.

'I wish I could tell you.'

'One of these days hopefully.'

'This is not like us is it? I've always told you everything, you've always told me, I feel bad about that.'

It's like the honesty between us is gone, Alva thought. She was miserable. What was she to Naomi now? Something had happened to the love they had felt for each other and she couldn't imagine a life without Naomi. Although they didn't live in each other's pockets these days, they were always there. To be relied upon. At the end of a phone if either one of them needed to talk. To unburden themselves of a problem they needed to tease out. Or impart some wonderful news.

'I must tell you before I burst. I can't make a decision. I'm standing on a cliff edge. Teetering. There's no one here to tell me what I should do. I'm relying on you to send me on the right road.'

Now Alva had allowed something to cut between them. She didn't know where that division had come from. And worried that she had taken Naomi for granted. Yet Alva's life always included her friend. And she valued her support and friendship which still existed like a bubbling stream. Twisting and turning through deep cuttings in ditches, singing, warbling, and whistling. A cascade of sound.

She looked at Naomi in longing. Needing to know her again. She always thought of her as a sister. That closest of relationships. Someone who was missing in her own life. She loved her two brothers. But Naomi was that person who fulfilled her in the absence of her mother.

Housekeepers had taken Julie's place, and although she knew now that the last one had been in a relationship with her father, it wasn't something she knew about when she was young. Now she missed Naomi.

Unexpectedly, Alva's phone rang, and she looked at the readout delighted to see Carlos's name there.

'It's Carlos,' she said to Naomi with a broad smile. 'Do you mind if I take it?'

'Not at all, go ahead. I've a few things to do in the kitchen.' She left the room.

'Hi,' Alva was surprised to hear from him so early. It was only half past nine. 'How are you?'

'I am fine, querida, are you still working?'

'No, I'm here with Naomi.'

'I engineered things this evening so we could have some time together.'

'That would be great.'

'I'll make dinner, bring Naomi with you,' he suggested.

'I'll ask her.'

Alva invited Naomi, but she didn't accept.

'I think you two need some time to yourselves, Alva, so I won't go along as a gooseberry. You don't need me,' Naomi laughed. 'Get yourself home. Make the most of it. You haven't seen Carlos home early in ages and now here he is. Go girl, go.' Naomi hugged her.

Alva did exactly as Naomi advised, so glad to find Carlos in the kitchen.

'Querida,' he turned away from the cooker when he heard her come in, and put out his arms towards her. They hugged closely.

'It's so good to see you home,' Alva whispered.

'I've been feeling guilty that I spend too much time at the hospital, so I've had a look at the schedule and cut a few corners.'

He kissed her gently.

'It's wonderful to see you.' She was tearful.

He put his arms around her and drew her close to him. 'And I you, my love, I want to give you my life. I'll always be yours.' He kissed her again, his lips soft and she responded ardently, wanting him so much.

They forgot that the paella was cooking on the stove until she smelled a burning aroma and realised that the rice was probably sticking to the pan.

'The paella,' she shouted.

Carlos turned to pull the pan off the stove.

Alva stirred the mixture.

'Forget about it,' he laughed. 'You're more important to me, it's almost cooked anyway.' He lifted Alva up in his arms and she burst out laughing as she hung on to him. He carried her to the bedroom. 'Let's eat later,' he said as they rolled on to the bed.

'My love, you are so beautiful,' he whispered, and kissed her again and again, and began to take her clothes off. She did the same and within minutes they were making love at a ferocious pace. 'I couldn't bear to lose you,' Carlos gazed at her, his dark eyes dragging her into his heart. So true and determined, she found herself believing him completely.

Chapter Fourteen

Back in Spain, Julie rose very early in the morning to attend to the packing which had to be done for their trip to Cadiz. At this time of the year, Seville was like a bowl in the land, the heat pounding, the breeze hardly effective particularly in the city. The temperature at this time in the summer often crept close to forty degrees and many people headed to the coast for their vacation. Julie and her partner Pedro had decided that they would move out to their summer property in Cadiz in the next couple of days. Although Pedro never spent much time there, except at weekends.

Julie was looking forward to having Pedro's daughters, Pacqui and Nuria, come out to Cadiz, and hopefully that Carlos and Alva would manage to spend some time with them this year, and had asked David and Sarah and their children, and Cian and Natalie as well. But initially, it would just be herself, Pedro and perhaps Pacqui.

She met Pedro coming out of their bedroom.

'Querida,' he embraced her as soon as he saw her, and they kissed. 'I will have breakfast, and see you later.'

'I won't be long.'

She followed him down in a few minutes, glad to see that he was still eating at the table with Pacqui.

'Buenos dias,' she kissed Pedro again, and Pacqui as well, and then helped herself to a cup of café con leche from the sideboard, and some fresh bread rolls.

'Have you got the packing done, Mama?' her step daughter asked.

'Si, and I'm looking forward to going to Cadiz tomorrow, are you both coming?'

'It will be the evening,' Pedro said.

'We will be together,' Pacqui added. 'And we'll bring Abuela with us.'

'It will be lovely to have her.'

'I've arranged to send the horses over in the morning,' Pedro said.

'Good, I'm looking forward to riding on the beach,' Julie said with a smile.

'And be very careful, my love, always have someone with you. You don't want the horse to bolt like that last time, I shudder to think of it,' Pedro warned.

'I'll take one of the stable hands.'

'I will feel more confident if you do, promise me.' He put his hand on hers for a minute.

'Don't worry, I will take no chances.'

'We'll ride with you on Sunday,' Pacqui said. 'You know you're very precious to us.'

'I know, but I have been riding quite a lot since the operation, so I'm back to normal surely?'

'We always worry, that will never change,' Pedro added.

'I'd better go, the vet is coming to see one of the horses,' Pacqui rose from the table.

'I'll come with you, I want to talk to him too.' Pedro stood up as well and followed her.

'I'll see you at lunch,' Julie said.

To their relief, the weather in Cadiz was much cooler than Seville, and as she had arrived first Julie was delighted to be able to spend time at the pool, lying on a sunbed under a striped umbrella, reading a novel just to pass the time. Later in the day she walked to the beach which was close to where they lived. In the bright sunshine, miles of white glimmering sand stretched away into the distance, not a person to be seen. Crashing waves thundered on to the beach and enticed her into the sea. She walked out through the shallows and when the water was shoulder height, she dived in and swam out to where it was calm. It was warm, and she enjoyed swimming backstroke staring up at the blue sky loving the feeling of the water curling around her, and as she swam back towards the beach being tossed by the waves as they crashed in. It was delicious.

Pacqui, Pedro and Abuela arrived in the evening and they sat out on the veranda and enjoyed their dinner. Julie topped up their wine glasses, but only poured water for herself. She didn't drink alcohol, and hadn't done so since she had arrived in Spain. Having been an alcoholic when she was married to her first husband, she had managed to finally quit after she had left home, never taking a chance to find herself in that position again. It had destroyed her life, and was the reason why she had lost her husband and children.

'Who's coming from Dublin this year?' Abuela asked.

'I don't know, I'm hoping Carlos and Alva might come, but he's always so busy he may not get time. I don't know whether David and Cian can come either.'

'That's a pity for you,' Pacqui commented.

Julie nodded, but said nothing. There was an Annual General Meeting of Purtell Vintners happening in a couple of weeks, but she had to broach the subject with Pedro soon. She was nervous about that, as he wasn't keen for her to visit Dublin so much, she knew that, and had to bide her time before she told him. But now she decided to mention it. He mightn't say anything with the others present.

'I'll be flying over to attend a meeting in Dublin so I'll see them all then.'

'But you were only there a few weeks ago?' Pedro said, a rather surly expression on his face.

'It's the AGM and important.'

'This business is taking up a lot of your time,' he growled.

'I have quite a large shareholding in the company now. I must take an interest in it,' Julie insisted.

'Maybe I'll go over with you,' Pacqui said. 'I'd like to see Carlos and Alva, particularly as they mightn't be coming over.'

'Would you?' Julie was surprised.

'Yes, let me know when you'll be going.'

'I haven't booked a flight yet.'

'Let's do that later.'

'I wish I could go as well,' Abuela said. 'How lovely to visit Dublin again. It has been many years since I was last there, I think Carlos was only studying for his degree then.'

'Mama, you would never be able for the journey at your age,' Pedro said.

'No, you are right, but it doesn't mean I would not like to go.' She stood up to him immediately. While he might have been her son, she never let him ride roughshod over her.

'I am glad you are not thinking of doing something so crazy.'

'I was eighty-five when I went last time and I had no problems.'

'You are not that age now.'

'And I know it well. But for ninety-five I am doing all right. Don't you think so?' she smiled.

'You are amazing.' Julie covered the wrinkled hand with hers and gently pressed it.

'Of course she is. It is in our genes. All the generations have lived long lives. Let us hope we'll follow in their footsteps,' Pedro grunted.

Julie was sorry she had mentioned going to Dublin at all as it had brought out Pedro's annoyance once again. Although she was glad that Pacqui was coming along, she would be company. And Pedro had not really complained too much in front of the others and she was delighted about that.

'I wish you didn't have to go to Dublin again,' Pedro muttered when they were in the bedroom that night.

'I'm sorry but I must play my part.'

'Why?'

'I want to be involved with my family.'

'You left them when they were children without a thought, have you no guilt about that?' he snapped.

'I have of course, and I'm trying to make it up to them.' Julie struggled to find excuses for Pedro.

'Do you think they appreciate it?' he asked, a hint of sarcasm in his tone.

'I hope so.'

'You sound uncertain.'

'I can't be sure of their feelings towards me. They were very young when I left.'

'I wish you luck.'

'Thank you.'

'When will you go?'

'Next week, and I'm glad Pacqui will be with me.'

'You're leaving me on my own.' Pedro seemed down.

'Paqui doesn't realise how much it means to me.'

'I wouldn't expect that she does.'

'Our children have no idea of my position really.'

'They lost their own mother around the same age as your Irish family.'

'I've tried to explain, but I'm not sure if they had a grasp of it at all. You know what it was like when I tried to explain to you,'

Julie said.

'I do, and because it's so difficult I don't expect anyone else to understand.' Pedro climbed into the large bed. 'Come in, querida, let us sleep.'

'I'm sorry the whole thing seems to upset you.'

'I can't help myself, I'm a man. What do you expect?' he laughed and put his arm around her.

'I love you.' She moved closer towards him.

'I'm glad to hear that, sometimes I've wondered if you might have gone back to Ireland to be with your other family.'

'No, I would never do that. You've been so good to me since I came here, and I love you.' She kissed him. 'You're my Spanish family. It's as if the children are mine, they always were right from the beginning. And they know it.'

'To have you in our lives means everything to us,' Pedro hugged her.

Chapter Fifteen

Alva closed the door behind her and stood there for a few seconds in a daze. The expression on her face was puzzled to say the least. She walked slowly down the corridor to the reception desk. Took her credit card from her purse and paid the girl, and then went out to her car. She sat in and drove home. In the apartment, she stood staring out the large picture window into the distance of a blue sky.

What was Carlos going to say, she wondered.

Would it fit into his plans?

Was it something he would welcome?

Questions burst through her and she had no answers. A feeling of dread gathered inside. She took her phone from her handbag and glanced at the time. It was just after five. Hours before Carlos would be home.

She opened up her laptop and tried to put what had just happened out of her head. They had talked about it. Something which they hoped would happen. But it was down the road. Further away. And they weren't in a rush. And because of how things had been recently, she wondered would he ever come around to agreeing to such an intrusion in his life.

It was after eleven when he came in.

'Alva, querida?' He looked into her eyes, and gathered her into his arms.

She had made some tapas, and they sat down and ate, talking

for a while about the day and then went to bed. Alva felt that she should have told Carlos immediately, but somehow wasn't able, just yet. She would have to choose the right moment, and that wouldn't be easy. There were so few opportunities to talk these days. So little time together. And she hated that. Hated the worry around not knowing whether he still loved her. Sure, he assured her that he did, but she still knew moments of uncertainty.

She didn't know why she was in such an indecisive mood. She couldn't believe herself. She loved Carlos. He was the person in the world she relied upon the most. What was wrong with her. He deserved to know. And she would have to give him time to decide if it was something he really wanted. That most of all. But, unexpectedly, things changed.

'Querida, I've been feeling so guilty about working such long hours, I've decided to make an effort to take you away for a break. These are the dates.' He opened his phone and showed her. 'And I hope that you can take the time off too. I thought maybe we could go on Friday, and return on Monday. Four days altogether. What do you think?' He cupped her cheek in his hand, and kissed her.

She stared at him, taken aback. 'How did you manage to arrange it?' she gasped, smiling, hardly able to believe what he was saying. Taking Naomi's advice, she had planned to arrange something herself but hadn't done a thing about it, too uncertain about Carlos's reaction.

'I've made changes to my schedule, so that we will be alone.' He held her close.

'Where will we go?' she asked.

'It's a secret, I want to surprise you,' he kissed her.

'I'm looking forward to it. So much. Thank you, my love.' She was really delighted. 'And there's something I want to tell you,' she whispered.

He looked suddenly worried. His eyes quizzical. There was silence between them.

'I hope you'll be happy,' she said softly.

'You always make me happy.'

'We're going to have a baby,' she said, glad that it was out now. She waited hesitantly, unsure of his response.

'His eyes widened with astonishment. 'What? You're pregnant?'

She nodded.

'I can't believe …' he stuttered. 'I don't know why I didn't expect it so soon. It's wonderful, querida.' He put his arms around her and held her close. 'A baby,' he sighed. They sat together for a moment. Then he looked down at her. 'Tell me, how are you feeling?'

'I feel fine, no morning sickness. I'm amazed.'

'Gracias a Dios,' he murmured.

'Are you happy?' she asked, still needing to hear that this was something which he really wanted.

'Of course I am, querida, this is fantastic news, to be honest I've been so busy since we came back from our honeymoon it didn't occur to me.'

'Me neither. I wasn't even sure until I went to the GP, I'm only about eight weeks so it's still at a delicate stage. I don't want anything to happen.'

'I'm sure everything will be fine.' He hugged her again.

'We won't mention it to anyone yet, just in case, if that's all right with you? Although I'll tell Naomi, couldn't keep my mouth shut about it if I'm with her.'

'Of course, it will be our secret,' he smiled and kissed her. 'And I'm going to have to look after you very well, you cannot take any risks. And maybe you shouldn't work such long hours?' he asked, and suddenly she could see how much he cared, and was reminded of how much she loved him. Imagine, he wanted this baby as much as she did. That meant everything to her.

'I'll try.'

'Promise me you'll already be in bed by the time I get home every night?'

She nodded with a smile.

'And I promise I'll try to be home earlier too,' he said earnestly.

'This is going to change our lives,' Alva said.

'A baby,' he said and smiled.

Alva was really pleased at Carlos's reaction to her news. Her worries had receded and now they were going into a new phase of their lives which was totally unexpected. She prayed her pregnancy would be uneventful, and that there would be no trauma which could put the life of her baby at risk.

'Would you like a boy or a girl?' she asked him later that night as they lay in bed.

'I don't mind. Either would be wonderful.' He wound his arms around her.

'I keep seeing a baby in pink or blue.'

'You can dress him or her in any colour you like. And maybe there will be more than one. Are there any twins in your family?'

'No, not that I know of. What about you?'

'No.'

'Maybe one would be enough. I can't think how I would handle two anyway. Imagine the sleep deprivation. Feeding and sleeping nearly run into each other, and I must have sleep if I'm to look after a baby properly and be a good mother. And you need a decent few hours' sleep every night too, you can't put your patients' lives on the line.'

'We may have to get someone to help initially.'

'Mum will do that I'm sure.'

'Of course she will.'

'We'd better tell her she's going to be a grandmother again.

She's coming over for the company AGM next week.'
They laughed and curled up together.

Chapter Sixteen

'Naomi, it's Darren.' He stood at the entrance door.

'Come on up.'

He went into the foyer and took the lift to Naomi's apartment.

She stood waiting in the doorway, and immediately threw her arms around him. 'How are you, my love?' She kissed him.

'For you,' he handed her a box of chocolates.

'Thank you.' She led the way inside and he closed the door.

'It's so good to see you. I've missed you. It's been too long.' He kissed her.

'Sorry, you know my schedule.'

'Who would want to have a Garda for a partner,' he laughed.

'A partner?' she echoed.

'Why not? I love you, and I hope you love me,' he said. 'Anyway, I'd give anything to live with you. Maybe one day we'll be together?'

'Who knows,' she smiled, opening the box of chocolates. 'Have one.' She held out the box.

'Thank you.'

'Would you like a drink?' she asked.

'Sure would.'

'Gin?'

'Thanks.'

'Tonic?' She poured their drinks.

'Cheers.' They clinked glasses.

He reached across and his arm slowly encircled her shoulders. 'Let's go out some evening for dinner.' He suggested.

'I'd love to, but you know how I feel about going out.' She had to say it.

'Is that because you're afraid we'll bump into Alva?' he asked sharply.

'I suppose,' Naomi hesitated.

'We can't live like that. Afraid to meet someone. It's ridiculous.'

'Alva is my closest friend.'

'So what?'

'I don't want to hurt her. She will be very upset.'

'We're finished, she doesn't give a damn about me. She threw me out, bag and baggage.'

'I know, but you'll have to make allowances.'

'You're saying I'm the one who has to do that? We'll have to live a normal life from now on. I want to go out when we feel like it, have a few jars, a nice meal, or a cup of coffee, whatever.'

'So do I, but ...'

'Our relationship is going nowhere if you're going to insist we live hidden inside this apartment. It's like being in a cave. Or one of your prisons.'

'It's not that bad,' Naomi laughed. 'I just want to be here together.'

He walked over to the doors which opened on to her balcony. 'I want out.' He stood at the edge and looked over.

'Come back inside,' she ran over to him. 'You could be seen.'

'I'll have to get a disguise,' he retorted.

'That's crazy.'

'Come here to me.' He reached and pulled her close. His arms tight around her. 'I want you.'

She flung off her top and shorts, and they threw themselves on the couch, and she dragged his clothes off and within minutes they hadn't a stitch on them. Wildly they made love. For Darren it was something so satisfying he could never resist her. Naomi had hidden sides to her that he hadn't known existed. While he hated the secrecy of their relationship, he enjoyed the chase. Enjoyed taking her from Alva. And had every intention of getting his own back on his former partner.

He never stayed all night, always slipping out in the small hours and driving back to his own flat. Now when he arrived home, he stood in the narrow hallway and wondered what he was doing. If he hadn't been so stupid about his relationship with that woman, and Alva hadn't thrown him out of their apartment he wouldn't be here now. And the way that Naomi was going on about staying in all the time was getting on his nerves. Why couldn't she have just let it go on the way they had begun. In the early days, they had gone out occasionally, but then Naomi had become very worried that Alva would see them together and refused to go out at all. It was ridiculous. Although in one way, he almost wanted Alva to see them. Wanted to get back at her. And to take his revenge.

Chapter Seventeen

'I'm pregnant, Naomi, can you believe it?' Alva was so full of joy she could barely express the words.

'Is Carlos happy?'

'We're both delighted.'

'I'm jealous.' There were tears in Naomi's eyes. 'I've always wanted a child, although I don't think I've ever told you that. It always seemed to be too selfish.'

'One of these days it will happen when you meet the right guy. Maybe this secret man is the one,' Alva smiled. Hoping that maybe today Naomi might reveal something about him. 'Now tell me, does he make you happy?'

'Of course he does.' Naomi blushed.

'There, you're showing how much you care about him.' Teased Alva knowingly.

'I do care, he's an amazing person.'

'When am I going to know who he is?'

'One of these days,' she said with a smile.

Alva sighed.

'Tell me how you are feeling. Have you had any morning sickness or anything like that?' Naomi asked.

'No, I've been fine, can you believe it?'

'There are lots of women I know who have an awful time.'

'I'm lucky.' Alva ran her hand over her stomach gently.

'You are,' Naomi agreed.

'It's hard to imagine, isn't it,' Alva said, smiling.

'Of course, it's going to be a major change in your life. Although you won't be able to take maternity leave as such,' Naomi said.

'I can work from home.'

'But how about sleep? You'll be on your own completely. And Carlos will be no help, he'll hardly be able to take paternity leave either and he can't work from home.'

'I'm hoping Mum will be able to come over for a week or two.'

'I can give you a hand as well if you like.'

'Thank you. That's so generous of you. But it could be tricky, your hours are very long.'

'I'll work around it. Maybe take time off.' Naomi's phone rang. She always had to reply no matter where she was in the event it was something to do with a case she was working on. So now it was no different and she picked it up. 'Yes?' she asked. But immediately hesitated. Then she nodded listening intently.

'I'm busy at the moment. Can you call me later?' The person who was at the other end of the line continued talking for a moment. 'Thanks.' She turned the phone off. 'Work,' she said briefly. 'It's always the same isn't it. Both of us are controlled by our jobs,' Naomi said. 'You'll have someone else who will control you soon,' she laughed.

'A little person I'll have to attend to. Feed. Cuddle. Dress. Change. And do a million other things I suppose too. And I hope I'm able for it.' Alva felt suddenly lacking in confidence.

'Do you think Carlos will be good at doing all that sort of stuff as well?'

'I haven't a clue. The two of us are first timers.'

'Most men are very good now apparently. Compared to what they were like in our father's time. Men wouldn't be seen dead pushing the pram in those days. They went to work and there was no such thing as paternity leave, and the women did everything.'

'Now everything has to be shared as every couple have two jobs.'

'I don't see how Carlos will share anything, except at weekends. He's got a bit better at taking time off on Saturday and Sunday. But during the week it's impossible. He's got clinics. Operating days and nights. And there are so many emergencies you wouldn't believe, and he's always on call because of his speciality.'

'You'll have to tell me what I should buy as a present. I'd like to get something nice. Maybe the cot or the buggy or something like that. I've so little time I'll have to be looking out for it while I have a chance. Anyway, I'd like you to tell me what you would like. Maybe go along to one of those baby shows. We could go together? What do you think? You'll get lots of ideas there.'

'Not at all, Naomi, something like that would be far too expensive, thank you for the thought. But I wouldn't want to buy too much at this stage, you know, just in case something goes wrong.' Alva looked doubtful.

'I'm sure that won't happen. Anyway, you can just look, and collect brochures, and then order on line when the time comes.'

'I think you're going to enjoy this more than me.'

'Why not. It might never happen to me. I will enjoy it. And I'm going to keep a close eye on you. Make sure you're doing all the right things. And no alcohol, remember.'

'Thanks Mammy,' Alva giggled. 'I haven't had a drink since I discovered I was pregnant. As you know, Carlos doesn't drink so I just said there was no point opening a bottle of wine for me to have one glass.'

'Have you told your Mum?'

'No, she's coming next week with Pacqui and I'll give them the news then.'

'They're going to be so happy, especially your Mum. It's

wonderful news. When is the baby due?'

'November.'

Naomi put her arms around her and hugged.

Chapter Eighteen

Alva was feeling very excited as she saw her mother, Julie, and Pacqui come through the doors at the airport, waving enthusiastically as soon as they noticed her. Julie threw her arms around Alva, hugging tightly. 'It's so lovely to see you,' she smiled.

They stood together for a moment.

'Pacqui,' she kissed her on both cheeks as they did in Spain. 'How are you?'

'I am fine,' she smiled, so pretty, dark-eyed, her skin with that lovely sallow sheen.

'Come on, let's go,' said Alva. 'I'm sure you are tired from the journey.'

'It was only a couple of hours, we didn't notice the time.'

'I always take a nap when I'm travelling,' laughed Julie.

'I'm glad.'

They left the airport in Alva's car, and it didn't take long to get to the apartment.

'Carlos will try to get home as early as he can,' she explained. 'He works hard.'

'We know that,' Julie replied. 'He's a workaholic.'

'He has never changed, our Carlos,' Pacqui sounded sympathetic.

'She loves her brother,' Julie turned and put her hand back to grasp Pacqui's who sat in the back of the car.

'Of course I do,' she retorted.

'We all do,' Julie laughed.

Alva stopped the car outside the high wrought iron gates and used the remote control to open them. After she had parked, she climbed out of the car, and took the bags from the boot. Then they took the lift up to their floor and she opened the door of the apartment and welcomed them in.

'Mind you, I know that both of you have been here many times before I met Carlos, so I suppose it's a bit strange to you that I should welcome you here.' She felt embarrassed.

'It's your home now.' Julie put her arm around Alva's shoulders.

'Would you like coffee and something to eat?' she asked.

'Yes please, we'd love to have a snack,' Pacqui said. 'We didn't have anything on the plane, the food is so tasteless.'

'I have some tapas. Would you like to freshen up while I prepare them? You know where to go,' she smiled.

'We will, thanks.' They went into the second bedroom.

Left on her own, Alva cooked the hot tapas, and kept them warm in the oven. The cold dishes she placed on the table.

They enjoyed the meal, and the afternoon drifted along as they caught up with the news and found out how everyone was doing.

'How are Pedro and Nuria and of course Abuela?'

'They are all well.'

'I hoped maybe Pedro might have come with you,' Alva said.

'No ...' Julie's face had a sudden expression of disappointment.

'He couldn't drag himself away from his horses,' added Pacqui. 'He adores them.'

'I was surprised to see you leave them to come with me,' Julie said, with a smile.

'I just decided to have a break, and I wanted to keep you company. They won't mind.'

'If you could talk to your horses on the phone, I know you

would.'

'Secretly I whisper to them.'

'That's a real talent. Whispering,' Alva murmured. 'It's all about communication.'

'Absolutely,' agreed Julie. 'And Pacqui can train our horses so well. She can read the body language and psychology of the horse instantly. They know she loves them.'

'I take after my father. His talent with his horses is astonishing. I'm still learning.'

'It's such an amazing ability,' Alva said, remembering the time she rode with Carlos and Julie in Spain.

'I wonder if you will ever have another life, Paqui?' Julie asked slowly. 'What will you do when you fall in love with a man and want to move away with him? Can you imagine what that will be like?'

'He'll have to take me with my horses,' she giggled. 'I'll never be parted from them.'

'Pick some guy from the stables. That's your only choice. Then he'll share your love of horses. And I hope he's not the jealous type. Who do you love most in the world, is it me or the horses he might ask,' Julie laughed.

'He won't be jealous of a horse,' Alva smiled at her.

'You don't know how Pacqui feels about her horses, and that's since she was a very small girl,' Julie pointed out.

'I think I understand. I can see it in her eyes,' Alva said.

'When she looks at them in the paddock and they come towards her as soon as she appears. They want her to put her arms around them and hold them close, gently touching them as if to reassure them,' Julie added.

'They know me and will do anything for me,' insisted Pacqui.

'Particularly in dressage. Stepping out so beautifully in perfect time.'

'I love dressage. Especially when the women ride side saddle, wearing top hats, and veils, all in black,' Alva said excitedly. 'I'd love to learn.'

'I'll teach you,' Pacqui immediately offered.

'Since my basic riding isn't all that great, it would be a very big step to tackle side saddle.'

'When you come over next time, we'll start.'

'You will come over to Cadiz to see us, won't you?' Julie asked.

'I'm not sure, Carlos is always so busy.' Alva didn't say anything about Carlos taking her away for a break in case Julie would be annoyed they had not gone to Spain to see the family.

'He spends too much time at the hospital,' Julie said sharply. 'He should remember he is a married man now.'

'It's his life.' Alva tried to explain, although she found it difficult. She still felt very emotional about the hours he spent away from her, even now. Julie and Pacqui rested for a while as Alva prepared dinner. For starter, she decided on gazpacho, for the main course she chose to cook sea bass, fried potatoes, and grilled vegetables. For dessert, she made a chocolate and cream flan, and hoped that her guests would enjoy it. She didn't know what time Carlos would be home, and prayed it mightn't be too late. If it was then Julie might have something to say. There had been a very critical sound in her voice when she made that remark earlier and it made Alva feel ashamed about Carlos's working hours, as if it was all her fault. And now that she was pregnant, it would be even worse.

She checked her phone, but there had been no texts from him. She prayed he would come in the door at any moment.

Dinner was ready to be served at about nine-thirty and still no sign of Carlos.

Julie and Pacqui appeared to be very much refreshed, and Alva served up a dry sherry as an aperitif, and just as she had poured it, to her relief the door opened and Carlos appeared.

'Querida,' he put his arm around Alva first and kissed her, and then welcomed Julie and Pacqui enthusiastically holding the three of them in his embrace. 'It's wonderful to see you, forgive me for being so late. I hope you had a comfortable journey and are not too tired?'

'No, we had a couple of hours rest, and so we have plenty of energy now,' Julie laughed.

'I'm glad.'

'And dinner is just about ready, so your timing is perfect,' Alva said, delighted that he had arrived home early.

'Just give me a moment to freshen up and change and then I'll be with you.' He went into the bedroom.

Alva insisted that Carlos join Julie and Pacqui and catch up with the news from home while she plated up the dinner. But there was something on her mind and she would have preferred to discuss with Carlos when and how they would announce their news about the baby, but didn't have an opportunity to do that and hoped she might get a chance later. In the meantime, she said nothing.

'This is a delicious meal,' Julie smiled at her.

'Yes, it's lovely,' Pacqui added.

'Alva is a very good cook,' Carlos said, 'And she loves Spanish food, so I'm very lucky.'

'You're not a bad cook yourself,' laughed Alva.

'I had to cook for myself all those years when I was studying here. Had to work from scratch. Couldn't depend on staff which I didn't have,' he smiled.

'Bet it was probably all junk food in those days. When I was over here, I'd cook for him, so at least he had something decent to eat, but I knew once I had gone, it was back to junk,' Julie smiled.

'Now I have Alva, there is no more junk. We eat together in the evenings, and I eat in the restaurant at the hospital and the food is quite good.' He reached out and held Alva's hand.

'And there is something we want to tell you,' she said softly. Glancing up at Carlos, glad to meet his eyes which had that warm look of agreement in them.

'We are going to have a baby.'

'How wonderful.' Julie stood up, as did Pacqui, and threw their arms around Alva and Carlos too.

'Congratulations,' Pacqui exclaimed.

'When is the baby due?'

'November.'

'It's going to be so exciting.' Julie was overjoyed.

'You're going to be a grandmother again,' Alva said, hugging her mother.

'Do you know whether it's a boy or a girl yet?' Pacqui asked.

Alva shook her head. 'No, and we don't want to know,' she smiled at Carlos.

'It will be a nice surprise for us when the baby arrives,' he said, holding her hand.

'I have to admit I think you look good, you have that glowing look,' Julie smiled.

'Everything is going well, nothing wrong according to the doctor.' Alva was delighted that she had told her mother and Pacqui.

'How do you feel about becoming a grandmother again?' Carlos asked Julie with a grin.

'It's going to be amazing. I can't believe it. But I'm going to hate being so far away.' Her expression was suddenly glum.

'I hope you can be here to help when he or she arrives. I don't know how I'll manage.' Alva held her mother's hand.

'I'll be over as soon I hear the news. I hope I remember everything, it's been a long time since I was a Mum.'

'You were a wonderful Mum,' Alva assured.

'I'm so sorry I wasn't around for long,' she said softly. 'This time I want to look after your baby, and when you need to sleep, I can take over. You'll need someone here as Carlos has such a full schedule,' Julie said. 'I'm not going to worry too much at this stage, everything will pan out. The most important being that the baby is all right.'

'Everything will be, querida, never worry.' Carlos put his arm around her and held her close.

The following evening David and Cian and their families came to dinner, and enjoyed another reunion. When they announced the news of their expected baby, there was much congratulations and happiness and they celebrated the good news with a bottle of champagne, all looking forward to the arrival of this baby.

Julie and Pacqui stayed on for a couple of days, principally because of the company AGM which Julie had to attend. Alva and the company accountant presented the previous year's accounts, explaining to those present how well they had performed.

For Alva, she really enjoyed seeing the families together, and spending time with her mother. She didn't see enough of her.

Chapter Nineteen

Alva glanced at her phone. She had forced herself to leave work earlier than usual. Listening to her body telling her that she had to take care of this tiny being who was growing inside her. When she looked at herself in the mirror, as her Mum had said, she felt she was glowing like the petals of a flower which had just opened out in the heat of the sun. She closed down the files on which she had been working. Took her diary and turned the page to tomorrow. She ran a pen down the list of items she had entered beside the various hours of the day. Her to do list. It kept her time in order. It was the only way she had control over the hours. Carlos insisted she go to bed early, and she did. Worn out.

She had an appointment for her twelve-week scan. It was the first big date and she was hoping that Carlos would manage to get away from the hospital, arranging it around lunchtime which hopefully would suit his schedule on the day he would normally be seeing patients in his clinic. Unless there was an emergency, he should manage to get there.

And to her great relief he hurried into the office in which she waited about five minutes before she was due to meet with her consultant. They were on time and she was glad that he was an acquaintance of Carlos as it immediately put them at ease. Then they were taken in and the ultrasound commenced. The consultant explained exactly what they were seeing on the screen, and that the baby was fully formed from the head to the toes. Alva found it very emotional to see her baby there in front of her moving around in the fluid of the womb, and held on to Carlos's hand tightly as they both looked at the screen. The consultant went on to explain that they can take various measurements and check for abnormalities. Alva was particularly apprehensive about that but was reassured when the consultant pronounced that all seemed well with their baby and there was no need to worry at all.

'There's a possibility that it's a boy but we can't tell for sure until the next scan.'

'Once the baby is all right we don't mind whether it's a boy or a girl,' Alva said, 'Sure we don't,' she smiled at Carlos, who squeezed her hand.

'And that you are all right too,' he added.

'I will be, I'm sure.'

'We will look after you,' the consultant said, and nodded to Carlos with a professional glance.

They parted outside the hospital, and while Carlos took a taxi back to Beaumont, Alva walked to her office which was quite close. She felt on cloud nine, glancing down at the white envelope in her black leather tote bag every now and then, and longing to take it out and look at the picture again.

She found it very hard to concentrate on work for that afternoon, her mind on her baby. Every now and then she touched her stomach gently as if to remind herself of its existence. Her phone rang constantly and she was forced to respond, having no Personal Assistant now. She hadn't been able to replace the very nice girl who worked for her previously, whom she had been forced to let go when their company had almost gone into liquidation. Now, without her, it was always busy.

Alva left early, looking forward to seeing Carlos later. Did some shopping and prepared one of their favourite meals, with a summer salad. She enjoyed preparing the meal, and set the dining table with candles, just to add a romantic ambience. This was a very special day for both of them, and she wanted to celebrate.

Everything ready, she lay on the couch and rested. In the last couple of weeks, she had put on a little weight, and it had made itself felt today. It wasn't much, but it signified the arrival of her baby. And seeing the little one on the screen had meant a great deal to her. Now she took the scan out of the envelope and looked at the grainy image again. Tears flooded her eyes and she found it hard to believe that it had actually happened and that this little one was living inside her. It was attached to her by the umbilical cord and all the goodness in her body was giving her baby sustenance until eventually he or she would come into the world.

She closed her eyes briefly, and it was only when some noise disturbed her that she opened them again, and realised that Carlos was standing over her.

'Querida,' he leaned close and kissed her.

'Hi my love,' she pushed herself up. 'Lovely to see you. I have most of the dinner prepared.'

He put his arms around her and held her close. 'How are you feeling?'

'Fine, although I didn't expect to fall asleep,' Alva laughed.

'If you need to sleep then you should, what do you call it?' he smiled.

'Catnap,' she laughed.

'These are for you querida.' He took a bouquet of red roses from the counter, and handed it to her. 'To celebrate this wonderful day, the first time we saw our baby.' He kissed her again.

'Thank you, my love.' She took the roses and breathed in their aroma. 'Beautiful. I must get a vase.'

'I'll plate up,' he said.

'The pork is in the oven.' She clipped the stems and arranged the roses in a cut-glass vase on the table.

She took the salad from the fridge and placed the bowl and the bread on the table.

They sat down and enjoyed the meal.

'How did you get away so early?' she asked.

'It's not that early, it's ten o'clock now,' he laughed.

'Earlier than usual.'

'As this was a very special day and there were no emergencies, I left.'

'But the team were there?'

'Yes, but it depends on the condition of the patients. But luckily the man I operated on yesterday is doing well.'

'It's a tough job.'

'You married a doctor, and that was a tough decision,' he smiled.

'You just looked at me then and I was lost. I couldn't resist you,' Alva admitted.

'I'm the lucky one, and I want to make you happy. I know you have had doubts about me, but I promise that I will change as much as I can.'

'That makes me feel so guilty, I shouldn't have told you of my fears,' Alva admitted.

'Of course you should, that's very important to me.' His dark eyes met hers.

'I won't complain again,' she said, hating herself. 'I'm just a moan.'

'Querida, don't say that. If there is anything you want to say to me, then say it. And I will do the same, so that we have complete honesty between us. We love each other, and that's all that counts.' He kissed her again.

She felt so much better on the following morning. It seemed they had swept away all the junk between them, most of which had been in her own head and she was glad of that. But she was dragged back in time, when her phone rang on the way into work. The call was from her solicitor, John, who wanted to discuss the case against Darren for the assault on her.

She thanked him, but as she drove on, her mind was in a daze. How could she deal with the case now that she was pregnant. Somehow it accentuated her vulnerability, and she felt isolated. But she knew he had admitted his guilt and that meant that she wouldn't have to be interrogated in court by his defence team. But still even to come face to face with him again would be as if she was being attacked all over again. It was a terrible thing to have done to her, and she hated him for it.

Chapter Twenty

'Bring some warm clothes, it's sometimes a bit cold at night,' Carlos said to Alva.

'Tell me where?' she asked with a grin.

'It's a secret.' He put his finger on his lips and smiled.

'Will it be warm during the day?'

'Yes. I'll give you a clue, we're taking a flight there.'

'Lovely. I'm so looking forward to getting away with you. No work. No patients. We won't know ourselves. And really I don't mind where we are going, I know it will be wonderful. To have you all to myself is going to be like our honeymoon all over again.'

As she said that, she wondered whether Carlos might be bringing her over to Seville to see the family. But she would have preferred to be on their own wherever they were.

When they arrived at the airport for the early flight, she still wasn't sure where they were going, but when Carlos checked them in it was only then that she saw the name Madrid on his phone. She was delighted. It was Spain. They landed safely, and picked up a hire car.

'Where are we heading?' asked Alva.

'Back to the place we were intending to see when we had to cut short our honeymoon.'

'How lovely, we're going to Toledo,' she smiled at Carlos.

'Your guess is right,' he agreed.

It only took an hour to arrive and the hotel Carlos had booked was the Arabe Medina.

'I decided to book our first night as we have so little time. There are only ten bedrooms, and each one is different, with a theme,' he said, as they checked in and went up in the lift. They stepped out of the lift and Carlos opened the door of Suite Five. It was amazing. A very large suite with black leather couches. The theme was Moorish and the décor sparkled with a mosaic of silver tiles on the floors which reflected in the mirrored walls. There were tables with exquisite mother of pearl inlay as were some of the items of furniture.

They went out on to the balcony and sat for a while looking over the city. 'As we may only stay a day I think we should do some sightseeing and then decide if we're going to move on in the morning. What do you think, querida?' Carlos put his arm around her and kissed her.

'Sounds great.' She returned his embrace. 'Thanks for arranging the weekend.'

Within half an hour they were walking around Toledo. First stopping for a coffee in one of the cafes in the Plaza de Zocodover, the central square in the city. They sat there, watching people passing by, and afterwards, they followed the narrow cobbled streets up to the Alcazar fortress, and wandered in and out of old churches, and buildings, hand in hand, and any other places that took their fancy. Visiting the Jewish quarter and district of convents. Snapping some of the more interesting palaces. They saw some El Greco paintings and they stopped for lunch at a small restaurant sitting under the shade of a white umbrella from the afternoon sunshine, and enjoying various local tapas. Later they returned to the hotel, and enjoyed a swim in the pool. Carlos then decided to have a massage in the Arab baths, although Alva chose to have a rest until they went out for dinner.

Their restaurant choice was La Naviera, the best seafood restaurant in Toledo, and it was. They enjoyed their meal and strolled around the old city again, getting the feel of the atmosphere at night. It was so romantic, and Alva loved every minute.

'This is a beautiful place,' she murmured.

'And you are even more beautiful,' Carlos kissed her. Then he took a small box from his pocket and handed it to her. 'Just to remind us of our second honeymoon. I hope you like it.'

She opened the small black velvet box, amazed to see an exquisite bracelet. It was a simple band of gold set with tiny diamonds, very similar in style to her engagement ring.

'It's gorgeous, I love it,' she whispered, taken aback.

'It is just to tell you how much I love you,' he smiled.

He took it out of the box, opened the clasp and clipped it around her wrist.

'It's so lovely. Thank you.' She clung to him.

'Do you want to stay here another day, or will we move on?' Carlos asked the following morning.

'Where else did we hope to see on our honeymoon?' Alva asked. 'I think Segovia was one place, but there's lots more to see here so we could drive up this evening and see Segovia tomorrow and then somewhere else on Sunday and back to Madrid on Monday to fly home. What do you think?'

'Sounds perfect.'

They enjoyed the rest of their day in Toledo and drove to Segovia that evening. Found a hotel easily enough which was not too far from the ancient roman aqueduct, and had dinner in a restaurant which specialised in traditional dishes which were delicious. The following day they explored the old town leisurely, and drove on to Ávila which was an amazing picture of a bygone age. The town encircled by huge medieval walls and there were nine ancient gates. The walls were open during the day and Alva and Carlos explored them enjoying the walk over the town, and later visiting the Convento de Santa Teresa which was built on the site of the house where Saint Teresa was born.

Their break was very relaxing and they finished off by spending a few hours in Madrid before flying home. 'Wow, what a weekend.' Alva stared out the window of the plane as it rose into the sky above the city. Then she turned to Carlos, and held his hand. 'Did you enjoy yourself?' she asked.

'Of course I did, to have you all to myself for the weekend was fantastic,' he smiled.

'Let's plan another weekend soon. It's probably easier for you to organise a few days off than any longer.'

'We'll get away again soon, I promise.'

Chapter Twenty-one

Darren walked up the steps to the entrance of the solicitors' office. He had received a text asking him to present himself and now dreaded the thought of even speaking to the man about his case.

He pressed the doorbell. A woman answered and he gave his name. There was a click and he pushed open the door and stepped into the hallway. He walked up the stairs to the first floor and went into the office. The receptionist motioned towards some chairs which stood against the wall, and he sat on the edge of the leather upholstered seat nervously. He knew he was a man who had to depend on free legal aid, and this solicitor had been appointed to represent him. Rather than even think of paying his own legal bills, he would have to deal with this man. He wondered would the court find out that he was working now in a reasonable job and cut him off the free legal aid list. He didn't know how things worked in the court, and didn't have anyone to ask. He kept his own counsel.

The receptionist stood up, and indicated silently that he should follow her. She led him to a heavy mahogany door and knocked on it.

'Darren?' the solicitor glanced up at him. 'Take a seat.'

He did.

'I just wanted to discuss your case,' he said.

'I know.'

'As you have admitted liability, then there will be no need for cross examination of the victim by our team.'

'Team?' Darren asked, not sure what he meant.

'There will be a number of us in court defending. But, unfortunately, you will very likely receive a custodial sentence.'

'You won't get me off?' he just about managed to speak.

'I doubt it.'

'I thought you might.'

'We'll do our best.'

'Now I want you to sign a few documents.' He opened a file and slid the documents around to face Darren.

He didn't have much opportunity to read them through but trusted the solicitor and quickly scribbled his name where the man indicated.

'Thank you.'

It was the end of the meeting. The solicitor said nothing else. It left Darren feeling frustrated and somehow he knew that he would end up behind bars. He wished he had some money to employ another solicitor and barrister and whoever else he needed. While he had some savings he didn't want to spend it all on a solicitor who might or might not have interest in getting him off the charges. That man he had just met would do nothing to help him. He was useless.

He left the office and wandered the streets then. Doing no more work for the rest of the day. He sat on a bench in St. Stephen's Green. So jealous of the other people in the park who all seemed to be enjoying themselves. Couples holding hands. Families playing with their children. Young boys and girls dashing about, shouting and screaming. They weren't facing a jail term. They weren't expecting to spend years in a prison cell. They were free. And there was no one chasing after them. Threatening. Holding him responsible for an assault on a woman he loved. And he hadn't meant to do it. He just wanted her for himself.

But that Spaniard who was her boyfriend at the time had brought the Gardai before they had a chance to be together. They had misunderstood. He loved Alva. He just wanted to be with her again.

He lay back against the back of the bench seat and closed his eyes. He wanted to sleep. That above all. Just to sleep. To close his eyes against the world and try to forget everything that had happened. Maybe it was all a dream, he thought. Could he have imagined it? Was Alva already at home waiting on him? Cooking dinner. Opening a bottle of wine. Turning to greet him with a smile when he came in the door. Throwing her arms around him, and kissing him. And later, he would take her to bed, and make love. Proof that it was all he wanted. Why had the Gardai blamed him for loving his partner?

As he hadn't found out where she was living, he was thinking now that he might have a better chance of meeting her when she came out of work one night. If he could only talk to her for a few minutes he might have some success trying to persuade her to give up the case altogether. He thought then about chatting to Naomi, she must be in contact with Alva.

He invited Naomi around to his place one evening and they ordered in a Chinese take away. Afterwards, they relaxed and he took a chance on mentioning his court case.

'I was in a meeting with my solicitor about the court case, although he said it could take quite a while yet. Have you talked to Alva about it?'

'No.'

'But surely she has mentioned it?'

'Forget about Alva.' She kissed him.

'I have forgotten about her,' he lied. 'But I'm still hoping that she might give up the case and then the whole thing will collapse.'

'I don't know if you can depend on that, darling.' Naomi was very sympathetic.

'Surely it must happen occasionally, particularly if there isn't enough evidence.'

'I'm sure it must, but as I said you can't be certain about that.'

'You don't think I'm guilty, do you?' he asked.

'I wasn't there at the time.'

'But you'd take my word for it, wouldn't you?' he insisted.

'Of course I do.'

'I'm thinking of talking to Alva, do you think that's a good idea?'

'You have to know that the Gardai are taking the case against you, not Alva.'

'Her guy brought the Gardai.'

'I'll help you all I can, love, but there's not a lot I can do. It's not in my area.'

'But you could talk to people, couldn't you?'

'It would be risky for me.'

'I beg you. Please?'

'I'm sorry.'

He looked despondent.

'I love you, Darren,' she said.

'And I love you,' he kissed her. 'Let's go out at the weekend. I'll book a table for dinner. Can't we just take a chance?'

'I don't know,' Naomi was doubtful. 'You know how I feel about Alva seeing us together.'

'We'll go somewhere out of town. Maybe down to Wicklow.'
She still looked uncertain.

'You're being very weird,' he grumbled.

'I'm sorry.'

'She'll have to know sometime.'

'If she finds out, our friendship will be destroyed.' Naomi pointed out. 'Then what will I do?'

'Is Alva more important than us?' he asked.

'Well ...no.'

'And I've put everything into our relationship. Always here waiting for you.' He was anxious to keep her on his side. She was his one contact with Alva and vital for that although he didn't think she realised how important she was to him in that respect.

'How is she these days?' he enquired cautiously. Almost afraid to ask such a thing. Although he wanted Naomi to understand that he felt differently towards his ex-partner now, and by that he needed to know more about Alva. What was going on with her now that she was married to that Spanish guy.'

'She's very well.'

'And the man she's with?'

'He's OK.'

His stomach tightened. He felt as if that man had punched him again as he had on one of those nights he had called to Alva at her home.

'I've met him a couple of times,' he muttered.

'She mentioned that to me. And it didn't go very well I believe,' Naomi said with a grin.

'I took him on, the bastard, and gave him a hell of a beating. He didn't know what hit him. I had him flattened on the ground more than once. I don't know what she sees in him. What does he do anyway?' he asked.

'He's a doctor.'

'What sort?'

'Neurosurgeon.'

'If I ever have a problem with my head, I'll know who to go to,' he laughed.

'Let's hope something like that never happens my love,' Naomi put her arms around him. 'Health is the most important thing in our lives. We have to make the most of each day.'

'Yeah, and the more I see of you, the better I feel.' He kissed her. 'Maybe we might move in together one of these days? Then everyone will know that we're an item including Alva.'

Naomi looked at him.

'What about that?' he asked and kissed her.

'It's a bit soon, pet.'

'I'm tired of living in this little rabbit hutch.'

'But there is your court case coming up, you have to think of that.' Pointed out Naomi.

'But you'll be supporting me, won't you love?' he asked, a plaintive note in his voice.

'Privately.'

'Can I depend on you being there on the day? I'll need you. Although I haven't got a date yet.'

'I don't think so, it wouldn't be appropriate, and Alva will be there too. I'll have to say the same to her since I'm not actually involved in the case.'

'I still feel I'll manage to persuade her to change her mind.'

'Wouldn't be too sure about that. Her legal team won't be too pleased if she does such a thing.'

'Who cares about legal teams, I don't think much of my crowd. Useless.'

'You did plead guilty. And sometimes that can be a good thing. The judge will look favourably on you.'

'I don't know what I'd do if I didn't have you.' he kissed her. 'You keep me going.'

'I'll always be there for you, my love.'

Darren depended on Naomi. She was so loving. And he could see that she would support him as much as she could. That made such a difference to him. Although there was no court date yet, he felt that the time was growing closer, and he needed to contact Alva soon so that he could persuade her to drop her accusations.

Early in the morning, he went around to the apartment which

he had shared with Alva in the hope that she had moved back there with her new husband. If that man didn't have his own apartment and was renting perhaps, then the fact that Alva owned her apartment would have been very attractive to him, although the thought of him sleeping in their bed sickened him. He still had the key fob for the gates of the complex, so was able to gain entry. He drove around to their parking spot but found both empty. He was disappointed about that and decided to come around on the following day again, it was Saturday and perhaps she mightn't be working.

But there was no one there at that time either. The spaces empty. He was frustrated. How would he make contact with her? It had to be face to face. If he made a phone call, it would be far too easy for her to put down the phone if she didn't want to listen to him. He had to see her. That was imperative. Maybe he'd just go in to see her?

On Monday he reorganised his day and parked close to her office, watching as people went in and out. Two men crossed the foyer and began to talk to the receptionist. Now he took his chance and quickly opened the door and walked up the stairs to the first floor. Delighted the woman hadn't spotted him. Outside Alva's office he stopped and opened the door. His heart thumping as he saw her working on her laptop at the desk.

'Alva?'

She turned around and stared. Her eyes wide when she saw him. Immediately she stood up. 'What are you doing here?'

'I just came to see you, I want to talk,' he said, feeling somewhat awkward.

'I don't want to talk to you,' she replied abruptly. 'There's nothing to say.'

'I want to say I'm sorry.'

'For what?'

'Everything.' He thought that might have been the best

approach. While he didn't feel sorry as such, it was more regret that he had been so stupid.

'It's a bit late for that,' she snapped.

'Can you forgive me?' he asked.

'No.'

'But that's all I want.'

'You don't get what you want just by saying a few empty words. They are meaningless. And you'll have to pay the penalty for what you did.'

'I want to ask you not to give evidence. If you don't do that, then the Gardai will have nothing.'

'I think you've asked me to do that before, what makes you think that I'm going to change my mind now?'

'I thought you might have felt differently towards me, when you think of what we had in the past.'

'The past is the past,' she said.

'But I don't want to lose it.'

'It's already gone.'

'I can't accept it.'

'You'll have to.'

'Why?'

'Because that's the way it has to be. I'm married now. You're not part of my life any longer.'

'You could leave him. Tell him you're going back to me.'

'That's not going to happen, Darren. You'll just have to forget me.'

'But I can't, don't you understand?' he insisted.

'You'll have to, there's no choice.'

'Please give me another chance,' he begged.

'There isn't another one available. You've used them all up.'

'That can't be.'

'It is. Our life is gone. I've got another one and it doesn't include you.'

'I can see that. Congratulations.' He indicated her bump with an air of sarcasm. 'I thought we were going to have a baby. That was our plan. But of course the time was never right was it?'

'I think you should go. You'll have to accept things the way they are.'

'I can never do that.' He shook his head.

'You will have to. And it would be so much better if we could be friendly at least.'

'That's what I want,' he barked.

'And I do too.'

'But you're going to accuse me of all sorts of things when we meet in court.'

'I'm only a witness, and will have to answer the questions I'm asked by the legal people. And I have to give my word to tell the truth and nothing but the truth.'

'That's rubbish.'

'Whatever, Darren. Anyway, I have work to do now, so I'd prefer if you let me get on with it.'

'Could we meet for a coffee or a drink?' he asked.

'No,' she said bluntly. 'And by the way, how did you get in here?'

'I just walked in,' he smirked.

'Please go Darren.'

'I'll call in again.'

'Don't bother.'

Chapter Twenty-two

'Bye, see you soon.' Naomi hugged Alva, and waved to her as she drove out of the complex.

She went back upstairs then feeling confused. Guilty. And a myriad of other emotions. Memories of Alva when they were children together. Thoughts of Darren and how much she loved him. How could she measure her feelings for him as compared to how she loved Alva. It wasn't possible to do that now. Alva was part of her. Like family. Darren was part of her. And she couldn't differentiate between them. To love Alva. To be in love with Darren. What to do?

She called him. But she had to leave a voice mail. He called back later.

'Everything OK?' he asked. Sounding worried.

'Yes, thanks, when can I see you?' she asked.

'How about tonight?'

'Great, I'll see you then.'

'It will be about eight by the time I'll be there, I have a meeting.'

She was glad to see him when he arrived. She said nothing, but just embraced him silently.

'This is a surprise,' he said. 'Unexpected.'

'I just had to see you,' she murmured.

'Is there a particular reason?' he looked at her quizzically.

'I've missed you.'

'And I've missed you.' He kissed her.

'Glass of wine? I've white cooling.'

'I'll chance a small glass.' He came into the kitchen and grinned at her.

'You won't be going home too early I hope?' She took a bottle from the fridge.

'I've no intention of that.' He put his arms around her and hugged her tight.

She squealed. 'Darren, stop. I'm pouring the wine.'

He laughed.

Naomi handed a glass to him.

They sat down.

'To the future,' he said.

'It's lovely just to relax here together.' Naomi sighed. 'I love you so much.'

'That's why I want to be with you all the time,' he added, and kissed her.

Unexpectedly, the doorbell rang.

'I wonder who that could be?' Naomi asked.

'Don't worry.' Darren dismissed it. 'If it's important they'll ring a second time.' He kissed her again.

'No, maybe it's one of the neighbours.' Naomi stood up and went to the intercom. 'Yes?'

'Naomi? Did I happen to leave my phone with you earlier? I can't find it in the car.' Alva sounded worried. 'I'll be lost without my phone. Would you mind calling me and if I've dropped it in the car then I'll hear it.'

'No, I didn't see it around,' she said. 'But I'll call you now and hopefully you'll hear it.'

'Thank you, Naomi. Just give me a minute to go back out to the car, it's outside.'

'That was Alva, she's lost her phone. What are we going to

do? She can't come up here and see you. Look around, will you?' In a panic, she began to search the room. Frantically dragging the cushions off the couch. 'I can't see it at all, can you?' she asked Darren who was looking for it as well. 'I'm ringing it now so we'll probably hear it if it's here, or she will.' She pressed Alva's number. 'It doesn't seem to be ringing at all. It's just silent. Maybe it's turned off?'

He stood up and looked around. 'Can't see a phone. I have mine in my pocket.'

'I hope she doesn't come up.' Naomi was very worried. 'She was sitting on the couch, but I can't see it anywhere.'

The doorbell rang again.

'There she is. I'll go down. You go into the bedroom so that she doesn't see you if she decides to come up to look for it.'

'I'm not hiding in the bedroom,' he retorted.

'You'll have to. Please?'

'If she comes up then I'm going to stand here and she can do what she wants.'

Naomi went out on to the corridor and closed the door behind her. Then she took the lift down and opened the front door where Alva waited.

'I can't hear it ringing, it's not in the car.'

'It's not in the apartment either.'

'Do you mind if I go up? Maybe you might have missed it.' Alva was anxious.

'I'm sorry, there's someone up there.'

'Someone?' Alva looked puzzled.

'My boyfriend.'

Alva realised what she meant.

'Look, I don't care who he is, Naomi. But I must find my phone. There is so much information on it, and all my contacts, and you know how difficult it is to get all that stuff on to a new phone.'

147

'It's not good timing, and he doesn't want to see you either.'

'Is he a famous person?' Alva demanded, becoming angry.

'No, he's not,' she said.

'Then what does it matter if I see him? If he is someone I don't know at all then what of it?'

Naomi looked very awkward.

'You're inferring it could be someone I do know?' Alva asked bluntly.

'Not necessarily.'

'Naomi, I don't know what you are saying. I might know this guy?'

'Well, yes.'

'Will I have to wait until he's gone until I get my phone?' she asked, seeming irritated.

'It could still be in your car.'

'It isn't there.'

'Let's not have a row about it, Alva. I'll search for it again. Go home. I'll leave a text with Carlos.'

'But I can't phone him either, and he can't get in touch with me.'

Let me look in your car. It may have slid down the sides of the seats or underneath or somewhere else.' Naomi began to walk towards Alva's car.

'I've searched it.' She sounded helpless.

'Let's have another look. Did you just sit in the front? You didn't put anything in the boot or on the back seats?'

'No, no. I didn't.'

'Alva, just drive around the block for fifteen minutes, he'll be gone by then. And we can look in the apartment.'

'OK, I'll do that. Thanks.'

Naomi hugged Alva. 'We'll find it, don't worry.'

She drove out of the gates, and Naomi went back upstairs to find

Darren sitting on the couch.

'You'll have to leave,' Naomi said. 'We can't find the phone in the car and Alva wants to come up. She's gone off for a short time but she will be back.'

'I don't want to leave,' Darren grumbled.

'You'll have to. You know how I feel about her, if she should find out about us then it could be disastrous.'

'All right then,' he agreed reluctantly. 'The night's ruined,' he said.

'It isn't, don't be ridiculous. Just sit in your car and I'll call you when she has left.'

'I hope it won't take too long,' he grumbled.

'We'll find the phone,' she said. 'Otherwise we'll have to tear the place apart.'

'That could take all night.'

'Darren, these things happen, it's life. How would you feel if you lost your phone?'

'I'd buy another one, what of it.' He shrugged.

'But she has everything on her phone, all her contacts. I wouldn't want to lose mine, if I did I'd be in a state as well.'

'I'll go now but hope to see you soon.' He pulled her close to him and their lips met.

It was like a melting of softness, she thought, and was irritated by all this fuss about Alva's phone.

'I'll wait to hear from you,' he said, and left.

Sorry about all of this, Naomi, I've really messed up your evening.' Alva hurried in, very apologetic.

'Let's have another look around for your phone,' Naomi said. 'You were sitting on the couch so it must be somewhere around there.'

Together they pushed the couch along the tiled floor and suddenly the phone appeared.

There it is,' Naomi exclaimed with excitement.

'Thank God.' Alva picked it up.

'I didn't think of pushing the couch over. Sorry.'

'Why didn't we hear it ring?' Alva was puzzled.

'It must have turned itself off or something when it fell.'

Alva threw her arms around Naomi, and hugged her. 'Thank you, that's such a relief.'

'All that business of trying to get all your stuff back is a pain. As far as I can see when you buy a new phone they can never manage to get everything transferred. The last time instead of being alphabetical all the contacts were mixed up and I had to go back into the shop to get them to change them.'

'Now I don't have that hassle,' Alva grinned, delighted. 'Thanks to you.'

'If only I had moved the couch sooner. I feel stupid,' Naomi said, feeling guilty.

'Don't worry, it was my own fault, it must have slipped out of my bag and in doing that it switched off. And so sorry to have spoiled your evening, I hope your boyfriend wasn't too put out. I'll make it up to you. Maybe we'll get together next week, let me know what nights you are available.'

'I'll check my schedule. Look forward to that.'

'Thanks again.' Alva hugged Naomi.

Darren's phone rang. It was Naomi. 'Hi?'

'We found the phone.'

'That's good.'

'You can come back now.'

'I've just met someone, so I'll be a while. See you later.'

'Don't be too long.'

Darren had moved his car further away from the entrance door. This was his best chance, he thought. There shouldn't be too much traffic and it would be possible to follow Alva home, wherever that was now. He had slumped down in the seat when she had arrived, and was relieved that she parked closer to the entrance than he was himself. He was nervous as he waited, hoping that she wouldn't be too long, and also that Naomi wouldn't come down with her and spot his car.

But no, his fears weren't realised, and Alva came out of the building and climbed into her car not too long afterwards. He waited a moment before moving behind her. She didn't know who he was and hopefully, wouldn't realise she was being followed. She turned left and he took the same route, leaving a distance between them because there wasn't much traffic.

To his surprise he found that she was heading for the East link bridge to the North side of Dublin city. He was able to keep one car between hers and his own and luckily that person was going in the same direction. She turned along the road following Dublin bay towards Howth and turned after a time into an apartment complex. Now he continued to drive further on as she waited at the entrance gates. He spent some time driving around and returned after a few minutes and pulled up outside. By that time, she had gone in and he wondered whether her husband was already inside or would arrive later. Betting that he might do that, he sat in the car as darkness gathered. He had no idea what type of car he drove, but could remember how he looked. He was a tall man with dark colouring.

He waited. Time passed. He dozed off, but awoke when a car passed and the lights dazzled. It was a jeep and it drove up to the gates. He sat up and climbed out of his car. There was a gap in the bushes behind the wrought-iron fencing and he peered through. The lights in the carpark lit up as the driver of the car got out. It was him. The husband. He knew him instantly. Now he could see that he drove a black jeep so he'd know him in future. He stayed where he was until the man went into the entrance and out of sight. He was going into Alva. Who was his partner and should have been waiting for him, not this other guy.

He felt insanely jealous. He would get his own back at him. Somehow. Somewhere.

He rang Naomi.

'I'm sorry, love, but I met my boss, and we're still here in the bar.'

'Come back, it's not that late.'

'I'll try.'

But he didn't.

Chapter Twenty-three

It was late when his phone rang. Carlos answered it, dropped a kiss on Alva's lips, and slipped out of the bed. There was an emergency with a patient. The same young man he had operated on before he went to Spain. He threw on some clothes, jumped into the jeep and drove to the hospital. His patient was in ICU, and he met with his team and together they examined the MRI and other scans which had been carried out.

'We'll have to go in again,' Carlos murmured.

'We have not removed all of the tumour,' the other doctor said.

Carlos was subdued. 'I was so sure we had.'

They had used image guidance computer technology. And during the first operation had discussed the procedure with other consultant surgeons around the world. But now there was no time to confer with them. Speed was of the essence as it was a very delicate technique and always risky, but it had to be done for the sake of their patient. Carlos was worried now.

'We'll go ahead as soon as the team is ready,' he said.

A short time later, he was dressed in his green scrubs. The anaesthetists, and nursing staff were in attendance, and the patient had been prepped. In the theatre, the lights were bright, and large monitors showed the vital signs of the man, heart rate, blood pressure, respiratory rate, etc., and as he was anaesthetised, on a monitor they could see where they had operated previously and now began to repeat the procedure. Hours went by as they worked through the primary pathways into the brain. It was slow, painstaking work. Laser arrows showed the path which the surgeons must use to reach the tumour. Tiny endoscopic cameras give depth perception and better visibility and showed the position of blood vessels before they may be touched and cause danger to the patient. It was warm in the operating theatre despite the air conditioning and they worked carefully, every movement so precise in the effort to save this man. It was hours later when they finally finished the procedure, and Carlos prayed that they had removed all of the tumour now. The patient was moved to the recovery room, and Carlos stayed there keeping a sharp eye on all of his vital signs. This was an important time in the recovery of the patient and he was very concerned that as the hours passed, his condition would continue to be stable.

He sent Alva a text later on that night, apologising for his delay, but saying that he would have to stay with his patient, he hadn't done an all-night stint for some time and regretted that this had happened, but he couldn't do anything about it. Alva would understand, he was certain about that. He spent the time watching over his patient although the ICU nurses were there all the time. Checking the various monitors. The drips. Blood pressure. Temperature. All the usual things. As the hours passed, the man continued to be stable and he wasn't so worried about him.

It was just after dawn when one of the alarms on the monitors gave off an unusual sound. Immediately, he checked it and was desperately worried to see that the patient was suffering cardiac arrest. He pressed an alarm and there was a rush of medical personnel into ICU, and all of them began to work on the patient. He was put on a ventilation machine to help him breathe, and Carlos watched the screens to judge the sound waves of the heart in motion, worried that sudden increases in intracranial

154

pressure might lead to severe hemodynamic disturbances. There were so many possibilities now that could lead to unforeseen complications after the procedure they had carried out earlier, and while he had been aware that any of them could have occurred, cardiac arrest hadn't been top of his list.

Various specialists in different fields were working on the patient now. Heart, lungs, and other organs which had been affected. Carlos still watched the screens which showed him how the patient was responding but wasn't encouraged by what he saw. The cardiac surgeon now changed the various medications which needed to be administered, and he hoped that they would be effective and save the life of his patient. His heart hadn't stopped beating for very long, and Carlos hoped that he wouldn't be affected permanently. He was a young man and didn't deserve that after all he had gone through. Carlos had been his doctor over the past few years and every fibre of his being was with those laboured breaths which kept his patient alive.

The day was long drawn out for the medical teams involved and Carlos. He texted Alva a couple of times when he had a chance and explained briefly why he was delayed. This was the part of it he hated. Leaving her out there on the edge of his life. He wished he could just call and spend some time explaining what was happening. Not only to get her support, but to ask what she thought and sense her love for him down the line and be the better of it.

Deciding to stay at the hospital for another night, he managed to get a chance to sleep in the late afternoon for a couple of hours, and was refreshed. It helped him focus. He was glad no one on the team called him to ICU then, thinking every hour his patient lived without intervention meant that his chances of a complete recovery improved.

The night darkened. It was like a cloud had surrounded him

and there was a heaviness about it that weighed down on him. In the later hours he sat by the bedside of his patient. The man's family had been in and out as they were allowed by the staff, and were very glad to see that their son and brother was holding his own and praying that he would make a full recovery. Their prayers so loud, the Lord just had to listen to them. Carlos was out there on the periphery of their prayers. Wondering how he could help. Was what he did even going to save that young man? The question was big, and tall and loud, and demanded an answer. Could he give the family an answer? What a question. He thought. And prayed that he could do exactly what his patient, and family wanted. Was that ever going to be possible? Was it like a miracle? Was he expected to perform a miracle? Self-doubt swept through him. He had never thought he could do such a thing. If his decisions regarding medication and surgeries were correct, then something akin to a miracle was possible. But if not, then what was left to him?

Chapter Twenty-four

In Seville, Julie threw her arms around Pedro as soon as she arrived at the house. 'Isn't it wonderful news about Alva and Carlos.'

'I was talking to Carlos, he rang to tell me,' he smiled widely.

'You must be so happy, we are,' Julie said. 'Isn't it wonderful. Our first grandchild.'

'I can't wait.'

'How will it feel to be a grandfather?' She hugged him again.

'It is another generation in the family.'

'We are all looking forward to it,' Julie said. 'I will have to go over to be with Alva, she doesn't have anyone to help when the baby comes.' Thinking that it would be good to mention in advance that she would have to go to Dublin at that time.

'Surely she will have help. Her family. Friends?' Pedro asked.

'It's possible. But everyone works so people don't have much time to help.'

'She could employ a nurse.'

'The best person to do that will be her mother,' Pacqui said. 'Or her cousins.'

'You can come over as well, and grandfather too,' suggested Julie.

'I am not good with babies,' Pedro admitted.

'You will be good with your first grandchild,' Pacqui said.

'Are you sure?' he laughed.

'You were good with us when we were babies,' she smiled.

'Your mother took care of you. She was wonderful.'

Pacqui didn't say anything.

Julie was also quiet. Pedro didn't mention his first wife very often, always giving Julie the benefit of being the mother of his children. She was always grateful to him for being so generous. His children became her children.

That evening, Pedro, Pacqui and herself took the horses out for a ride. It was cool at this time, and they raced along the deserted beach. They always brought their own horses out to Cadiz. The stud which had a large number of horses and foals was big business and took up a lot of their time, although Julie wasn't involved in the stud itself other than on the PR side they had many clients who needed attention, and she enjoyed dealing with them.

They rode into the surf and the horses seemed to really enjoy the flying spray as they cantered along. Julie was very confident about riding now, the fear which had dogged her since her horse had bolted and thrown her the summer before last had diminished and she was very happy to be up on her horse once again, loving the feel of him beneath her carrying her along in the sea. She rubbed her hand along his neck and whispered words encouraging him. His ears pricked up, and he was obviously happy galloping with the other horses. They slowed down and went back on to the sand again. Hooves pounding like drumbeats on the hard wet surface at the edge of the surf. She glanced across at Pedro and Pacqui and they both laughed back at her. Heads down, hands gripping the reins, their horses racing too.

Back at the stables, the stable hand took their horses in. Julie decided to spend some time with her horse, rubbing him down after his exertions, but after a while she followed Pedro and

Pacqui to see a new foal which had just been born. They were in one of the other stables, and were bending down to see the little black foal which lay in the straw his mother licking the wet coat.

'He's beautiful,' she whispered. Any little animal always appealed to her but especially the foals.

'He is worth a lot of money, I am so glad he is safe. I must call his owner,' Pedro said and took his phone from his pocket.

'His mother is really taking care of him,' Pacqui murmured.

'That's so important,' Julie replied.

Chapter Twenty-five

Darren felt a great sense of satisfaction as he saw the black jeep drive into the apartment complex. Any night he had time he could be found watching the place. He hadn't decided what he was going to do but he had every intention of persuading the man to leave Alva. He wondered what it would take. He could write to him. Threaten him. But where did he work? Which hospital? It had to be on the North side of Dublin probably. If he was a neurosurgeon as Naomi had said, then there was a chance he worked in Beaumont. He looked up the list of consultants on Google. Carlos. It sounded familiar. He remembered that night he went around to see Alva when she was staying at her father's place, and the boyfriend, as he was then probably, arrived back and prevented him from getting into the house. She had called him, and yes, his name was Carlos.

He wrote a letter that very evening.

'I am watching you.'
'Leave Dublin.'
'Or else you will have no life.'
'Nothing to call your own.'
'I will take everything you value.'

He read it over again, folded it, and put it in an envelope. He felt good about that. Instead of watching them all the time, he was doing something much more constructive. He wondered what affect his words would have on this Carlos. What sort of man was he? How might he react to the letter? Would he be scared? Would he report him to the Gardai immediately? Insist that they arrest him? Drag him into prison? He suddenly thought of his situation with the Gardai. Would this latest action mean that they would treat him differently? No. He dismissed it. Carlos would do nothing at all, he was certain of that. And how would he know who had written the letter anyway? That was the most important thing. He wouldn't have a clue. Darren stared at the envelope in his hand. A wave of doubt suddenly in his mind. Was he doing the right thing, he asked himself? Was this the only way to get Alva back. The only way?

Other than by persuasion. To dig deep into her heart. To wind around that organ which beats loud and sure and tells him that they can go back in time and find the love they once knew. Pure unsullied love. Something he had defiled with that woman. How stupid he had been. Had a cloud darkened his eyes and prevented sight revealing the future and the pain he would have to endure. How had he not known the truth. How had he not learned his lesson after that first time. When he should have apologised and promised that he would never be unfaithful again. All it took were a few words. A simple promise. I will never be disloyal to you again. And with this pledge he would open himself up to her and hope that she would forgive him. But how many times would he have to ask her, he wondered. Would Carlos tell her that he had received the letter. And what would be her response? That question floated across his mind. And he had no idea what she would say.

He kept the letter. And waited. That was all he did. Waited. Looking at it every day and thinking about what he was doing.

Then a thought. What if the Gardai should find out that it was in his handwriting? He was shocked. They could do that so easily and discover he had written it. His plan was shattered. What was he going to do now?

In the end, he decided that he would create it using letters cut out from a newspaper. Yes. That was the answer.

He had to buy a newspaper as he didn't get his news that way these days and chose a couple of the papers which had a selection of different size fonts. He wore gloves as he pasted the letters on to a sheet of paper and so hoped that no one would be able to tell who had sent the letter. Although he printed the name and address on the envelope using his laptop, he felt more confident now. This should work.

Chapter Twenty-six

Carlos stayed in the hospital attending to his patient. His condition hadn't improved unfortunately, but Carlos changed his medication and treatment methods in any way he could. But nothing seemed to help him recover. And then to his shock, he suffered another cardiac arrest. And in spite of everything the medical team did, they lost him.

Having to explain to his family what had happened was particularly difficult for Carlos. This hadn't happened to him before, and he blamed himself for everything. What had he missed? That question constantly pounded through his head. Had his choice of medications been so wrong that he had made an error? Was that what happened? Had he made some grave blunder in the original operation to remove the tumour?

The family were brought in then, but their son had already gone.

Carlos took them to another room, and a support team was arranged to help the family in this awful situation in which they found themselves. But it was Carlos whom the mother and father approached in their distress.

'What happened to our son?' they asked, in between their tears.

'It was a cardiac arrest ...a heart attack,' he said. His voice soft, and he hoped, sympathetic.

'But he had cancer,' the mother said, trying to dry her eyes. 'I thought you said he had a tumour?'

'That is true, and we operated to remove it, but we couldn't prevent the heart attack. There may be a number of reasons why that happened.' He couldn't mention the list of possibilities, although he knew them. But the words would frighten the life out of these good people.

'His heart was always strong.' The father came into the conversation.

'We cannot always explain the reasons.' Carlos found this whole process very difficult, and sat down beside the parents.

His brother spoke then. He was angry. 'Did you make a mistake? Did any of you do something you shouldn't have done and is that why he died? Can you explain to us why it happened? He was so young. Too young to die.' He put his arms around his younger sisters and turned away from Carlos.

As he did, the mother lay her head on the shoulder of the father. He embraced her and silently they wept for the loss of their son.

Carlos checked on the condition of other patients before he left the hospital, worried about all of them because of what had happened. Eventually, when he was satisfied that they were stable, he left to go home. He should have been exhausted but instead of that he felt numb. As it was in the small hours now, Alva was already in bed asleep and he just slipped in beside her reluctant to disturb and lay there, his mind back at the hospital with the grieving family. He felt responsible. It was his fault. The guilt cut through him. He couldn't escape the implication. And what that meant for his future. He thought about the other patients who needed care, and whether he would manage to do what he was supposed to do. The vision of his scalpel cutting through tissue, avoiding blood vessels, and removing tumours suddenly filled him with terror. He couldn't understand himself.

He had been a surgeon for a number of years specialising in the field since he had qualified as a doctor, and now he felt like it was his first day in theatre. He couldn't sleep.

When the alarm went off, he awoke. Aware that he must have dozed for a short while. But immediately he turned towards Alva, put his arms around her and kissed her. Her eyes opened and smiling she kissed him back.   'How are you, my love?' she asked. 'It's been so long since I've seen you. How is your patient?'

'He died,' he said slowly, as tears welled up in his eyes.

'I'm so sorry, my love.' Alva held him close to her.

He hung on to her, needing solace.

'It must have been terrible for you, Carlos, I wish I could have been there for you. You should have told me how serious it was.'

They lay there and he felt comforted by her touch and her soft whispers.

'How are you feeling this morning?'

'I'm all right,' he said.

'You must be exhausted. Can you rest a while before going into the hospital again?'

He shook his head. 'I did grab a couple of hours sleep.'

'When?'

'I was home about three.'

'It's only six now. Three hours? That's nothing.'

'It's enough,' he said.

'You have a shower, and I'll make breakfast. Have you enough time for that?'

'Of course I have, querida, I just want to spend some time with you now.'

'And I with you.' She hugged him tight.

He felt a little better after talking with Alva. Knowing that she understood meant everything. But as he drove to the hospital, that grim presentiment of dread grew ever more threatening and he found it very difficult to face into the day. Even the simple act of walking into ICU and finding another young man lying in the bed where his own patient had died a few hours before was particularly difficult. He would have liked to call the parents and ask how they were but hesitated. They would be involved in making funeral arrangements now, and getting together with family and he wouldn't have wanted to interfere in any way, and didn't think they would appreciate it.

He looked at his schedule, and could see he was operating today. Knowing every one of his patients very well, he could immediately judge their condition and the next step he would have to make in their recovery. His patient was a woman, and he dreaded the thought of the procedure he would have to carry out.

He worked slower than usual. Taking every care. Aware that he was shaking inwardly and hoping that the other members of the team did not notice. With the other surgeon on his team, they succeeded in removing the tumour and he had a great sense of relief when they made the final moves and the monitors showed that her life signs were all good.

The next patient was wheeled in and he remembered him. An older man. He prayed that with this procedure, and after all he had endured by undergoing treatment over the past few months, he too would make good progress.

That first day was horrendous. He thought it would never end. To his relief there were no urgent matters in the evening and he was able to get home earlier than usual. So glad to turn his key in the lock of the door and walk in to feel Alva put her arms around him, and reassure him that she had been waiting for him.

'It's wonderful to see you,' she said.

'There were two operations but we got through.'

'I hope you weren't nervous,' she said.

'You know me too well,' he smiled. 'I was very nervous. It was the first time I've had a patient die and it's affected my confidence. I don't know how I actually went ahead with the operations today.'

'I'm sure that will never happen again. Let's not talk about it. We'll have a relaxing evening. Maybe take a walk in Howth and have dinner somewhere,' she suggested.

'Good idea.' He kissed her.

They drove out, and walked along the pier. The sea in the harbour was calm, the blue sky reflected in its green blue depths. The clinking of metal stays on the aluminium masts of the yachts berthed there echoed atmospherically as they made their way to the end of the pier and sat with feet dangling near the Harbour Lighthouse. They went to a small restaurant nearby for dinner and sat at a window as twilight faded and pinpricks of light brightened Howth Head behind them.

Chapter Twenty-seven

Alva was worried about Carlos. After the death of his patient, his mood had changed, and she found it hard to jolly him along. Each day it was harder. Even though she had said that they wouldn't talk about it again, she felt perhaps it was the wrong decision. It would have been much better to talk it out at that time and get it out of the way. Now, it rose between them like a forbidden subject and she just didn't feel she could open it up again.

She rang her mother, Julie, every few days, letting her know what was happening with her and the baby who was growing larger and making its presence felt inside her. Kicking and moving about and reminding her that it would be here in the world in another couple of months. While she would have loved to talk to Julie about Carlos and his low mood, she didn't feel she should break a confidence and so said nothing. Julie would only worry too much particularly as she wasn't planning to come over until the baby arrived. Also, she was disappointed none of her family had managed to come over to Cadiz and join them at the beach. David's business was going well but he needed to work very long hours. Sarah was also working in the company and really they didn't feel they could spare the time. Her brother, Cian, who worked with Alva in the family firm, and his partner, Natalie, were also busy so had to regretfully decline. Cian was trying to persuade Alva to leave the office at five in the evening and so reduce her hours as the arrival of her baby grew closer, but Alva would never agree. She enjoyed work. She was addicted to it, and freely admitted that, so there was no way she was going home any day at five o'clock, it was far too early and would have felt like a half-day. And as Carlos wasn't home in the evenings either, she was never too keen to work at home. The hours crawling by as she waited for him to arrive. She could of course have met Naomi, but her hours were just as bad and they could only manage to meet occasionally.

Over the summer she had gone walking along the coast road occasionally, but while it was good exercise, she really didn't enjoy it on her own. But work always came first. This was something she inherited from her father, and the new company she visited while in Spain on honeymoon was proving to have some very good quality wines which were already selling very well and she enjoyed dealing with the owners, who were delighted to have new business in Ireland. Alva had the full agency for Ireland, so as the sales grew, so did her profits. It was always good to sell some new wines as she hated producing all the usual ranges to her customers. Some just wanted the same ones, but others were always interested in something different. And this company produced organic wines which these days were popular, although slightly more expensive, but that didn't seem to matter to her customers.

This evening when she arrived home, she found Carlos already there sitting on the couch and staring at the television.

'Hey, you're here already. Why didn't you phone me? How long are you home?'

'Not so long,' he said.

'I would have had dinner ready if you had. Now it will take a bit of time.' She went towards him, and bent to kiss him. But it was awkward with her bump and she couldn't quite reach. Surprised too that he hadn't stood up to kiss her when she arrived as he usually did.

'Are you hungry?'

'Not particularly.' He shook his head.

'You seem a bit out of sorts, are you feeling all right?' She was suddenly worried, and put her arm around him.

'I'm fine, don't worry,' he said. And then stood up. 'I'll do the dinner, Alva querida you relax, sorry, I don't know what I'm thinking.' His mood changed unexpectedly.

'It's a casserole and just has to be heated,' she protested. 'I'll put it in the oven.'

'It's a heavy dish.' He took it from the fridge, opened the oven door and slid it inside.

'I'm used to it. I'm not an invalid,' she laughed.

'No, but you must take care and not put strain on yourself.' He hugged her and seemed much more like himself. After they had finished dinner, she was delighted to notice that he seemed to have cheered up a bit, and everything was more normal.

But it didn't last and she had to deal with those changes in his personality on a daily basis. Never quite sure what mood he would be in when he awoke in the morning, or when he came in from work. All the time, she put it down to the death of his patient. It had to be that. He was a very sensitive person and she knew that he had been very upset by the incident, and that there was nothing which he could have done to change the outcome. But for how long would it continue? And what could she do about it?

She looked forward to the arrival of their baby and hoped that it would help Carlos to handle what was troubling him now. Since she had known him, he had always been very upbeat about everything, so this new side to him was very strange.

Naomi called one evening, and also noticed the change in Carlos when he came home.

'He doesn't seem himself at all.' She was astonished.

'Since he lost that young man, he doesn't seem to be able to cope,' Alva remarked.

'It's a terrible responsibility for any surgeon. I can't imagine operating on someone.' Naomi shuddered.

'He's always been very confident since I've known him.'

'Don't worry yourself too much, you've enough to think about with the baby coming.'

'I miss the support he used to give me. I'm wondering now if he regrets that we got pregnant and that our lives are going to change radically when the baby arrives.'

'But I thought he was delighted,' Naomi said.

'He was, but maybe the more he thought about it has had a negative effect on him. And he's coming home earlier these days, like he can't bear to stay in the hospital longer than necessary.'

'Well, that's a good thing. The hours he worked were crazy, and yourself as well.'

'Cian is giving me grief over that, and taking on as much of my work as he can.'

'You're lucky to have him. I hope you'll take off some time when baby arrives. You can't be bringing he or she into work. I can see you do that, you know,' said Naomi, laughing.

'Obviously I'll take off some time initially, but I can work from home. That's no problem.'

'You should have a complete break, just to get to know your baby. You'll never manage the feeding, the changing, the sleeping, motherhood is tough going. Anyway, I'll take a few days off and be with you. At least I can let you sleep. Although I don't know a lot about babies. But I'll try my best.'

'That means there will be two of us trying to find out how to look after one baby,' Alva laughed.

'We'll probably find Carlos is better than either of us,' they giggled.

'I'll be very glad if he takes to the baby.'

'Men are so hands on these days.'

'Hope so. Only six weeks to go.' Alva touched her bump gently. Suddenly tears moistened her eyes.

'Why are you crying?'

'I don't know, it must be hormones. At the least thing I can burst into tears. When Carlos is in a mood that's when it happens. You wouldn't believe, it's not really me.'

'Not usually, but then a pregnant Alva is someone I don't know either. You're a different person.'

'It's the first time,' Alva sighed. 'The first time for everything. Maybe I won't be able to cope either. What do you think, Naomi?'

'You will be able. Don't be ridiculous.'

'It's good to see you, Naomi. How are things going?' Carlos came into the room.

'I'm fine, Carlos, and looking forward to our big event,' she smiled.

'Let's have supper,' Alva stood up. 'Come on, Naomi, sit down.'

'Thanks, that looks really delicious,' she said.

'Carlos put it together.'

'Thank you, Carlos, I love tapas, and cold meats.'

'Enjoy, Naomi,' he smiled.

Chapter Twenty-eight

Carlos went through the post on his desk. A bundle of envelopes which he slit open with a paper knife. The last one contained just a single page of A4, but the lettering was very strange. It seemed they had been cut out of a newspaper and stuck on. Even the edges had partially peeled away. He read down the sentences.

'I am watching you.'
'Leave Dublin.'
'Or else you will have no life.'
'Nothing to call your own.'
'I will take everything you value.'

He was shocked at the threatening tone. Who would want to send him such a menacing letter? What was it all about? He was puzzled. He replaced the letter back in the envelope, and put it into his briefcase. Certainly, he didn't want anyone else to see it. But all day he found the image of the letter stayed in his mind and wouldn't let go. While he had a clinic today and was meeting various patients, some new whom he hadn't met before, and others who were regular and he knew quite well, he had to concentrate and force the image out of his mind and not let it take over. Before he left his clinic, he read the letter once more, but was no nearer to finding out who may have sent it to him.

Afterwards he went around the wards and checked on his

patients. It was something he always did both morning and evening. Discussing their progress with the doctors and nurses who would be on duty over the next few hours. Driving home, he wondered if he should tell Alva about the letter, but decided against it. It would only worry her unduly and probably not be good for her in her present condition. But that night, he lay in bed going over and over the circumstances of receiving the letter. He could see it in his mind. It had to have been sent by someone from Dublin. The postage stamp was Irish but then he realised that the frank on the envelope said it had gone through Portlaoise Mail Centre and was dated the day before. He had checked that Mail Centre and saw that it covered Munster and Leinster outside of Dublin. Now he wondered if it was just a joke being played on him by someone? If so, they had a very strange sense of humour. Who on earth could it have been? Maybe it was one of the staff at the hospital. Maybe they had some dislike of people from Spain. But then unless they could see his reaction to receiving it, what was the point? He began to think he was over-reacting and decided to put it out of his head altogether and forget. It was nonsense. He had more to think of than crazy stuff like this.

But he couldn't. It continued to bug him and worst of all he found he was unable to sleep properly. Tossing and turning during the night, always conscious of disturbing Alva and often getting up and sitting in the lounge reading medical journals just to pass the time. While normally he only slept for a few hours which was adequate, this broken sleep was disturbing and he hated its affects. He needed to be on top of his game every day. Requiring a great amount of concentration to handle the cases which were under his remit and he was very aware of his responsibility to all of these people and their families.

'Carlos?' Alva came into the lounge.

He looked up.

'What are you doing out here? It's only four o'clock.' She stood looking at him, concern etched on her features.

'Couldn't sleep,' he said.

'Come back to bed.'

'I'll only disturb you.'

'I won't be able to sleep because I'm on my own. Come on.' She put out her hand and he took it. 'Why can't you sleep, I don't think you've had a decent night's sleep for the past couple of weeks, I'm a bit uncomfortable because of the baby, as you know, so I'm quite aware that you're not sleeping well.'

'I'm sorry about that.'

'It's not your fault.'

He shrugged.

'Come on.'

They went back to bed, but he felt neither of them slept well, and he was guilty about that. Alva needed her sleep, now especially.

'Querida, maybe I should sleep in the other room,' he suggested. 'Then I won't be preventing you from getting a good night.'

'No, love, there's no need for that. I want you in the bed with me. I'd miss you too much,' she persuaded.

He agreed, not keen to argue. He still couldn't sleep, and now, he just lay there his mind going around in circles, thinking about that letter he had received.

'Are you worried about me?' Alva asked him.

'Of course, I am.' He put his arm around her.

'You shouldn't be. I'm going to be fine. I have my bag packed. I've bought some things for the baby. All we have to get is the baby basket, we can get everything else we need later. Although Naomi would have the place stocked with stuff if I let her. And I know she has already bought lots of things but she hasn't brought them over yet.'

'I can understand that you don't want too much at this point.'

'I'll enjoy it better afterwards, when he or she has arrived.'

'It's going to be wonderful.' He kissed her.

'Our lives are going to change radically, you do know that?' she asked, teasing him.

'I do,' he said, smiling.

'Not to worry, I don't expect you to give up your career.'

After that conversation, Carlos felt he really had to help Alva in the run up to the baby's arrival. It was all very well for her to say that she would do all the shopping needed after the baby arrived, but that meant she would need time and he knew how tired she could feel these days, and shopping was the most tiring thing of all. Still, she might shop online, but he knew she liked to touch and feel before she bought anything particularly for the baby. He checked his schedule, and noted he had a clinic on Saturday. He usually saw people in his rooms, and needed two days each week to get through his list as quickly as possible for the sake of his patients. He knew there was nothing worse than having to wait for appointments particularly when they were worried. Sunday was his day for catching up with admin, although these days he was trying to spend more time with Alva. So now he had to look at the list of appointments he had and see where he could trim the times so that he could free up some availability on Saturday afternoon. When the office made contact with the patients, he managed to bring some people in earlier in the morning which made a big difference. Then an appointment cancelled and he knew he would be able to leave about three o'clock.

'Let's go shopping on Saturday afternoon,' he suggested.

'Shopping?' Alva looked at him, her expression astonished.

'Yes, for baby,' he smiled and kissed her.

'Where would you get the time?' she laughed.

'I managed to re-arrange my schedule.'

'On Saturday?'

'Yes. And can you manage time off from your job.'

'I certainly can.'

'Sorry I can't make lunch but we could have dinner later and maybe go to see that play you mentioned.'

'They serve food before the play and if we're not finished before the play starts it doesn't matter. We could eat at six and the play starts at seven. I can't remember the name but someone in work mentioned it was very good and it's on until Saturday which is perfect.' Alva seemed really excited.

'That's a date,' he said.

'We'll have to arrange a few more dates like that, because there will be no more opportunities when baby arrives.'

'I should have made more of an effort up to now, but thinking about the baby has forced me to look at my schedule. Of course, before we met all I thought about were my patients. And I always tried to keep on top of my list so they wouldn't have to wait too long. I think now I'll have to put you and baby first, patients can't be first, however hard that's going to be.'

'You must have a life, Carlos, you can't work those hours for ever, it's crazy. I know I'm not much better but if you were home then I'd be home. I don't even notice the time I spend in the office usually. And I haven't any hobbies other than walking or going to the gym which I don't do at the moment.'

'I think having our baby is going to change everything in our lives.'

'For the best.'

Chapter Twenty-nine

Carlos was in the office early and picked up the bundle of envelopes on his desk. He slit open the first one and opened it. His heart almost stopped as he saw the misshapen letters on the page. He whispered an oath and read through the few lines. The wording was similar to the first. Threatening. Hateful. As before, he couldn't imagine who would send such a letter, and felt that he should probably bring it to the Gardai and see what they could do about it. But then, as he had no idea who might be the culprit, how would he help them to find such a person. It would be like searching for a needle in a haystack. He sat down in the chair and stared at it blankly. As before, he put it away in his briefcase and tried to put it out of his mind. But as he worked through the day, it came back, and wouldn't let him be.

Back in his office before he left that evening, he took out a sheet of paper and looked through his schedule for the last month. Were any of his patients living outside Dublin. He checked the addresses and there were a number. He went down the list and thought about what treatment he had given them. Procedures he had done. And there, in the middle, was the one patient who had died. He clenched his fist. Could it be one of the family who hated him for not saving that young man. They were angry with him, he remembered that day. Particularly the father and the brother. Was it possible that they felt strongly enough to send him these letters? Very anxious to get rid of him. Or maybe they intended to take a legal case against him, and this was part of that. But he had not received any solicitor's letter informing him that they were taking such action so far. He was perplexed. Now that he thought he had pinpointed the person or persons who might be behind the two letters, he thought about what could be done about it. Should he approach the family. Ask if there was anything which he could do? Did they need counselling? There were bereavement counsellors on the staff and available to anyone who needed such help and he didn't get involved usually. They dealt directly with the family. But now he could see that the parents of the young man may have expected him to help them through the bereavement process. Although he had attended the funeral and sympathised with them, he hadn't made any other overtures towards them, and they might hate him for it. He felt very guilty and could immediately understand that they felt strongly enough to possibly send him those letters. But what to do now? Had he identified the person? He didn't know. But because he wasn't searching around in the dark aimlessly, and had some idea, he decided to call the father of the young man who had died.

'I was just wondering how you are all getting along,' he asked gently.

'Oh, you know how it is, good days, bad days,' the man replied.

'And his mother? And his brother and sisters?'

'They're much the same. We must get on with life. That's all we can do.'

'I understand. Have you attended the counselling service?' Carlos asked.

'Oh no, that wouldn't be for us. We'll manage.'

He sounded quite self-possessed and calm, Carlos thought.

'If you ever need help, you can call me any time,' he offered.

'Thank you for saying that. We always liked you and we were very grateful for everything you did for our son. We heard you flew back to Ireland when you were on your honeymoon when he got a bad turn.'

'That was nothing.'

'I'm sure your new wife didn't think it was nothing,' the man laughed.

'She understood.'

'You're a lucky man.'

'I am.'

There was a silence between them. Carlos didn't know what else to say for a moment. 'Don't forget what I said, you can call me,' he emphasised.

'Hopefully, we'll get on OK. He's up above looking after us all the time.'

'That's a nice way to think of him.'

'Apple of his mother's eye.'

'I hope she is all right.'

'She does a lot of praying, and visits his grave every day. It keeps her going.'

'I'm glad to hear that.'

'Thank you again for phoning, it was nice to hear from you.'

'Take care of yourselves.'

'We will.'

'Goodnight, I'm sorry for calling so late.'

'We're very glad to hear from you again, Doctor.'

As Carlos put down the phone he immediately felt that this man certainly didn't appear to have any grievance against him because of the loss of his son. But perhaps his other son or even his wife, the young man's mother, may have secretly harboured some hatred deep in their hearts about which the father was unaware. But he was glad that he had phoned and spoken with him. That at least. But it left him still feeling frustrated. How would he ever find out who had sent the letters?

But when he was home, he found it very hard to hide this burden on his heart, in spite of the joy both he and Alva felt about the arrival of the baby. It was on this weekend that they would go shopping, and that in itself was a novelty, particularly for him. He picked Alva up at home and they went to a large centre in Coolock to see what accessories they carried in their different ranges.

'I've made a list, and top of that is a travel system, a buggy with a car seat and other bits and pieces. I'll have to buy one of them as if I have to go anywhere with the baby in the first couple of weeks, I'll need it.' Alva glanced at the note in her hand.

'Of course we will. And we'll need to buy two car seats as otherwise we'll have to be swopping them from one car to the other which will be awkward,' Carlos pointed out.

'Yes, you're right, didn't think of that,' Alva smiled at him. 'And we'll need a Moses basket for the bedroom, and one of those bottle heaters.'

'But I thought you said you wanted to breast feed?' he asked.

'Yes, I hope so, but just in case it doesn't work out, I'll need a bottle heater somewhere along the line. And bottles. I've looked up this website and they have some nice things. Come on, Daddy.' She took his hand and they walked in. They spent some time browsing, and saw most of the items they wanted.

'I like that buggy,' Carlos said pointing to one.

'Most of the colours which are fashionable now are quite dark. Black. Grey. Navy. But I like the grey as well.'

'It is nice.'

They looked at the mechanics of it and decided that it would suit. 'I'll take a photo of it and then we can order it on line and they'll deliver.' Alva was so glad Carlos was with her. To share the choice of all the things they needed for their baby meant everything to her. While Naomi was very keen to shop with her, she really preferred Carlos to be there. Afterwards, they went into another store in town, and picked up some of the other items they needed.

'Carlos, that was great to get everything, and to find it was all in stock,' Alva smiled at him. 'Thanks so much for arranging to get time off, I really enjoyed today.'

'I've decided I'll be doing that much more often now,' he said. 'You and our baby are too important to me. You'll be tired of looking at me.' He put his arm around her.

'That will never happen,' she smiled, looking very happy.

'Right, we've chosen everything, so let's go eat and catch this play,' he suggested.

They went over to Dawson Street to the Glass Mask Theatre, booked their seats and went in. It was very atmospheric, being quite small and intimate. There were only a few rows and the seats were a mix of armchairs and couches with small tables in front and were arranged in a semi-circle in front of an area where the actors would present the play.

The waitress came over and handed them a menu.

'I'm glad there's a menu, and they don't point us to the QR code on the table mat,' laughed Alva. 'I hate trying to decide what I'm eating on my phone.'

'So do I, as we don't eat out very much I haven't noticed it here, although I'm sure there are lots of places who do now.'

'It is mostly in Spain. And they have those robots in restaurants as well, someone was telling me. It was like a little man and it moved across to their table carrying the desserts. It was hilarious apparently,' they laughed.

'But that's where it's going, you know. There will be no waiters or waitresses in restaurants after a while. It will be all robotic, and completely impersonal.'

'At least we have a proper menu to look at now. Let's see.'

Alva looked down the list. 'How about Antipasto - a platter of salami, and ham, and olives etc. That sounds nice with bread. Tasty. What do you think?'

'Let's go for that.'

They ordered. Their meal was brought to their table quickly, giving them enough time to enjoy it by the time the lights softened and the play began. It was a three-hander about some rather downbeat people on the edge of life, trying to save themselves from a grim reality. Sitting quite close to the small stage, they were both swept up into the actors' dilemma and enjoyed the drama.

'That was really good,' Alva said. 'These plays are all new work which is amazing. When I was at college I was really involved in theatre, but unfortunately, when I qualified I had to go full time into the business and that was the end of my career on the stage. I even had hopes of going on to take a course in the Gaiety School of Acting and put myself out there into the world of being a professional actor. But sadly that never happened.' She seemed rather down about it.

'I'm sure you would have been a great actor.'

'Chances to do exactly what you want only come once in your life,' she admitted.

'I suppose I was lucky. I always knew what I wanted to do although my father had to be persuaded, and that took some effort between my Mum and myself to force him to let me go to Dublin to study. He wanted me working with him in the stud with the horses of course.'

'But you were going to do a degree and have a job at the end of it at least. Acting is a bit more uncertain and it's hard to make a living if you even get a couple of parts a year.'

'You never know where you could have ended up, you might have been on film and a famous movie star by now.'

'No chance of that,' she laughed. 'I was committed to my

Dad, and as I was already working part-time in the business I couldn't have turned around and told him I was going to do something else altogether and forget about the company.'

'Of course, you couldn't. You're a very unselfish person. I'm sure your father appreciated you. I'm sorry I never met him.'

'Although Mum was never happy with him,' Alva said slowly. 'It's so hard to know what's going on in people's lives. You can never tell.'

'She did talk to me about it,' Carlos said.

'You would have got on well with my father, he was a man's man I suppose you could say, and what went on between himself and Mum was their business really. Although it was because he died that I met my Mum again, and you and all your Spanish family,' she smiled at him, and touched his face gently.

'It was an amazing coincidence we met in that way,' he admitted.

'It was wonderful.'

'Knowing you has changed my life. And very much for the better, can you believe that?'

'And mine,' she agreed. 'I never could have imagined that I would be so happy.'

'Me neither.' He kissed her.

'I hope there will be many more days like this.'

'There will be.'

Chapter Thirty

With gloved hands, Darren carefully cut out the letters from the newspaper so that he could compose another message. It was similar to the first two but this time he wanted it to sound even more threatening. Make this Carlos feel that he was in danger. Darren wasn't sure exactly what he was going to do but tried to create something which would frighten the life out of the man. He enjoyed writing the messages and sometimes spent an entire evening working on them. He would go on a spree. It would take him only a few minutes to write each one and then he had a selection to choose from. He would have liked to send them all together but he forced himself to hold back and chose days which would be appropriate. It was far better to do that and imagine how receiving the letters would affect this Carlos fellow. Was he the worrying type of person? Would the letters freak him out as they had done to Alva when he sent her all those threatening letters a couple of years ago? He laughed, imagining what this Carlos would say to Alva. Or would he say anything at all? Maybe he wouldn't even know exactly what Darren meant by the lines in the letters? That he wanted him to break from Alva. The baby she was going to have should have been his. Was it clear enough? But he decided to keep the words vague so that they would be even more unsettling.

He would have loved to tell Naomi what he was doing, but held back. She wouldn't approve, he was sure of that. And she might even try to prevent him from doing it, or tell Alva and Carlos, which would spoil the excitement of it. He kept it to himself. All the time planning his next steps, anxious to force this Carlos into such a state he certainly wouldn't be able to support Alva the way Darren thought she should be. He was the one who should be taking her to the hospital and being there when she gave birth. Sometimes he was angry as he thought about everything. It even came between him and his own job which was very demanding. Keeping up with the targets set by the company which had increased sales recently to levels he had thought previously were almost impossible to achieve. He could have looked for another job as he found the general hardware products so dull compared to Purtell Vintners. Selling wines had something glamorous about it. It had been a great job. But on the other hand, the clients he had now all wanted everything he sold and it was so easy to sell the range he always reached his targets. He got to know them, and now he was welcomed in as an old friend, brought into the back office and offered coffee or tea, or even a drink if he had felt like it, and always a new order for whatever he had to sell. New products were eagerly taken, examined, tried out, and even shown to customers in the shops to get their feedback. It was very satisfying.

But there was something else bubbling in the back of his mind. It was just a kernel of another plan. Lately, he had been looking at houses for rent. Particularly out on the edge of town. If he could find somewhere isolated and quiet it would suit him. He was tired of living in the apartment. But anything he saw had long queues of anxious tenants waiting to view the property, and even though he was often near the top of the queue, was never lucky enough to be offered a tenancy. This evening he went around to an area on the outskirts of Dublin beside the sea. He parked some distance away and walked to the address he had noted in his phone. The house was an old cottage overlooking the beach which looked as if it needed some repair, but that didn't matter to Darren. He didn't know how long he would be living here. He just wanted a place to rent for a while. He expected that he would be joining another queue to see the property but probably because it was so far out of the city he was the only person there.

He was met by the agent, who quickly took him inside. The house was actually very small, but that didn't matter either. He was glad that the garden which stretched out on either side was even a bit wild. They couldn't ask that much for the rent. The man took him around, and while there were some basic items of furniture, again they were rough and ready. There was wood flooring, and the paintwork had been touched up fairly recently. The bathroom and kitchen were in reasonable condition, as was the en-suite bathroom.

'It's just yourself?' he was asked.

'And hopefully my partner.'

'Well, we're looking for about €1,200.00 a month. The landlord knows that it needs renovation but he's not in a position to begin that yet, so in the interim he will accept that amount.'

Currently, Darren was paying €1,000.00 per month for his modern apartment, so this rental was certainly achievable.

'That's fine,' Darren agreed.

'If you can call to the office tomorrow, I'll have a lease drawn up for the first three months as the landlord wants to renovate. I'll need the rent for next month in advance and a deposit for the same amount.'

As he left, Darren met a couple coming up the path and a few cars were already parking and their owners approaching eagerly. He grinned to himself, he was so lucky to have been here first and beat the rest of the prospective tenants. Anyway, the fact that the lease was only for three months wouldn't appeal to a lot of people who would want a more permanent rental.

Darren called to the estate agent's office the following day and signed the lease. This rental would take some of his savings, but as he had been working on his plan for a while now, he could afford it and the place was exactly what he wanted. The rent on the apartment just rolled over so he could give notice at the end of the week and move in here then. He had done well in the company, and had signed up quite a lot of new accounts and each time had received €1,000.00 in commission. His boss was delighted with his progress. And he was doing so well he was considering looking for another job. Companies were finding it hard to get staff so that wouldn't be hard. This would be important if he was going to get his plan off the ground.

He called Naomi to make an arrangement to see her. But he was very disappointed when she said no. She was too busy. So much going on.

'But Naomi, I miss you, when are we going to get together? You know I love you,' he persuaded.

'Soon, it's just I can't see you at the moment. We'll have to wait.'

'What's going on?' he asked, annoyed.

'The baby will be arriving soon,' she said.

'Alva's baby?' he gasped.

'Yes.'

'What is it, I mean, a boy or a girl?'

'We don't know yet.'

He grinned to himself. This is the child who should have been his. Alva and his son or daughter. All happy families. Darren thought to himself sarcastically. Bloody hell. Where did he fit in? He had to have a position in this set up. And he would. He vowed. Angry that he was being pushed around. Naomi didn't understand him. She had no idea how important this child was to him. But then he supposed it would be better if she didn't know. She never mentioned his name to Alva he was certain about that.

Her own relationship with her friend meant too much to her to reveal the fact that she was connected with her ex-partner.

Chapter Thirty-one

Alva watched Carlos. He seemed preoccupied, and had slipped back into that mood again since their day out yesterday. He was reading a medical journal, something which he did regularly if he had a few minutes to spare. Sunday was their only day off now, and even then Carlos could be called into the hospital if there was an emergency so at any time his phone might ring and that would be the end of their day of relaxation. She pushed herself out of the armchair with difficulty. Heavy now with the baby and feeling that it would arrive any minute. But she wasn't due for another week, but was aware that the date was unreliable. First babies were very likely to be late rather than early. She put her hand on her bump and could feel the little one move. Twisting, turning and kicking. Reminding Alva that he or she would arrive soon and not to be complacent. Everyone was so excited, particularly her mother and Naomi. Julie couldn't wait until she heard the news that her grandchild had arrived. While Carlos wasn't in a position to book time off because of the uncertainty of the date, he had cleared his schedule somewhat so he could be with her. Naomi had also offered to come over and stay for which Alva was very grateful.

At the office, her brother Cian had insisted that Alva leave two weeks before her expected date. While she had agreed, she still worked from home which was easy and gave her something to do. Anyway, what else would she do if she didn't work as she waited for Carlos to come home, she thought. But she was nervous as the time grew closer. While she had attended all the antenatal classes about childbirth, she still didn't want to think about too many details just yet. Anything could go wrong, she was aware of that, but prayed all would be well with her and the baby.

'You'll be fine,' Naomi said confidently. 'If you look at statistics.'

'I don't want to think of statistics,' she said grimly.

'Sorry, I shouldn't have mentioned it.'

'They're not usually accurate and often put a negative twist on things. Anyway, the doctor said everything seems OK.'

'How about Dr. Carlos?' Naomi grinned.

'He's worried, I've noticed that.'

'It's only natural. Come on, let's go out for a walk, the fresh air will do us good.'

'I'll just finish off this report.' Alva turned back to the computer keyboard.

'You're not supposed to be working at all.'

'A few minutes.' Alva did what she needed and before long the two were driving along the coast road. They parked the car, walked along the harbour and sat on a bench to watch the waves churn in towards them. The weather was surprisingly mild and it was very pleasant.

There were quite a few people walking, but very few working on the boats and many of them were up on the quayside for the winter. A short time later they were sitting in a cosy café sipping coffee, and eating buttered scones with blackcurrant jam and whipped cream. It was busy, patrons chatting amid the clinking and clanking of cups and saucers and cutlery, chairs being pushed back and forward as people came in and left.

Naomi's phone rang. She took it from her handbag and glanced at the readout. 'No need to reply,' she said and put it back.

'That special person?' Alva asked with a grin.

Naomi nodded. Her cheeks pink.

'You're embarrassed.'

'I suppose,' she admitted.

'Every time you mention him you get like that. All confused and blushing like a little girl.'

'Go on with you.' Naomi made an attempt at denial.

'It's true. How long has it been?'

'About ten months.'

'Going steady,' Alva smiled.

Naomi shook her head.

'Why not move in together? It would completely change your life. Look at Carlos and me? You could say that was unexpected.'

'Not yet.'

'At least you'll have to tell everyone who he is then,' Alva quipped.

Naomi was silent.

'Go on, tell me his name?'

'I can't.'

'You won't,' teased Alva.

'You're always giving out to me,' grinned Naomi.

'Me, never,' Alva smiled. 'Oh,' she exclaimed, and put her hand on her bump.

'What is it?' Naomi looked at her anxiously.

'A twinge, it could be the start,' Alva said.

'We'd better get back,' Naomi waved to the waitress, asked her for the bill and paid it.

Alva pushed herself out of the chair and straightened up. Naomi took her arm and together they left and walked to where her car was parked.

Naomi turned to Alva. 'Do you feel that you need to get to the hospital now?'

192

'No, not yet. If I do that, then they could send me home again and say I'm not far enough along and to come back later. I don't want that to happen. Then I'd have to let Carlos know and I don't want to create a problem for him if that happens. It doesn't feel bad enough anyway. I'm sure the contractions should be much worse and closer together. I haven't had another twinge yet and it's about ten minutes since that happened so it mustn't be that urgent.'

'The baby isn't due until next week anyway, but let's get home now. We'll wait together,' Naomi said.

'I don't feel it's imminent yet,' Alva smiled.

'I'll stay with you. I'll call my boss and explain.'

'Thanks a mill,' Alva felt another dart of pain, this time in her back.

'Is that another one?' Naomi asked.

Alva nodded.

'Maybe we should time the contractions.' Naomi glanced at her watch.

'I'll do that.' Alva looked at the time on her phone.

Naomi drove a little faster. 'I don't want to be caught speeding by one of my friends, that would be embarrassing,' she laughed.

'I'm sure there's time enough,' Alva said with a smile. 'And the pains are not too close at the moment.'

Naomi turned into the apartment complex, and Alva clicked the remote to open the gates. Naomi drove up to the main door.

'I'll go up with you and come back down to park the car.' She climbed out of the car, ran around to the passenger side, and helped Alva step out, and go upstairs to the apartment.

'Sit down and relax, I'll be back in a minute.'

Alva went inside and sat down on an armchair.

While there hadn't been another contraction in the last five minutes, she was sure there would be another along in a minute. This was it now, she reminded herself nervously. Just then there was another contraction, this time more severe than the first few and she clenched her teeth as it cut through her. She looked at her phone just to keep track of the time and judge when she should go to the hospital.

Naomi sat beside her.

Alva took a deep breath as another contraction cut through her.

'How long has that been?'

'About four minutes I think,' Alva said.

'That baby is definitely on its way. Let's go.' Naomi suggested.

'I'll text Carlos and tell him, and send one to the team leader as well, he'll give him a message. Alva sent the texts but it was frustrating as she would have preferred to talk to Carlos and tell him their baby was on its way. Another contraction took her mind off what she was thinking.

'Come on, where's your bag?'

'In the hall press.'

'I'll get it. Now put on your jacket and take my arm.'

'Oh my God, my waters have broken,' Alva exclaimed.

'Let's go quickly then.'

They went downstairs, and almost immediately Alva had another contraction.

'I feel as if the baby is about to pop out at any minute,' she said.

Naomi didn't reply, and just sat Alva on the chair in the foyer and rushed out to bring the car around. She helped Alva climb into the car. It was difficult for her.

'Give me the remote,' she asked, and Alva did so. As the gates slowly opened, she shot through them and turned on to the main road.

'Are you all right?' she glanced at Alva.

'Hanging in there,' Alva grimaced. The contractions were happening now on a regular basis and she could feel the baby

194

moving down through her. But she bit her lip and kept as quiet as she could.

'Right, here we are. Stay there for a minute and I'll get someone to help.' Naomi pulled up outside the main entrance to the hospital and rushed in the door, reappearing in a couple of minutes with two nurses, one of whom pushed a wheelchair.

'I think the baby is almost here,' Alva gasped.

'Relax, we have you.' They helped her sit into the chair.

'I'll park the car,' Naomi said. 'See you soon.'

The nurses pushed Alva inside, and rushed her straight through to the birthing unit.

A few minutes later, Naomi came back in and was allowed into the unit to be with Alva as Carlos had not arrived yet.

Alva was in the throes of childbirth, and immediately taken by another contraction and cried out loud. Naomi took her hand and stood behind. The two midwives there were encouraging her. 'Push now, Alva, you're nearly there. Breathe deeply. Breathe.'

She groaned out loud. There wasn't time for an epidural. She could feel beads of perspiration dribble down her forehead at the effort of pushing and dealing with the pain.

'It won't be long now, your partner is here.'

She twisted her head just a little and could see Carlos out of the corner of her eye. His hands reaching to hold hers.

'You're doing good, querida,' he murmured, pressed his hand on her forehead, and kissed her.

'Push now, push now, we can see the head of the baby. The last contraction worked its way through her and she screamed and could feel the baby slide out, to be quickly gathered up by one of the midwives as she cried, 'It's a lovely little boy.' She cleared his airways, and then she placed him on Alva and he gave a little cry. Alva stared at him, and could not believe that she had given birth to such a beautiful baby. She burst into tears as Carlos put his arms around her and they both cried with emotion. Even Naomi was in tears.

'Gracias por darme un hijo tan hermoso,' he said. 'I love him. And I love you my Alva for giving me such a beautiful son.' He kissed her again.

The midwife helped Alva sit up a little, and positioned the baby on her.

'Te amo, Alva, querida,' he murmured. Hugging her and curling the baby's cheek in his hand.

'Would you like to cut the cord?' the midwife asked.

'I really want to,' he said. And took the scissors held by the midwife.

She had already clamped the cord which was actually quite hard to cut.

'He's beautiful,' Naomi whispered, overcome with emotion as well.

'Thanks so much for being with me,' Alva smiled.

'It was a wonderful experience. I'll never forget it.'

'Thanks so much for taking my place, Naomi.' Carlos seemed very grateful. 'I'm sorry for being so late, I was only just in time. My team leader got your text and so I was able to finish up the procedure with his help.'

The midwives left the three of them together with the baby for a while, then they returned and one of them took the baby away for a few minutes to check him out.

While that was happening, Carlos made a few phone calls. 'Your mother is over the moon, and Papa and Pacqui. And your brothers and their families are thrilled as well.'

'Let the word go out. I want everyone to know,' Alva smiled.

'You should be proud of yourself,' said Naomi.

'There are a lot of women who are giving birth today. I'm

nothing special and it was all very quick for me.'

'We are still very proud of you,' insisted Carlos.

'A perfect little boy, a good size.' The midwife handed the baby to Carlos who cupped his little head which had soft dark hair.

'Look at his perfect hands.' Naomi touched them. 'He's a little pet.'

'Exquisite,' murmured Carlos. He couldn't hide the tears in his eyes. The baby's hands waved around and he seemed to reach for Carlos's face.

'Look, he knows his Dad,' Alva giggled.

'I can't believe he's here at last.'

'Why don't you hold him?' Alva asked Naomi.

'Can I?'

'Of course, you can.' Carlos gave him to her.

'He feels so warm and cosy,' she smiled down at him. 'What have you decided to call him?'

Carlos and Alva smiled at each other.

'We haven't decided yet,' Alva said.

'Will it be Spanish or Irish.'

'He will be Irish, so maybe a Celtic name. There are connections between the two countries,' said Carlos.

Naomi handed the baby to the nurse who helped Alva position the baby to latch on to her nipple. 'Oh …' she exclaimed.

'Is that painful?' Naomi asked.

'A little.'

'You'll get used to it,' the midwife smiled.

'Thanks. I hope I'll be able to feed him. I really want to breastfeed if I can, it will be so much better for him.'

Alva's phone rang. Carlos handed it to her. 'Smile,' he said and took a few photos on his phone.

'It's Mum,' she smiled. 'Hi there?'

'How are you my love?' Julie asked.

'I'm fine.' Alva was in tears all over again.

'I'm so happy for you. A little boy. I'm looking forward to seeing my grandson, when will I come over?'

'Naomi is staying with us for a while so that I'll be able to get some sleep in between feeds.'

'That's very good of her.'

'I don't know how long she's going to stay. I'll let you know. But I'm really looking forward to seeing you.'

'I'll try and persuade Pedro to come with me.'

'Yes, do, I hope he can come.' In her heart she would have preferred that he didn't come. Pedro was so critical and would insist that they do everything he felt they should do, and she didn't know if she could deal with that.

'When will you be home from the hospital?' Julie asked.

'In a day or two.'

'Carlos seems so excited.'

'He is, we're both very happy. Our baby is beautiful.'

'I'm looking forward to seeing you.'

'I'll call you tomorrow and we can have a longer chat.'

'Yes, you must be very tired.'

'I don't want to sleep, I just want to keep looking at our baby. Carlos has just taken some photos so he'll send them to you.'

'Please do.'

'We'll talk tomorrow. Love you.'

'Carlos, sit beside Alva and the baby and I'll take some more photos of the three of you,' Naomi instructed.

He put his arm around the two of them, and hugged.

'Our new family,' Naomi smiled.

A midwife came in.

'I think our Mum needs some rest, if you don't mind?' she said pointedly.

Carlos bent to kiss her, 'Sleep well, querida. I love you both.' He cupped the baby's cheek in his hand, and kissed him too.

'We'll see you tomorrow. Love you.' Naomi hugged her.

The nurse stood waiting at the door and, reluctantly, they left.

Alva was alone now, and she cuddled the baby close to her. He only had a light blanket over his baby grow, and a white wool hat, but he was warm against her body, and that feeling was so wonderful she almost burst into tears again but was suddenly thrilled to see Carlos put his head around the curtain.

'I mentioned I was a doctor and persuaded the nurse to let me in again for a few minutes,' he said with a grin, and sat close by her. 'How is baby?' he smiled down at him.

'He's just drifted off to sleep.'

'I was thinking about what name we will give him.'

'So was I.'

'We'll have to decide soon, can't keep calling him baby.'

'I was thinking about Roberto which is easy to pronounce for both the Spanish and Irish families. What do you think?'

'It was one of our choices.'

'And there was Antonio which is nice too.' Alva looked down at him.

'I think Roberto is good, that was my grandfather's name.'

'You mentioned that.'

Carlos nodded.

'Let's go for that then. I like it,' Alva smiled.

'Our son, Roberto.' He kissed the baby's forehead, and then Alva. 'I love you both so much.'

Chapter Thirty-two

Naomi gazed down at the baby. She adored him and would have given anything to have him for herself. She had always hoped to have a family, although her relationships to date had never led to that possibility. Some of the men she met on line were supposedly single, but none had any interest in taking their relationship any further. Another was a married man in work and while they had been close, they had to keep everything very secret and she was forced to break up with him, hating the secrecy, but now she found herself in the same situation, although Darren wasn't a work colleague at least. But the secrecy still got to her. Watching every word she uttered in Alva and Carlos's presence. It was very difficult, but she did love Darren and she wanted to be with him. Live together soon, and have their own family. But all of that depended on whether she could persuade Alva to see how important Darren was to her. Was that ever going to be possible, or would it destroy all of those years she and Alva had known together?

She looked down at the baby again. His eyelids were closed, the lashes were dark and soft, and far too long for a boy, she thought with a smile. The little hands clenched and then opened wide suddenly, and clenched again. Naomi curled her index finger into his hand loving that warm feeling she felt when he gripped it. She was so happy to have this opportunity to spend time looking after little Roberto. So glad that her team in the

Gardai had just concluded a case, which hopefully would result in a conviction, and so give her the chance to take some of her unused holidays to spend time with Alva.

Her phone rang and she left it go on to voicemail. It was Darren. She could see his name come up on the readout from where she had left the phone on the coffee table. Anyway, she didn't want to tell him where she was. He wouldn't be very happy about that. Even when she had mentioned Alva had had the baby, she could sense that he wasn't too interested in knowing that even though he had asked if it was a boy or a girl. Naomi had told Darren she couldn't see him and felt somewhat guilty. But her first responsibility had to be for Alva now. As she was breastfeeding the baby then she had to be available to him whenever he wanted a feed, and that meant that her time to herself was very short. 'Are you a very hungry little baby?' Naomi asked him softly. He slept heavily now but for how long? That was the big question. The last feed was only about three quarters of an hour ago and that didn't give Alva very much time to sleep if he awoke soon. She held him close to her and hoped the fact that she was warm would help him to stay asleep. In the Moses basket he never slept for very long, so she always just sat with him in her arms.

'Hi?' Alva appeared from the bedroom. 'How is he?'

'Fine, still asleep.'

'That's good.' She looked down at her son.

'You didn't sleep very long yourself, why don't you go back to bed and doze a little.'

'Couldn't really sleep properly. I'll catch up,' she smiled and just sat beside her friend and looked at Roberto lovingly.

Naomi thought that she was seeing the old Alva again. So caught up with the baby during her pregnancy, when he had arrived at last she had to give him every minute she had in her life. Maybe she was making up for the fact that Carlos couldn't be there as much as Naomi felt he should be. While he took a week off after the baby was born, some of that time was broken up with the fact that he was on call, and had to attend his patients no matter what was going on. But still she could imagine that if this baby in her arms was hers then she would be absolutely over the moon and refuse to let anyone else near him. She cuddled him even closer and moved him a little in her arms. Slightly disturbed, he made a cry but to her relief didn't wake up.

'I often wonder is he getting enough milk,' Alva asked.

'He seems happy enough.'

'But it's so hard to know.'

'He would soon let you know,' Naomi smiled down at him.

'I suppose.' She didn't seem convinced.

'And it's important to eat plenty, the baby needs it.'

'Don't worry about me,' Alva whispered. 'I'm not a good mother.'

'What do you mean? You're a perfect mother.'

'I can't love him like he should be loved.' Tears flooded Alva's eyes.

'Of course you can. Look how he loves you. So bright and beautiful.' She looked down at the sleeping baby.

'He loves Carlos better than me. I can see it.'

'He's only a baby, he loves everyone who smiles at him. Even me.' Naomi tried to explain.

'He doesn't love me, Naomi,' she seemed despondent.

'That's only the baby blues talking, Alva. It's your hormones. They're all over the place. It's normal.'

Alva shook her head. 'I thought I had everything covered. And that I knew all there was to know about being a mother. Now I'm not sure what I should do.' She wiped away the tears on her cheeks.

'You couldn't know it all. You only learn by experience.'

'But it seems so slow, each day I wake up and hope that it will be better, but it never is.'

'Your Mum is arriving from Spain tomorrow, you'll feel much better when you see her.'

'In one way I'm looking forward to seeing her and in another I'm afraid to admit how I feel.'

'Maybe you should just try to explain. And when you see Carlos tonight do the same, he will understand exactly how you are feeling. He is a doctor after all.'

'I can't do that. He'll think so little of me. He's been looking forward so much to the arrival of our baby and now I'm so miserable it really isn't fair on him.'

'You must tell him.'

'It's too difficult.' She shook her head.

'A few sessions of counselling might help.'

'I'm not going to counselling,' Alva snapped.

'Maybe you should, before it gets any worse. It could get very bad and it will affect baby and Carlos too,' Naomi emphasised gently.

'No, I won't let that happen.'

'You mightn't be able to stop it. It's an illness.'

Naomi held back from describing the symptoms of postnatal depression. But knew very well what it involved and was very worried about Alva.

The baby suddenly began to cry out loud.

'He's hungry. He mustn't have had enough earlier.' Alva bent to pick up Roberto and immediately put him to her breast. 'I'm not even sure I'm doing it right,' she said worriedly.

'Of course, you are, see how he latches on,' Naomi reassured. 'What would you like for dinner this evening?'

'I don't know,' Alva said vaguely.

'I'll have a look in the fridge. We have to eat. Relax there for a while and feed our little man.' She disappeared into the kitchen, and reappeared a short time later. 'Dinner is all sorted. How is Roberto doing?' Naomi came close to look at him.

'I'm not sure.'

'Well, he's not crying so he must be all right.'

Alva sighed. 'I'm very tired.'

'That's normal, you're not getting enough sleep.'

'Let's hope Roberto will sleep longer after he has his feed this time. I hate putting him down, and then trying to sleep myself. I want to keep him by me all the time, that's why I can't sleep.'

'You must sleep, that's why you're not feeling so well. Sleep deprivation has some very harsh side effects.'

'I won't take sleeping pills,' Alva warned. Anger in her tone. 'And don't suggest that to me.'

'No, I haven't suggested that. It would be too drastic. I'm sorry to have given you that impression, I didn't mean to.' Naomi was immediately apologetic as Alva's response was most unusual. 'You'll be fine after a couple of weeks,' she reassured.

Chapter Thirty-three

Darren moved into the rented house by the sea. He felt guilty about keeping his move to this place a secret from Naomi, but he knew such a run-down old cottage would never appeal to her. He picked up his phone and called her, but she didn't reply and all he could hear was her voicemail. He left a message but hated doing that, his words echoing into the ether, like a meaningless rant. Now he wondered whether she ever listened to his messages. She never said she did, so he decided to stop in future, that would make her think twice. But then, to his surprise, she returned his call later.

'Sorry, I missed your call. I'm with Alva.'

'How is she?'

'She's fine.'

'And her son?'

'He's good.'

'Do you think I could come and see her?'

'I don't know.'

'Would you ask her? I want to ask her for forgiveness. Say I asked you to intervene.'

'I'm not sure whether she would agree at this point.'

'But you can persuade her, I'm sure you could.'

'There's a lot happening at the moment with the new baby.'

'But now's the time I want to talk to her, and I want to see the child.'

'Carlos might not be so keen.'

'You don't have to say anything, I don't want him to be there. Go on, Naomi, do me a favour. It's just once. Have I ever asked you to do anything for me before?'

'Well ...'

'I might have, I suppose, but do this for me. It's very important. Or maybe I could meet her outside somewhere, what about that?' he was excited at the thought. It would be perfect.

'She's not going out much.'

'Surely she takes the baby out for a walk for some fresh air.'

'I'm sure she will do that soon.'

'Let me know and I can go there at that time.'

'I'll think about it,' she was doubtful.

'You know how much I love you, Naomi. And maybe if Alva forgives me then there is a chance for us.'

'I suppose you have a point. If I'm ever going to tell her that we are in a relationship, it would be vital that she has forgiven you.'

'There, I'm so glad you understand. Then we can move in together and start our own family. Would you like a baby?' he asked gently.

'Of course I would, even taking care of little Roberto is wonderful. I almost feel he is mine already,' Naomi explained. 'The thought of having our own baby is something I really want. And I'm ready to commit myself to you.'

'I wish I could see you now. I'm so lonely for you. When will we get together?'

'Alva's mother is coming tomorrow.'

'Let's get together one evening. We can have dinner somewhere nice. There won't be a chance of bumping into Alva now.'

'No, probably not. Let's do that.'

'I'll book a table.'

'I'm looking forward to seeing you.'
'Can't wait.'
'Love you.'

He was excited about his plans for the cottage. He would have to do some work on it to make it as secure as he needed it to be and ordered some wood through his own company. He measured the windows and asked the men in the wood department at work to cut the lengths to size so he wouldn't have to cut it himself. He had a drill, bits, nails etc. from his stock of samples so he didn't have to go out and buy them. So every evening he worked, and before long had the place exactly as he wanted.

He liked living there. In the evening, he strolled on the beach. There were very few people around at this time of the year. He was reminded of his home in Waterford where his parents still lived. He felt guilty that he hadn't seen them in some time, but planned to drive down one weekend soon. He was ashamed to tell them that he had split up from Alva, they had really liked her, and hadn't the courage to tell them he had had to resign from Purtell Vintners either. They would be very disappointed in him.

He sent another letter to Carlos. This time it was even more threatening.

'I'm still watching you.'
'All the time.'
'Your career will crumble.'
'Don't think you will escape me.'

He booked a table for dinner, and picked Naomi up at her apartment in a taxi.

'This is wonderful,' he embraced her. 'To be able to go out without worrying too much about seeing Alva is amazing. It's so good to relax.'

'I'm looking forward to it. Where are we going?'

'Secret. I want to surprise you.'

It was a restaurant he had heard about recently online and it sounded really amazing. A place in Dalkey which was nowhere near where Alva lived and he was glad that there was absolutely no chance that she would go there now.

The wine waiter came to the table and served them both champagne. He had planned all that in advance.

'I love you,' he said, and raised his glass.

'Love you too,' she clinked his glass. 'To us.'

'To the future,' he smiled. 'And I've got good news,' he announced with a broad grin.

'Tell us?' she asked.

'This is a celebration.'

'The champagne is gorgeous.' She sipped the bubbly liquid. 'Go on, what's the news?' she asked.

'I've just started a new job.'

'Where?'

'Impression & Co in Santry. They're owned by a French group.'

'What do they sell?'

'Stationery. They're a big company.'

'You never told me you were changing jobs.'

'I went for the interview a few weeks ago, but didn't want to tell you at the time in case I flunked it. But then they called me a couple of weeks ago and asked me to start immediately.'

'What did your boss say?'

'He wasn't too pleased, but he had no choice.'

'Are you in sales?'

'Yeah, and there are good prospects for the future, so that's very important to us. Good salary. Commission. A new car too. Another Toyota, silver this time. Cool.'

They clinked their glasses together.

The waiter brought the menus, and they spent some time perusing the dishes, and eventually decided on what they wanted to order. Starters, main courses and desserts.

'This is delicious,' Naomi tasted the rolled pork with bacon main course dish.

'My steak is perfect,' Darren agreed.

The waiter topped up their champagne, and brought the dessert menu. 'I don't think I could manage to eat any more,' Naomi sighed. 'I'll just have a cup of coffee.'

The manager ordered a taxi for them, and they were driven back to Naomi's apartment.

'It was great to drink as much as we want and not worry about driving,' giggled Naomi.

'We'll have to go out more often,' Darren said. 'You know how tired I am of secrecy.'

'I am too.'

'I must see Alva soon. Did you think of asking her if she would see me?'

'There was no opportunity, and Julie is arriving on Tuesday.'

'How long is she staying?'

'I don't know.'

'I hope it's not too long. She will interfere with our plans. I'm running out of patience.' He rapped the table.

'Give it time. We're not in that much of a hurry, my love.'

Chapter Thirty-four

Carlos bent over Alva and dropped a kiss on her hair. Then he looked down at Roberto who lay sleeping in the Moses basket. He was so beautiful he just didn't want to disturb him. Let him sleep as long as he needed. Because Alva was so insistent on breastfeeding him, even expressing her milk and letting Carlos feed him during the night wasn't something she would consider for even a moment. She was exhausted from lack of sleep and no matter what Carlos said she insisted on feeding the baby herself. He was worried, and wished he had more time off when he could have helped. But Alva's mother, Julie, was arriving from Spain later and he hoped that Alva might listen to her mother's advice. Also, her brothers and their families had called around when she came home from hospital, and he knew she was very glad to see them all, particularly her niece and nephew, Sisi and Jon. But in the last few days, she seemed very tense and anxious. Although, when he asked if she was feeling all right, and happy, she dismissed his fears and wouldn't admit there was anything wrong.

He went into the gym for a swim on his way to work. Dived into the deep end of the pool, and swam for the length, kicked and returned to the other end. He did that twenty times and when he climbed out and stood under an icy cold shower, he felt refreshed, and ready to start the day.

In his office, he checked the appointments in the diary. It was a full day, and he didn't see himself finishing before six o'clock unless there was a cancellation. He sighed. Thinking that there wasn't much chance of that. He flicked through the envelopes in the bundle of post from the previous couple of days he had been out of the office. Slitting them open with a knife, stopping suddenly when he noticed something familiar about one of them. He compressed his lips, angry, as his heart fell into his stomach. Not another one of those letters, he muttered, dreading the thought of opening it. He wondered if he shouldn't bother at all, but something made him pull the single page out of the envelope and read the words which had been stuck on to the white page. It was much the same as the other letters, and once again, he was puzzled as to which dissatisfied patient might have sent it. He had not responded in any way and maybe that was frustrating the sender. Was it someone close to him who would expect him to tell them what was happening and ask advice? What did they expect him to do? He wondered. If he had gone to the Gardai how would the sender have known? He probably should have done that. But he hadn't wanted to tell Alva about the letters. It would only unsettle her and she would have worried too much, thinking that he was about to lose his job because one of his patients had died under his care. and he couldn't have taken that risk. It was every doctor's fear that he would be found negligent. Of course, every medic had insurance, as he had himself, but there was always the fear that the insurance company would not pay the full claim, and then the unfortunate doctor would be compensating the claimant for the rest of his life.

But Alva couldn't cope with something like that now. He knew that. She was suffering from postnatal depression since the birth of the baby. He hadn't made any comment about her moods but had been very aware of them. He would have to leave it for now. He replaced the letter in the envelope, and put it in a file in his briefcase with the others he had received. He would have preferred to burn the letters, but something held him back and he didn't do that. Putting them out of his mind as much as he could.

The most important people in his life were Alva and Roberto, and he needed to care for them protectively. And would have dreaded to let them down in any way. They were all he had.

When he arrived home, he was delighted to meet Julie in the hallway.

'It's wonderful to see you,' he embraced her.

'Congratulations, little Roberto is beautiful,' she said. 'They're both asleep now.'

'Alva isn't finding it easy,' he said.

'Yes. She seems very tired and worries all the time about the baby. I've been here a few hours and offered to help, but she insists on doing everything herself and so the burden lies on her. I feel useless and wish I could do more.'

'But I'm sure she was very glad to see you, Mum.' They walked through into the lounge. 'She doesn't want me to do anything either, even change him or bathe him if I'm here. I'll look in on them.' He went into the bedroom and sat beside Alva. The baby was tucked up beside her and her arm encircled him. He smiled but didn't disturb her.

He sat and talked to Julie.

'It's wonderful to have our little one finally, but very worrying that Alva isn't well.'

'I hope she will improve soon.'

'Now that you're here I'm sure she will.'

'We need to boost her confidence,' Julie said.

Carlos and Julie went into the bedroom and sat by Alva until she awoke later.

'How are you, querida, did you sleep well?' He kissed her.

She nodded.

'And do you feel rested?'

'Yes.' Immediately she looked down at Roberto, and gently stroked his little face. He opened his eyes with a tiny cry.

'He's hungry.' She lifted him up into her arms and put him to her breast where he latched on. She kissed the top of his head.

'My little grandson,' Julie whispered.

'I'm not a very good mother,' Alva murmured.

'That's crazy,' Julie insisted.

'I'm trying hard, but every time I look at him I see disappointment in his eyes.'

'Querida, you are a wonderful mother and he knows it. Look how he clings to you.'

'No, I can't give him what he wants.'

'Of course you can,' Carlos smiled at her.

She shook her head.

Carlos looked at Julie, his dark eyes filled with worry.

'He's such a beautiful baby, Alva, you mustn't worry so much. Look how happy he is to be so close to you. It means a great deal to him, I can see it. I'm so glad to be here with you both. I hope I can help in some way,' Julie smiled.

'I'm very happy to see you, Mum, I've been looking forward to having you here.' There were tears in her eyes.

Chapter Thirty-five

Naomi called over to see Alva, and Julie.

'I'm so glad to see you,' she hugged Julie.

'I'm so happy to be here and to meet my grandson for the first time. Isn't he beautiful?' She looked down at the baby.

'I was so lucky to be there at his birth,' Naomi smiled.

'You were great to be here with Alva in the first few days, thank you so much,' Julie said.

'Alva really needs you now, Julie, although a couple of days ago I persuaded her to take a walk so that Roberto can get some fresh air and it has seemed to improve her mood. The weather is quite mild which is great. I'm due back at work this week so I'm hoping she'll go out on her own with the baby. It will boost her confidence, and maybe you and she could go together.'

'I hope so.'

'She's not eating very much and if she becomes upset in any way, she bursts into tears. She definitely feels inadequate and thinks she is a bad mother and that Roberto doesn't like her. Which I think is crazy as he seems to be so happy whenever she looks at him.'

'Has she seen her doctor, do you know?' Julie asked. 'I mean, apart from Carlos.'

'He understands how she feels but doesn't want to try and persuade her to see someone.'

'We can only pray.'

'I don't know if that's going to be enough.'

'I am very worried,' Julie admitted.

'The walks will do her good I'm sure.'

Julie's phone rang.

'Excuse me, do you mind if I take this call,' she looked at the screen. 'It's Pedro.'

'Give him my love,' Naomi said.

Julie nodded.

'I'll have a look in on Alva.' Naomi left the room.

'How are you, Pedro,' Julie smiled as she spoke to him.

Naomi gave her a few minutes to talk with Pedro, before knocking gently on the door. She opened it slightly and was shocked to hear Julie sobbing. She pushed it open fully and went in. Julie was still sitting on the couch, her face hidden in her hands. 'What's wrong Julie?' she asked, concerned, sitting down beside her.

'Abuela has died.'

'What?' Naomi was puzzled for a moment, wondering if she had heard correctly. 'How sad, what happened?'

'Pedro didn't say, he was too upset.'

Naomi put her arms around Julie and hugged her. 'I'll get you a cup of coffee.' She hurried into the kitchen, and quickly poured a cup from the percolator, added sugar and milk, and rushed back. 'Drink this, it'll help.'

She took it and sipped.

'Can I do anything for you?' Naomi asked.

'I must tell Carlos, he is going to be very upset to hear that his grandmother has died.'

'Do you want me to call him for you?' She took out her phone.

Julie nodded, dabbing her eyes with a white handkerchief. 'I am sorry I am so upset, but we are all very fond of Abuela.'

'I'll try Carlos,' Naomi said and pressed in his number. The phone rang out but it went on to his voicemail. 'He's busy. I'll send a text as well.'

'Should I tell Alva?' Julie asked.

'Maybe not yet, she needs every minute of sleep she can get.'

Naomi's phone rang. 'It's Carlos,' she replied, and handed her phone to Julie. Then she went into the bedroom. Alva was still asleep and Naomi sat near the window, worried about her reaction to hearing of the passing of Abuela and what that would do to her.

There was a tap on the door and Julie called her out.

'Carlos can come home, so he'll be here soon,' she explained.

'Thanks be to God,' whispered Naomi.

'I'll have to arrange a flight home.' Julie handed Naomi her own phone which she had given her to talk to Carlos, and then began to search in her bag for her phone in a frantic fashion.

'I can do that for you,' offered Naomi.

'Thank you, I'll have to get back. The funeral will be arranged soon.'

Naomi searched for flights. 'Tomorrow?'

'Yes please.'

'There's just a direct one at 17.25, that's all. Arriving in Seville about 21.20.'

'I'll have to take that.' She rooted in her bag again.

'Why not try Madrid, and take an internal flight to Seville?' suggested Naomi. 'I'll have a look.' She clicked on her phone. 'There's an earlier one to Madrid, leaving at 7.25, arriving 11.15. How about that?'

'Much better,' Julie said. 'Although we could take the fast train perhaps?'

'Let's see what connects with Seville. How about Iberia, leaving 15.55, arriving 17.05?'

'That sounds better although I have to wait a few hours between.'

'There is one about the same time you arrive but you'd never make the connection.'

'It's better than arriving late. I'll book that.'

Carlos arrived shortly after that, and he seemed very upset about Abuela.

'Have you told Alva?' he asked.

'No, she's asleep.'

'I'll go in,' he said, first checking on Roberto who was still asleep in the basket.

In the bedroom he sat on the bed beside Alva but didn't wake her. She lay in a deep sleep and he was glad she had managed to sleep as long as the baby was sleeping. It would do her good to rest. As he sat there, he thought about his grandmother and what a loss she would be to the family. Of course, she had been a great age and he had been very close to her and his grandfather when he had been alive.

When Alva opened her eyes, Carlos kissed her. She stared at him.

'What time is it?' she asked him.

'It's just after eight. But I have some bad news,' he said gently.

'What?' She sat up in the bed. 'Is something wrong with Roberto?'

'No no, he's fine and still sleeping, it's just,' he hesitated, 'Abuela has died.'

She stared at him, shocked. 'Oh no. Poor Abuela.' Tears filled her eyes. Carlos put his arms around her and held her close to him.

Suddenly, Alva found herself alone. Carlos had to take time off and booked the same flight to Spain with Julie and the two of them left very early the following morning. She would have loved to go too. She wanted to say goodbye to Abuela, but she

217

felt Roberto was too young. Anyway, funerals are held very quickly in Spain, between twenty-four to forty-eight hours after a death, and she hoped Carlos would be back soon.

She was feeding Roberto when Carlos and Julie left for the airport, and she waved to them from the window, and they waved back, before they climbed into the jeep. She was very sorry to see Julie go, as she had only been back in Dublin such a short time, and Alva hoped she would be able to come soon again. Although she knew that there was a celebration of the life of Abuela in the next couple of weeks and she would have to stay for that. But still Alva wanted to be in better form when she returned. She was very aware of her low mood since Roberto's birth. And she struggled to get out of its grip. Hating to see the worry in Carlos's eyes, and knowing that she was making life very difficult for him. Now that she was on her own, she decided that she was going to make an effort to shake off this dark cloud which hung over her.

Chapter Thirty-six

Darren rang the doorbell of Naomi's apartment, and was delighted when she answered the intercom.

'Hello?'

'Naomi, it's me.'

'Come on up.'

He let himself in and took the lift.

Naomi was already standing in the doorway when he walked up the corridor. 'How are you, my love? I've really missed you.' He threw his arms around her and they kissed passionately.

'This is a surprise. I'm only just back from work. Come in, come in.' She closed the door.

'It's great to see you.'

'And you too.'

'How's Alva and the new baby?' he asked.

'She's not so good, but the baby is fine.'

'What's wrong with her?' he asked curiously.

'Depression really. It sometimes happens after a woman has had a baby. It's very worrying.'

'She's lucky to have you as a friend.' He sat down beside her on the couch, his arm around her.

'She needs my help. I am encouraging her to get back to normal, and she does seem to be improving. I went with her and Roberto for a walk a couple of days ago, and I'm hoping she'll go out on her own now, and feel more confident about that.

Carlos and Julie went to Spain this morning as his grandmother has died.'

He put his arm across the back of the cushions. She curled into him and they kissed passionately. 'You are so sexy,' she murmured. His lips gripped hers and he began to open up the buttons on her shirt. 'I want you, Naomi.'

'And I you. Can you stay the night?' she whispered, her voice husky.

'Of course, I can, that's all I want.'

'I've an early start.'

'I'll keep you awake. There will be no sleep for you tonight.'

And there wasn't. They had been so long without each other that they had to make up for lost time. At least that was how it was for Naomi.

'I'm hoping with Alva tied up with the baby, this really frees life up for us.' Darren took off her shirt, and kissed her body with his lips. Slowly he removed each item of clothing. She responded and before long both were naked and he had carried her into the bedroom.

'That's to remind you of carrying you over the threshold on our wedding night.' He kissed her and gently lay her down on the duvet, then covered her body with his. He held her hands in his, and their lovemaking was intense, spiralling again and again over the night. They showered together when they rose, and once again their need for each other became apparent. And they quickly went back to bed to satiate their craving for each other one more time.

Chapter Thirty-seven

Carlos and Julie boarded the aeroplane, and both were very subdued.

'Are you all right?' Carlos asked as they searched for the numbers of their seats.

'Tired,' she replied.

'Maybe you might get some sleep on the journey,' he suggested.

She nodded.

'Here you are,' he pointed to the aisle seat. 'And I'm further up. Would you like anything when they come around with the drinks trolley, or food?'

'I might get a soft drink.'

'He saw her seated, put her bag in the overhead locker, and then sat down himself.

As the plane took off, Carlos lay his head back on the headrest and closed his eyes. He felt very sad about the death of his grandmother. Always spending a lot of his time with her and grandfather when he had been a boy. Remembering wonderful days spent at their house, and riding out with grandfather across the land. He had died some years before and now Carlos had another loss to bear.

He glanced out the window and could see the Irish coastline below and thought of Alva and Roberto and prayed that they would be all right while he was away. He was still worried about Alva, hoping that her depression would lift soon, even thinking that she might be better on her own for a few days. Was it his fault that she felt the way she did? He wondered. Was he taking much more notice of Roberto and not enough of her. Did she feel claustrophobic? He couldn't decide. As a doctor he imagined he should understand but now he felt helpless and hoped that he would be more supportive in future and help her get through this difficult time.

When they could walk through the plane, he went down to Julie but found her sleeping. He was glad of that. She needed the benefit of a few hours rest to be able to face into the stress of the next couple of days. He didn't disturb her and went back to his own seat. The flight was only just over two and a half hours and Pedro was waiting for them in Arrivals as well as Pacqui. They rushed towards the two and embraced them emotionally.

Pedro hugged Julie tight, and Pacqui burst into tears as she threw her arms around Carlos. They didn't say very much and walked together out to where the car waited.

'There are a few people at home, they are anxious to see you,' Pedro said, driving on the motorway.

'It's mostly the family, everyone is very upset about Abuela.'

'So are we, it's such a shock,' Julie said. 'I always thought she would go on for ever. She was so healthy and vibrant.'

'Has she been brought to the Chapel of Rest yet?' asked Carlos.

'We were waiting for you to arrive,' said Pedro.

'Thank you, we would not want to miss being with Abuela.'

When they arrived home, they were welcomed by the family, and barely had a chance to shower and change before the undertakers were to take Abuela to the Chapel of Rest which was a simple chapel decorated with white flowers and flickering candles.

Carlos took a moment to call Alva and was glad to hear that both she and Roberto were fine.

They gathered then and the cars slowly followed the hearse, which was a funeral carriage drawn by six black horses. It was their family tradition to carry the remains of their relatives to the Chapel of Rest. Once there, the open coffin was placed behind a glass screen and people were able to view Abuela, who looked very much at peace.

'I'll stay with Abuela over the night,' Carlos said to his father, Pedro.

'I will also,' he agreed.

Julie, Pacqui and Nuria kept a vigil with Abuela as well, and other family members also.

In the morning, they took an opportunity to go home for a couple of hours, and returned later when Abuela was moved to the cemetery. At this point, all the mourners left their cars, and followed the carriage on foot in procession. At the cemetery, there was a service and Abuela was laid to rest in a niche among a series of niches which was the way burial was conducted in Spain. Afterwards, the mourners were invited back to the house for drinks and food, and to remember Abuela's life. Carlos was glad to meet members of the family whom he hadn't seen in some time.

He called Alva a couple of times that morning and was glad that she still seemed in good form, planning to take Roberto for a walk in the afternoon. He was happy to hear that, and encouraged her.

'I love you and Roberto, just take care. I'll be home on Monday.'

Chapter Thirty-eight

Darren drove to Alva's apartment in Sutton, aware that her husband was away. He had to be quick if his plan was going to succeed. Naomi had told him that she took the baby for a walk most days so he hoped to catch her when she came out. He sat in the car all morning but there was no sign of Alva and her child. He cursed. Maybe she would go for a walk in the afternoon. He waited on. Where are you, Alva? Come out. He muttered. His mind swirling with thoughts of what he would do if he didn't make his scheme work. Opportunities darted like sparks from a fire. Red. Fiery. And in his imagination, he discarded them, one by one, as useless. He wasn't any clearer about what road he should take if he didn't see Alva today. But was ready to act as soon as he did.

He slumped in the driver's seat. Half hidden. He watched people come out of the apartment block. Most of them went to their cars and drove out through the high black gates. There weren't very many. And a couple of others took the pedestrian gate and walked down the road probably to catch a bus or walk to get to wherever they intended to go. Then, he sat up abruptly as he saw Alva push a baby buggy out through the door of the apartment building. His heart pounded. She was wearing a red coat and dark jeans, a striped scarf wound around her neck. Her dark hair blowing slightly in the wind as she pushed the buggy down the steps. He reached to clasp the door handle and held the door semi open. Calculating the length of time it would take her to come as far as the pedestrian gate. He casually stepped out of the car and waited near the railings. There were trees growing on the inside and he knew that she couldn't see him. She pushed the buggy ahead of her out through the gate and turned left along the road. There was no one around. Darren followed, with soft footsteps, until he caught up with her.

'Hello Alva,' he murmured, and pushed the weapon he held into her back. 'Stop.'

'Darren?' Her voice trembled.

'Just turn back.'

'What do you want?'

'I want you.'

She was silent for a few seconds and didn't turn back as he had told her to do. 'You can't have me,' she said.

'Then no one will have you. I will kill you. Just like that. One slash and you're gone. The same for your child.' Nervously he glanced around. But to his relief there was no one there.

'Don't do that, Darren, please, I beg you,' she asked him. 'He's only a tiny baby.'

'Then do as I say, turn back and hurry up.'

She swung the buggy around and he moved with her, digging the knife into her side.

'Give me your phone.'

'No.'

'Do as I say, give it to me and walk as far as that car,' he ordered. 'Quickly. Go on.'

They walked together, Alva pushing the buggy. The baby lying asleep inside it.

'The phone?' He put his other hand out.

Reluctantly she gave it to him. He put it into his pocket.

They reached the car. He opened the passenger door.

'Get in.'

225

'No.'

'You're coming with me.'

'I'm not.' She pulled away from him.

'Let go the buggy,' he muttered.

'No, you're not having him.' she cried.

He pressed the knife harder into her side.

'Don't hurt him, please?' she begged. In tears.

'Get in then.' He pushed her into the car. 'Stay there.' He went around, grabbed the buggy with the baby in it and pushed it along the back seat crookedly, and banged the door shut.

Alva pushed open the door and began to climb out of the car. 'You're not taking me or my baby,' she cried.

He pushed her in again and pulled the knife. 'Sit down.' He held the knife close to her throat.

She screamed.

'Shut-up,' he muttered, glad no one had appeared. Cars drove past, but none stopped to enquire what was going on.

He climbed into the car, started the engine, put his foot on the accelerator and the car shot away from the kerb up to the lights at the end of the road which were showing red. But to his satisfaction, the lights turned green, and he turned left and drove to the house by the sea taking a longer route in order to get there so that Alva wouldn't guess where he was taking her. She was still crying and her arm was over the back of the seat trying to reach her baby.

'He's all right,' muttered Darren.

'I can't see him,' she sobbed.

'We'll get him out soon.'

'Where are you taking us?' she gulped.

'To my place.'

'Where is that?'

'It's a surprise.'

He drove up on the gravelled pathway close to the front door.

As soon as he stopped, Alva moved to open the car door, but he had anticipated it and put his arm across her. 'Don't.'

'Get away from me,' she struggled against him.

'Quiet.' He held the knife close to her again.

She did as he ordered.

Quickly, he climbed out of the car and lifted the buggy with the baby in it and put it on the ground. The baby still slept.

Alva was almost out of the door again, but he pushed her back inside and pressed the central lock button. Now she was banging on the window, screaming. He ignored her. He pushed the buggy up to the front door, opened it, and brought it into the kitchen at the back. Then he went out to the car again.

She was still banging on the glass.

He opened the car, dragged her out and up the path into the house. He didn't think anyone would see them as there were trees and bushes growing around the front of the house. And it was winter anyway.

'Enough and shut up,' he snapped and pulled the knife from his pocket. 'Get inside.'

'Darren, stop,' she whispered, staring at the knife. Her eyes wide and terrified.

'Do as I say and I won't hurt you or him,' he muttered.

'Where is he?' she shouted.

He pushed the point of the knife into her back. 'Shut-up.'

She straightened up immediately, and he could hear her sharp intake of breath.

'Get in there.'

'My baby?' she screamed. He covered her mouth with his hand, pushed her down the hall and into a room. Then locked it. Immediately, he could hear her bang on the door, but couldn't hear the sound of her voice. He was glad about that. He went into the back room and looked at the baby in the buggy for a while.

He was a tiny chubby little fellow.

'Hello baby?' Darren was immediately charmed by the child. 'Hello little boy.' He lifted him out of the buggy and held him up. 'You're mine, aren't you?' he smiled at him. 'I'm your Dad, do you know that?' But suddenly, to his surprise he started to cry and for a moment Darren didn't know what to do. He lay him back down in the buggy and stared at him. Then it dawned on him that he could be hungry. He picked him up again and took him to the room where he had put her. He unlocked the door and holding the baby in front of him he pushed in. Alva put her arms out and took the baby from him. Gathering him up, and kissing his little face.

'What's wrong with him?' he asked, closing the door behind him.

'He's hungry,' Alva snapped. 'Can't you understand?'

'I thought that.'

'And you didn't bring him in to me?'

'He only started crying a few minutes ago, I wasn't sure what was wrong with him.'

She turned away from Darren and began to feed the baby. 'Go away.'

He did leave then, deciding that he should make dinner for himself and Alva. It was like he was living with her again. They were a loving couple. A family. He was so happy now and was looking forward to the future with Alva. She could forget about that Spanish bod.

He brought in a tray with two plates of food. Grilled fillet steak, vegetables that he knew she liked, spinach, and mushrooms, and oven chips. He wasn't a great cook, but could make a reasonable meal if he put his mind to it.

'Hope you like this,' he said, setting it out.

She shook her head.

But he had already left the room, automatically closing the

door behind him and pocketing the key.

He brought in some extra items, glasses of water and bowls of dessert. He had bought a trifle although he had to admit in his heart that it would not compare with any dessert Alva might make herself. But she would have to like it.

He sat down at the small table. 'Sit down and eat your dinner, Alva,' he encouraged.

'I'm not hungry, I want to go home.'

'You must eat your meal,' he said.

'I told you I don't want to eat anything. I want to go home, I've nothing for Roberto or myself.'

'I've bought clothes for you, jeans and sweaters and stuff. They're in the wardrobe. And there are nappies and clothes and other baby bits and pieces. See the nice cot I bought as well.' He pointed to it in the corner. 'And the lovely bedclothes.'

'He doesn't want anything you bought. You're nothing to him,' she snapped, walking towards him, the baby in her arms. 'Open that door, I'm going.'

'How do you think you're going to go, walk?' he smirked.

'If I have to.'

'Have you seen the weather. It's lashing rain now.'

'I don't care.'

'You're not taking the baby, I won't have him catch a cold. And do you know where you are?' he asked.

'I'm still in Dublin, I know that. We weren't driving for that long.'

'It's a big place, you'd never find your way back.'

'You can't keep me here. It's against the law to imprison me. You'll do more time for doing such a thing.'

'I'm not imprisoning you.'

'What would you call it?'

'I love you, Alva, we're partners.'

'I don't love you, Darren.'

'We'll fall in love again. If you just give me a chance.'

'You're crazy.'

Suddenly, taking care to hold Roberto tight, with her other hand she took hold of the table and shoved it towards Darren as hard as she could. As it hit him, all the dishes slid across and her plate of meat and vegetables fell into his lap, the glasses of water toppled over and soaked everything. Bowls of dessert slithered too as she kept on pushing and Darren fell back in his chair which tumbled over and crashed to the floor.

'Hey, what are you doing?' He shouted at her from where he lay.

Now she stood over him. 'You bastard, I want to kill you. Let me go home. Let me go home.' She kicked him again and again.

'Stop, you stupid bitch. You have me destroyed.' He tried to push himself up from the floor, but it was difficult to do that with the chair underneath him.

'I'm not staying here. Open that door and let me out,' she shouted. 'Where is the key. Give it to me.' She bent down and tried to search the pockets of the jacket he wore for the key with one hand, but that proved to be difficult and she couldn't get hold of it.

He put up his hands and grabbed hers, stopping her, and finally managed to push her away from him. Getting up he flung her towards the wall with a violent thump and she had to keep her arms tight around the baby so that she wouldn't drop him. Then he slapped her across the face a couple of times with such strength her head swung left and right.

'Bitch, you'll pay for this,' he muttered, and flung himself out of the door, banged it behind him, and turned the key in the lock.

In the back room, he took his own phone and Alva's and removed the sim cards. Throwing them into the Aga cooker where they should melt. Then he took a hammer and smashed the phones into pieces. Tiny pieces. Then he wrapped them in old newspapers, and left the house.

He drove to Dun Laoghaire. Walked along the East Pier and flung one of the parcels into the choppy sea at the end. Then he did the same in the West Pier, relieved that he had got rid of both phones. He knew that the Gardai could track phones so he was glad he was one step ahead of them.

Chapter Thirty-nine

Naomi was in great form. The last night Darren had stayed had given her the impression that marriage between the two of them might be on the cards. So far, he hadn't ever indicated that he was that serious so now she could hardly believe that one of these days he would propose. That they would go around to various jewellery designers, and choose a ring which would bond them together. She had often looked at rings in shop windows and particularly liked vintage designs and now was even more enthusiastic about her choices even narrowing them down to one final possibility which she was looking forward to showing Darren. Spending a lot of her time daydreaming about life with him. Would she sell her apartment and buy a house with him, she wondered? It would be the start of their life together. But Darren had no money and only received a salary from his job which when added to hers wouldn't cover a new mortgage for a bigger property. She didn't want to stay in an apartment block. Or raise her children in such a place. She was keen to have a garden for them to play in, and maybe to have a house near the country rather than in a concrete jungle. Since Alva's child, Roberto, had been born, and having spent so much time with him she would have given anything to have a child herself. Now all of these dreams had materialised and she almost couldn't wait until Darren asked that question she longed to hear.

Naomi was at home on Saturday, hoping that Darren would arrive. They hadn't made a definite date, but she phoned him, left a voicemail and sent a text, but he didn't call back. She cooked a meal, opened a bottle of wine, and changed into something alluring in anticipation of his visit.

She waited. There was no call from him. Growing more and more frustrated she turned on the television and switched through the channels vaguely without any interest. Every now and then, she stood up and glanced out the window which gave her a view of the road outside. Each set of headlights she saw made her peer ever closer in an effort to make out the colour of his car.

Time passed slowly. She picked up her phone and called Alva. But she didn't reply. The line was dead. Naomi listened, puzzled. It was unusual. Alva normally answered her phone immediately if she saw Naomi's name come up on the readout. Maybe she was sleeping, she decided. Yes, she probably was. She would ring in the morning just to check on her.

She didn't sleep well. Still expecting her doorbell to ring if Darren arrived. But he didn't come. She was disappointed. In the morning, she rang him again, but his phone seemed out of order as well. It was very strange as this was a Sunday and he wasn't working. But she put it down to something which had occurred unexpectedly. She also called Alva again, but it was the same with her. Now she was worried. Alva should definitely be at home, all she did was to take a short walk with the baby, and had told Naomi that she was doing that yesterday. On the way to work, she detoured just to make a quick call on her.

In the apartment complex she checked the car park and could see Alva's red Mercedes parked there in her usual space. Carlos's jeep wasn't there as she knew he had gone to the airport on Friday with Julie. Then she rang the doorbell, but there was no reply. She waited a few minutes aware that she didn't have much time. And rang again. But nothing. She pulled a set of keys from her pocket. Alva had insisted on giving them to her when the baby was due to arrive so that she could get into the apartment. She took the lift up and knocked on the apartment door. There was no response. She unlocked the door and pushed it open.

'Alva?' she walked down the hall into the lounge, but it was empty. 'Alva? Are you there?' she called again. Desperately concerned that she was ill or that something else had happened to her. She knocked on the main bedroom door and opened it. But she wasn't there. The bed was made, and Roberto's clothes were neatly folded on top of the tallboy. It didn't look as if she had left in a hurry. Naomi was relieved.

But maybe she had already gone out today. Perhaps she had felt better after going out yesterday, and decided to go out again. Naomi wasn't sure what to do. She looked around but couldn't see if she had left her phone behind and that it would explain her not picking up. She didn't see the buggy either, so assumed that she had taken the baby with her and gone out.

She rang Carlos straight away.

'Naomi, how are you? I've been trying to call Alva but I can't get in touch. Have you seen her today?' he sounded worried.

'I'm in the apartment at the moment, Alva gave me a set of keys before the baby arrived. But she's not here. Although her car is parked in the usual spot.'

'What?'

'I think she may have gone out for a walk early, and I'll continue ringing. I'll call again later. Her phone must be out of order.'

'I'm coming back as soon as I can. As I was at the funeral of Abuela yesterday I assumed she wouldn't call me yesterday evening because of that. I texted her a couple of times but with everything going on I didn't notice that she hadn't responded to me.'

'I certainly will, but I'm sure she will be here later.'

'She may have gone to visit her brothers. She didn't mention it, but she might have decided to go because I was in Spain.'

'Perhaps she's done that.'

'Possibly.'

'Have you phone numbers for David or Cian?' she asked.

'I'll text them to you.'

'I'd like to check if she has been in touch with them. Although she may have met a friend today either. We could be over-reacting.'

'Perhaps,' he sounded doubtful.

'I'll make a couple of calls,' she promised. 'And get back to you.' She did that, but neither Cian nor David had heard from Alva.

She called Carlos again.

'Perhaps I should report her missing?' Naomi asked. Feeling very uncomfortable even suggesting that to him.

'Oh my God, I can't believe that she could be missing, where is she and the baby? How is it possible?'

She could hear the distress in his voice.

Leave it with me, I'll do the report and come back to you.

'I appreciate what you're doing.'

'Of course, she may have had an accident. and I'll ask that they check the hospitals as soon as possible.'

'Yes, si, muchas gracias. I'm going to catch a flight as soon as I can today.'

Naomi went into work, and made the report. Praying that Alva would be found. During the day, she slipped out and went to the apartment again, but Alva hadn't returned. Thinking that she might be depressed and may have just wandered somewhere and forgotten her way home, Naomi then got into the car and began to comb the area. Stopping at petrol stations, shops, and bars, restaurants, anywhere she could think of. Driving up and down streets searching for a woman pushing a buggy. Unfortunately, she didn't remember what she was wearing, but thought she might have been wearing her winter coat which was a bright shade of red. Naomi wasn't sure about that, and was eventually looking for any woman pushing a buggy. But she had no success and couldn't find her.

Chapter Forty

Carlos couldn't believe what was happening. Naomi had shocked him with her suggestion that she report Alva as missing to the Gardai. He was frustrated that he was stuck here in Spain when he should be at home in Dublin searching for Alva. Julie had insisted on coming with him and they waited together at Seville airport for a flight to London, and then taking a connection to Dublin. He wasn't sure if Naomi had called David and Cian yet, but he did that now, just to obtain their help to look for Alva.

'David?'

'Hi Carlos.'

'Has Naomi been talking to you?'

'She mentioned that Alva is missing and that you are in Spain at the moment.'

'I'm on the way back now. I wanted to know if you had knowledge of any of her friends?'

'I know the way she works that she hasn't much time for visiting friends. It's family usually.'

'Maybe I'll ring Cian, he might know of someone.'

'I'll put my thinking cap on.'

'I'll be organising a search,' Carlos told him.

'I could make up some posters with her photo on, and go around putting them up. I took one at the hospital.'

'I'd be grateful if you could do that. Thank you. I'll give Cian a call now and see if he has any ideas.'

'Call me when you arrive and I'll meet you, I'll start putting the posters up as quick as I can.'

'She was a bit depressed, you know, so that may have affected her.' Carlos explained.

'I'll go around by your place in case she has got lost,' David promised.

Carlos rang Cian then and had much the same conversation with him.

'I could put it up on social media,' Cian offered. 'Facebook, Instagram and any of the others. What do you think, Carlos?'

'That would be fantastic, Cian, have you got a photo?'

'Yes, I have the one you sent me.'

'That's fine.'

'Someone might have seen something, you never know.'

'Thank you so much, Cian, I'll let you know what time we are landing in Dublin.'

'I'll begin straight away, what time are you due to arrive?'

'About six o'clock. Although we'll be going to the Gardai straight away.'

'David has been on to me and we'll begin to search immediately. Give me a call when you're here.'

As soon as Julie and Carlos arrived in Dublin, they went immediately to the local Garda station as Naomi had told him to do. She met them there and introduced them to the detective who was handling the case of Alva's disappearance.

After that, there was a long interview.

There were two Gardai there and Carlos was aware that he was being recorded.

'When was the last time you saw your wife?'

'On Friday morning when I left for the airport.'

'How was she then?'

'She seemed normal, although she hasn't been well since the

birth of our baby.'

'Did you talk to her on the phone over the weekend?'

'Yes a few times.'

'When was the last call?'

'On Saturday, about lunchtime.'

'What form was she in at that time?'

'Good, she was planning to take the baby for a walk.'

'Do you know if she took her phone with her?'

'Naomi went to our apartment looking for her and couldn't see it.'

'We'll have to conduct a search of your home. We'll call tomorrow morning.'

He nodded.

'Was there anyone who may have a reason to kidnap your wife.'

He stared astonished at the man and didn't reply immediately.

'Kidnap?'

'Yes, kidnap.' The man nodded.

'Her previous partner will be up in court for attempted rape,' he said.

'What's his name?'

'Darren Malone.'

'Do you know where he lives?'

'No.' He shook his head.

'We'll find out,' he said confidently.

They continued questioning him, often repeating the same questions in a slightly different way, and he found that very confusing trying to remember exactly what he had said the first time.

Afterwards, they informed him that a team had been put together and a search organised in the area of Sutton and Howth by the police and Civil Defence. Fire and Rescue were included. CCTV would be gathered so that Alva's last known position could be located.

Julie was waiting for him outside. She had also been questioned but her interrogation hadn't gone on for as long as Carlos, and he was glad about that.

'I feel strange,' he said, as they sat into the jeep. 'I've never had anything to do with the Gardai here, and I actually feel that perhaps they suspect me of doing something to Alva. You know how it is, the husband is often under suspicion.'

'Not at all, Carlos, how could they think that of you?' Julie dismissed it.

'How did you find the questioning?'

'Confusing. Asking over and over about every detail of our journey to Seville, and what we did there.'

'I'm sorry you had to go through that.'

'I don't care, I just want to find Alva. I pray nothing has happened to her.'

At home, Carlos called Naomi and told her what had happened.

'They're looking for Darren,' he said.

'Darren?' she seemed surprised.

'They asked me about that and think there might be a connection. And there is something else I mentioned to them. I've been receiving threatening letters in the post.'

'What did the letters say?'

'They were just saying that my life will be over and …' he hesitated.

'Have you any idea what might be behind them?'

'I thought it was connected with a patient I was treating.'

'What happened?'

'A man died after an operation.'

'I see.'

'But there was so much going on I did nothing about the letters.'

'Do you think there is a connection with the letters and

Alva?' She asked. Immediately, she remembered how Darren bombarded Alva with texts and letters after she threw him out of her apartment and they had split up.

'I don't know.'

'Have you had any phone calls demanding money?' she asked.

'No.'

'Keep your phone on you just in case,' she advised.

'I don't care if that happens, I'll pay anything to get Alva back. Any amount.'

Chapter Forty-one

Naomi felt shocked. The Gardai were looking for Darren. She couldn't believe that he was involved in this situation with Alva. She called him. But as before his phone seemed to be out of order. She had left messages on Saturday, but he hadn't responded. Now she was in a complete state of confusion, wondering why he hadn't been in touch. It was completely out of character as he often called to the apartment on the spur of the moment. Normally he rang or left messages every day and she missed that now, and felt he had suddenly lost interest in her.

But she needed to see him. Explain what was happening and that the Gardai had an interest in talking to him about Alva. What would he know about Alva? But remembered that she had told him Alva wasn't well and hoped she would get out and about on her own soon. Now, with Alva missing, her remorse grew and grew, and she didn't know what to do. But then she decided she would go to see Darren and let him know what was happening.

She drove to his apartment which was in an old Victorian house with apartments on each floor. She parked outside, ran up the steps and pressed Darren's bell. It took a while for someone to answer the intercom and she was surprised to hear a woman's voice.

'Yes?'

Naomi was surprised.

'Is Darren there?' she asked.

'Darren?'

'Yes, Darren Malone.'

'No, there's no one by that name here,' she said.

Naomi turned away and stood staring at the front door. Thinking for a moment that she had pressed the wrong bell by mistake. She pressed it again. There were no names on some of the bells, and Darren hadn't bothered putting his own name there either.

'I'm looking for a man called Darren Malone, he lives here.'

'I told you there's no one by that name here. I'm living here now.'

'I hope you don't mind, but could you tell me how long you are living there, he was renting an apartment in this house for quite a while before you and I thought he was still there.'

'Why should I tell you that? It's none of your business.'

'I'm sorry, but he's a close friend of mine and I would appreciate it if you would tell me. I'm very worried about him.'

'Maybe I'm living here with him now, so do you think he'd want me to tell you everything about us. Could be he doesn't want to have anything to do with you any longer,' she snapped.

Naomi's heart sank into her stomach. She hadn't been able to contact Darren for a couple of days now, and she couldn't imagine that he had already moved someone else into his apartment.

'Are you telling me the truth?' she asked suspiciously.

'I'm just having you on,' the woman laughed. 'Don't be so gullible.'

Relief flooded, and she relaxed.

'Look I'm living here about four weeks, and I don't know who was here before, so I suggest that you look somewhere else for him.' She banged down the phone again.

Naomi stared at the door. The black paintwork on the door was clean. The brasses shining. She felt rebuffed by the woman, and couldn't understand where Darren might be. She had been over to his apartment more than once, but both of them found her place more convenient. And he hadn't told her that he had moved out of his apartment and rented somewhere else. What was the reason for that? Was it that he was tired of her? Had he ghosted her?

She walked back to her car and sat in, wondering where she would find him. Then a thought. She knew he was working in that new job, but wondered if it might be very awkward for her to make enquiries about him there. And perhaps he moved to live in a new place as well and hadn't told her that. Her heart thumped with anxiety. Ghosted. Ghosted. The word continued to echo in her head.

She drove around the North side of the city. Searching for Alva, although didn't expect to see a woman pushing a buggy at this time of night. But still she continued to look for her friend. She had to be somewhere near here. If she was walking with a buggy then she couldn't get very far.

Naomi went to see her colleagues, and talked to the officer in charge.

'I know I shouldn't be involved in the case of my missing friend, but I know her better than anyone and I feel I could contribute. Have you identified any CCTV which might give some idea of where she was last?'

'Naomi, you can't get involved. You're involved in another case and don't work in the Missing Persons Unit. If we were ever to take someone to court for harming Alva in any way, then any evidence you may have might not be admissible. It's not worth taking a chance on that.'

'I understand. But could you at least let me know what's happening?' she asked. The fact that she wasn't working on Alva's case was frustrating, as she couldn't get involved in all aspects. Examine the evidence which had been gathered and make suggestions as to where she might be.

'No, it's not possible.'

He put her down sharply and she had to accept that.

Chapter Forty-two

Darren pushed into the room.

'Here, clean that mess up.' He threw down a plastic brush and pan.

'I won't,' Alva retorted. 'You can do it yourself.'

'Do it,' he yelled. 'It can't be left here.'

She stood staring at him until eventually he did it himself and brushed the food and broken glass into a plastic bag. 'That's the last dinner you're going to get. I'm not going to that trouble again,' he muttered.

'Don't bother yourself.'

He stomped out of the room again. Very angry.

Roberto was crying. He was red-faced from hunger and had tossed off the bedclothes. She had been afraid to have him in the bed with her as it was just a single and he could easily fall out or she could roll over him if she happened to doze off even for a few minutes. She reached for the baby and gathered him into her arms and held him close to her breast so that he could latch on. She lay back in the bed and was comforted by his warmth against her body.

The door was unlocked, and Darren appeared.

'Why was he crying?' he asked.

'He was hungry.'

'What do you want for your breakfast, oh no, I forgot it should be tea, or dinner or maybe nothing at all,' he smirked.

'I don't want anything from you,' she snapped angrily. On the first day which she knew was Saturday she had pushed the table against him and all the food and dishes fell on top of him. Now it was Sunday, and she was hungry.

'All right, but what about the kid?' Darren asked.

'I'll feed him,' she said.

'You won't be able to feed him if you don't eat.'

It was only then she thought she had better eat something. Otherwise, she would have no milk to feed Roberto as he had suggested. While she had been very down thinking that the baby didn't like her, and she was a very bad mother, she realised now that she had to make an effort to look after her baby even under these awful circumstances.

'You'll have to eat something. What do you want?' he shouted out loud, very aggressive.

'Whatever,' she retorted.

He brought in a boiled egg, toast, and a cup of tea later, and she forced herself to eat. It wasn't easy. When she had finished, she decided to try and talk to him.

'Why is it so dark, Darren?' There's no light in this place at all except for the bulb. I don't know whether it's night or day.'

'You don't need light.'

'But it's confusing.'

'That doesn't matter.'

'When will you let me go, Darren. You know everyone will be looking for me. A person can't disappear like that. I'm sure Naomi will be on the case as well and she will definitely guess where I am.'

'Nobody will have any idea. This is secret. It's our hide out. And we're going to live here as long as we like.'

'Where exactly is this place?' she asked curiously. 'I know it's near Skerries or Rush as I saw a road sign.'

'What difference does it make to you?' he asked with a grin.

'Are you going to keep me inside all the time? Surely, you will give me a chance to get out and take some fresh air. I hate to be inside, and you know that.'

'If you wouldn't run away, I might take that chance, but I want you here with me. And I love our little boy.'

'But he's not yours, Darren. He's mine and Carlos.'

'He's yours and that's enough for me. If we had a baby, he'd look just like him.'

'He looks more like Carlos than me.'

'Well, I like him. I want him.'

'You can't have him. You'll never get him,' she shouted, becoming angry.

'I'll get him,' he grinned evilly.

'I won't let you.' She held on tight to Roberto.

'Has he had enough milk?' he asked.

She looked down at him, and ran her hand over his head. 'He's asleep now.'

'Let me hold him.' He reached out his arms.

'No.' She held him tight against her.

Darren pulled a knife from his jacket pocket. He held the blade to her throat. 'Give him to me,' he muttered, menacing. His mood had changed suddenly.

'No.' She moved back from him.

The knife followed. The blade was inches from her neck. It came closer.

'Darren,' she whispered.

His hand reached, and his fingers gripped the baby's arm.

'Don't,' she warned. 'You'll hurt him.'

'I won't if you give him to me.'

'He's mine.'

The blade touched her skin. It was cold. Droplets of blood dripped on the baby's head.

Horrified, she immediately brushed it off with her hand. 'Look what you've done,' she shouted. 'Stop, you bastard.' She pressed her fingers against her neck to stop the bleeding.

'I'm taking him.' He put his hands out, caught the bloodstained white babygrow and dragged him out of her arms. The baby woke up and began to scream.

'Give him back to me.' Alva put her arms out but didn't want to hurt Roberto by grabbing him back from Darren.

He backed off towards the door. Opened it and went out. Locking it again behind him.

She ran after him and banged on the wooden door.

'Come back with my baby. How dare you take him from me.' She kept banging and furiously, she screamed out loud. But her voice bounced around her, and she knew that she couldn't be heard outside of the room. Darren had covered the window with wooden slats and although she had examined them when he brought her here, she still couldn't see how she might remove any of the nails which kept them together and try to escape. Still she searched the room, looking for something she could use.

Alva couldn't tell exactly what day it was. She slept when Roberto slept, so there was no night and day as normal. It was Saturday when Darren brought her to this house. Yesterday was Sunday and today must be Monday. She had tried to keep track of time, but because it was dark in this room it was difficult. What was Carlos thinking, she wondered. He must be home and had gone to the Gardai by now. Were they searching for her? They must be. But how would they know where to look? That was the thing which upset her most. Tears drifted down her cheeks, and she began to bang again on the door screaming for Darren to bring Roberto back to her. If Carlos knew what he was doing, he would kill him, she was certain.

She went into the bathroom and looked in the mirror. The cut in her neck wasn't much, but there had been a surprising amount of blood. She cleaned it with a tissue and was relieved to see that it had mostly dried up. Darren didn't come in again for ages and then pushed open the door carrying Roberto. The baby was crying.

'Feed him,' he said. 'He didn't like the bottle I gave him.'

She rushed to the door and took Roberto out of his arms. 'Of course, he didn't. I'm the only one who can feed him. I'm his mother.'

'I changed him anyway. I've plenty of nappies outside. And I put on a clean babygrow. There's more baby stuff in the wardrobe, and you can bathe him in the bath there.'

'Where is my phone, Darren? What have you done with it? I must ring Carlos, he is going to be so worried about us.' She tried again to talk to him. And deliberately forced a gentle tone.

'You're not making any phone calls,' he snarled.

'Please Darren, give it to me.'

'I don't have it.'

'I gave it to you,' she protested.

'Well, it's at the bottom of the sea now so you can't make any phone calls,' he laughed.

'What?' she was horrified. 'How did it get there?'

'How do you think? I got rid of it.'

'Why did you do that? I have all my info on my phone, how am I going to get it back again?'

'You won't need it.'

She stared at him, longing to punch his smirking face, but with the baby in her arms it was impossible. She pressed Roberto to her but still took the chance to push her shoulder against Darren. 'Let me out,' she said and tried to squeeze past him through the narrow gap at one side through which she could see the hallway. But he pushed her back, his fingers piercing her shoulders. 'Get inside,' he said, stepped back and closed the door with a bang. It

250

was the first time she had taken a chance to get out of this room, but it gave her courage to try again.

She checked the pockets of her coat but all she had was a small amount of money. She had left everything else at home, and of course Darren had taken her phone. She lay on the bed and as the baby fed, she relaxed against the pillows and tried to think of how she might approach Darren. If she was angry with him all the time, then he would be the same back. Perhaps she would be better talking with him gently. It hadn't worked a few minutes before but she would try again, giving him the impression that there may be some chance that they might be reconciled. Maybe they could behave in a normal way if he didn't think she might try to escape. She decided to try that tactic with him.

Chapter Forty-three

The Gardai called at seven o'clock in the morning. Carlos stood staring out the window of the apartment as one of the Gardai rang the bell, and he responded by pressing it and causing the high metal gates to open. They drove in, and again he buzzed them through until they came up in the lift and he met them at the door. He told Julie they had arrived and she stood with him as the Gardai came in.

It was very difficult to watch them go through all their possessions. Opening presses. Drawers. Looking under tables, chairs, lamps, and ornaments. Peering at photos. Flicking through books and magazines from shelves. He felt this was a terrible personal affront to him and Alva, but could do nothing about it. They took quite a while to finish and eventually they left carrying his computer and laptops. He also gave them the letters he had received. They took his phone but promised he could collect it later at the Garda station. They told him then they would begin the search in Howth at two o'clock.

He went into the hospital then, and talked to the department head. He felt lucky that his partner could handle all the urgent cases on his list. In his office he checked emails and post. His heart sinking when he saw another of those threatening letters. The person who had written it was now telling him that he was going to delight in his misfortune and that he would lose everything he cherished. He read it a couple of times to see if there was anything different in it and then took this latest one to the Garda station. He met the detective who was in charge of the case and he was very interested in seeing it. As Carlos had assumed that the writer of the letters had a connection with one of his patients it was only now he thought that this person may also have had some connection with the disappearance of Alva and Roberto. The detective brought Carlos up to date on the case so far. The search by the underwater team was completed and they had found no sign of Alva or the baby. He was relieved to hear that. Although he still felt that he could be the main suspect. But he had an alibi at the time and the Gardai had been able to see his airline bookings on the phone.

Now he told them that they had been putting up photos of Alva and Roberto and were searching for her. 'There are a group of people getting together later. Do you want us to check in with you before we go out?' he asked.

'Yes, that's a good idea.'

'We're intending to go up Howth Head first.'

'I will call you re the timing and we can organise that search. The Civil Defence will be involved as well. Everyone should have hi-vis jackets, and have photos. But we would also suggest that you raise awareness of Alva and Roberto's disappearance on social media platforms.'

'Her brother, Cian, did that last night and will continue posting. Thank you for all your help.' Carlos was very grateful.

'As regards this Darren Malone, he is not at his address any longer. He has also left his previous employment.'

David had printed a poster composed of a recent photo of Alva and Roberto and he, Carlos, Cian and Julie had already been around the streets during the night putting them up. And they would join all the staff members in Purtell Vintners who were going to distribute the posters as well and join in the search for Alva and Roberto that afternoon.

Carlos and the large group of friends and relatives gathered in Howth. There were even some colleagues from the hospital. The Garda returned his phone to him and also told him that so far they hadn't been able to track Alva's phone to find out where she might be. And there was no CCTV of her as she left the apartment.

It was a bright cold day, and they were split up into groups by the Civil Defence and given areas to search. Some of the people gave out copies of the poster and put them up on notice boards in shops, bars, restaurants, churches and a couple of hotels in the area. Other people in the group combed the green areas. Thickets. Shrubbery. Anywhere Alva could have had an accident. Perhaps she might have fallen and broken her leg and was so incapacitated that she couldn't have managed to walk. While she had her phone with her, she could have dropped it and been unable to get to it.

Carlos, Julie, Cian and David, and others climbed Howth Head. There were a lot of areas up there where she could have fallen as well. The Gardai had told Carlos that the air sea rescue helicopter would also search for Alva and Roberto, and he had told them that their group would be in that area as well. But they were unsuccessful and when darkness fell they had to abandon the search.

But for Carlos, Julie, and her brothers, they couldn't leave off looking for Alva and Roberto even in the darkness. They came back to Alva and Carlos's apartment, just had a quick bite to eat, and then put on warmer clothes and went back out again. Naomi had called Carlos and said she would join them. She hadn't managed to come along today as she was working and the Gardai were involved. She warned them to say nothing to the

Gardai, and that she would come along every night for as long as it took.

By now the weather had changed and it was raining. They struggled along under umbrellas trying to see where they were going, only occasionally noticing another person out on this night. But regardless of the weather, they lit the torches they carried and peered into the distance trying to ascertain if any of the people who walked past might have been Alva. But they found no sign of her.

When they eventually gave up for the night, Carlos just lay on the bed for a couple of hours and then went out again himself. He called the Gardai in the morning, enquiring as to whether there was any further information about Alva. Asking particularly if they had found out anything about Darren. And whether there were any results from forensics regarding the letters which he had been sent.

'Whoever sent the letters wore gloves,' responded the detective. 'There is no information regarding DNA.'

Carlos's mood was very dark. He had hoped that something would materialise from the forensic tests but he couldn't see past the ghastly possibilities that constantly went through his mind. Nightmares that took him into places of horror. Where were his darling Alva and Roberto? The question repeated over and over and he had no answers. He found the frustration of that almost impossible to handle. Had she left him with their baby because she didn't want to live with him any longer. What was he going to do if he couldn't find them? His whole life would be destroyed.

Julie tried to reassure him that Alva would never have left him. That her mental state must have been behind anything she might have done. And she would have had no control over her actions. But he wasn't consoled. This was the worst thing that had ever happened to him.

Chapter Forty-four

Naomi's mind swirled around in circles and all she could think of were Alva and Roberto. Where could they be?

She called Darren's company, and asked if she could speak to him, explaining that she was his sister. But the girl who answered the phone told her that normally he would be on the road but this morning he had called in sick. As she listened to her explanation she wondered if he was in hospital. He wasn't at his apartment. Or had he moved that woman in with him and was he there all the time. A sense of shock reverberated through her. She felt sick. Darren had almost promised to marry her. He had promised.

She went out to Sutton and could see that an area had been cordoned off, and there were a number of Garda cars parked nearby, so the underwater divers were already in position. The thought that Alva and Roberto had been drowned was too much for her and she continued driving, all the time trying Darren's number again and again but the line was still out of order. She couldn't believe he hadn't been in touch with her. It seemed so strange. And the fact that Alva and Roberto had disappeared was odd too, although she didn't think for one minute there was any connection. She was angry with him. All she wanted to do was to talk. Find out what was going on with him and why had he rejected her. Was that what he had done. She asked herself. It was a few days since she had talked to him. Prior to that all was going well and she had no reason to believe that suddenly he would ghost her without any warning.

That night, after searching for Alva, she drove to Darren's address and parked a few doors down the street. In the darkness, she lay back in the driver's seat and even though it was late her Garda eyes watched people walk past. Noting what they were wearing. Noting their demeanour. Wondering what secrets lay hidden beneath their eyelids. She felt like an author. About to write a book. And find characters which she could use to people the chapters and give them personalities according to the impression she picked up as they walked past.

She checked her phone. It was almost two o'clock now and he still hadn't returned here. She sighed. He must come soon. She was certain that he was living with that woman now. But then was he even inside the building? She gave up an hour later and went home. Grabbed a couple of hours sleep but came back at six in the morning again.

As she sat there her mind switched from Darren to Alva and her baby. Could he have anything to do with their disappearance? He had been very keen to see Alva, she remembered. He had wanted to meet her outside and talk. He wanted her forgiveness. More and more her thoughts took her back to those remarks and now she was certain he had to have something to do with it. Now she had to see him. It was the only way. She couldn't understand why he didn't made contact with her. If he had lost his phone, then surely by now he would have bought another. He couldn't operate without one.

She called Carlos and he confirmed Alva hadn't been found overnight.

'Her passport is still here. And there's no point checking the airports as she can't leave the country without a passport. And we've checked her credit cards, but she hasn't made any purchases at all since the day before she disappeared so ...' his voice broke up and he couldn't speak for a moment.

'Is there any possibility that she has gone to stay with a friend or family?'

'We've checked all the family and none of them have seen her. As regards friends, there could be someone she knows who offered to give her a home.'

'But they would have to support her as well. And that would be very unusual,' Naomi said.

'Unless it's someone from her past who is prepared to do that. Maybe even Darren.'

'Oh yes, Darren,' she said vaguely.

'The Gardai have checked him out but apparently he's left the company he worked with a month or so ago.'

'Oh,' she forced surprise.

'And he's also moved out of his previous accommodation and they don't have a new address for him.'

She listened attentively. Finding out more through Carlos than she could have herself as her colleagues in the Missing Persons Unit were not inclined to give her too much detail about their work.

Naomi was worried now about him. And why he hadn't made contact before now. She was frustrated, and felt so rejected by him. He hadn't many friends, she knew that, although his family lived in Waterford, he had never introduced her to them. She blamed herself now for the way their relationship had developed. Her deep friendship with Alva causing her to keep her love for Darren to herself. Alva had never talked much about her relationship with him. But they had loved each other deeply, Naomi knew that. And assumed that the attraction Alva felt for him was as strong as the attraction she felt herself.

She needed Darren. And even more so now that he had cut her off. Did it mean he didn't love her any longer? What did it mean? She just wanted him back. Above anything else in her life. And found herself going around to his apartment, and parking close by in case he was still living there with that woman and that her explanation was some sort of ruse to alienate her.

At the same time, she realised that if he had gone away with Alva and her baby she did not know where they might be. Should she mention that she had seen him recently to the Gardai? And if she told them that she knew him they would definitely take her in for interrogation, particularly as a Detective Inspector in her position shouldn't be in a relationship with someone who was due to come to trial for attempted rape. And she had huge guilt now around the fact that she couldn't tell Carlos or Julie what she was thinking, and was forced to let them continue searching for Alva although now Naomi was becoming more certain that Darren had taken her, or she had gone with him because she wanted to leave Carlos. She knew that Alva wouldn't be found wandering the streets with her baby.

Chapter Forty-five

Alva still wore the clothes she was wearing when Darren took her, and was very reluctant to use any of the clothes he had hanging in the wardrobe. While she had showered each day, finally she had to give in and changed into clean underwear, blue jeans, a white tee shirt and red jumper. Because of the cold, she put her red jacket on over the clothes. The heating came on and off. But she still found it very cold and spent all of her time with the baby in bed cuddled under the duvet.

When Darren unlocked the door, he immediately laughed out loud.

'Oh, you've changed. Hope you like my good taste.'

She didn't answer, but forced a smile. It was deliberate and really she would have preferred to glare at him instead. But she didn't.

'How are you?' she asked softly.

'I'm fine,' he said and immediately went towards the cot where Roberto lay sleeping. She had put him there to please Darren. 'I'll take him up,' he reached for him.

'Please don't, he's only just gone down for a sleep now. He'll be very cranky if we wake him.'

'He'll go to sleep again. He'll know it's me holding him.'

'I'd prefer if you didn't. We have to get him into a routine.' She used the word "we" deliberately.

He took no notice of what she said, leaned in and took hold of him. The baby woke up but didn't cry.

'You've disturbed him.' She couldn't resist saying that, even though it sounded like criticism and she knew that always annoyed him.

'There, there, little boy. You'll be all right with Daddy.' He held him up to his chest and walked about the room rocking him back and forwards.

'He loves me, can't you see it?'

Alva didn't reply.

'I'll take him out for some fresh air. It will do him good.'

'It's cold outside,' she pointed out, worried about the baby.

'Not that cold.'

'It's cold in here.'

'I've the central heating on,' Darren protested. 'Feel the heat of it.' He put his hand on the radiator.

'Could you put it up higher please, do you think?' she took a chance on asking him, as she had been afraid to do so before.

'I can't afford the oil bill. You know the cost of it now.'

'Are you going to keep us here in the cold?'

'No.'

'Well, what are you going to do. Maybe the other room would be warmer, where you spend most of your time?' she asked.

'I suppose I have the Aga cooker in there and that keeps the place warm. Maybe I'll take Roberto in there more often if you think he is cold.'

'What about me?'

'The baby is more important.'

'But I'll freeze.'

'I'll give you an extra duvet and you will be warmer.'

'Darren, why are you keeping us here anyway. What's in it for you?'

'I want you back, Alva, that's all. Don't you understand? Look

261

how happy we are now. Can you imagine how much happier we will be when Roberto grows older and we'll be a real family. And maybe we'll move house. We're by the sea and I love to walk along the beach every day and wouldn't mind having a house here where all of us could live together.'

'Maybe that's something we could plan,' she said cautiously.

'Do you think you might consider it?' he asked brightly.

'A new house at the beach, it sounds lovely,' she said.

'So romantic. Like it used to be between us when we moved in together first. Do you remember? We were so in love,' he smiled at her.

'We were,' she forced herself to go along with him.

'I'll have a look around the area. And when I find a house it will be a complete surprise for you.'

'I'm looking forward to it,' Alva murmured.

'Ah look, Roberto is asleep again,' Darren looked down at the baby. 'See how he loves being in my arms.'

'How soon will you let us go home?' Alva took a chance.

Immediately, he looked at her angrily. 'I'm not letting you go back at all, you're mine, and don't forget it.'

'Please don't be angry, Darren, I was just asking.'

'Don't ask again, remember that.' He stood up abruptly and marched outside with the baby, and locked the door again.

Alva was left there on her own. Feeling like someone in solitary confinement in a prison.

How was she going to bear being imprisoned with Darren in this place? She wondered how Carlos was and her Mum and all the family? She couldn't imagine how her loss would affect Julie, who had only found her a short time ago, and now had lost her again. Tears filled her eyes. She couldn't bear to think of not seeing everyone again. It was too much.

While Darren was in the other part of the house, she tried again to see if there was some other way she could break down the wooden panels and so find a way out of that room through them. There had to be windows outside. The bathroom was the same. The window there blocked up as well. But there was nothing she could see in either place which would help her to escape. She was frustrated. Darren was never much good at DIY, and she was surprised at the quality of the work. But obviously he had made a good effort to keep her here. Imprisoned. It was a weird plan he had concocted.

When he kept the baby outside, she was always worried that he was harming the child in some way. Darren wanted to keep her in his power. Under his control. But she wasn't going to let him. She had made up her mind. But would he kill her spirit eventually? She was in a dark place and struggled to withstand his smiling suggestions. She was like someone playing a part. To give him the impression that there was some chance of their relationship being rekindled, although she knew that it was impossible. But if she didn't play along with Darren then would she ever escape his clutches, and achieve her freedom and that of her child?

Darren came back into the room later holding the baby. Roberto was crying. His little face red and very cross.

'He's hungry,' she said to him and rushed to take the baby.

'Feed him.'

She took him into her arms. Trying not to show how annoyed she was with Darren. She held him to her breast and he latched on, immediately quiet. 'See, he's happy now.'

She found it hard. Wanting to scream and shout out loud, cry for help, or do anything at all, but could not. She hated Darren for what he was doing to her and her child. She hated him for wanting to have her back. What sort of person was he? How had she ever loved him? She didn't know.

Chapter Forty-six

It was Tuesday now and Carlos went to see the detective in charge of the case of Alva's disappearance again. He and Julie had continued searching for Alva and Roberto, and Naomi joined them as often as she could. There were a lot of posters with their photo in various places, and apparently the Gardai had said there were some responses, and people had seen both of them, but when they interviewed them, none of their information was worth following up. The timing was wrong. Their description was inaccurate. Some said she had a child with her. But the age was wrong. Some said she was on her own. In a car. On a bicycle. So far nothing had come of their information.

'I'm wondering should we offer a reward?' Carlos said.

'It might be worthwhile, but if your wife has gone away, do you think money will encourage her to come back? Or do you think it's likely she is being held against her will and therefore the person who is holding her is going to set her free for a reward?'

'It's possible her ex-partner has taken her or maybe she has gone with him voluntarily.'

'Then is there any point in offering a reward?' The detective seemed vague.

'I have to do something,' Carlos said. 'Whatever the situation.'

'Would you be prepared to go on television and make an appeal?' The man asked.

'Yes, I will,' he said immediately.

'I agree with that,' Julie said, when Carlos arrived home and told her. 'How much are you going to offer?'

'I was thinking about €100,000.00. I may as well make it quite a large amount otherwise it won't attract anyone.'

'Can you raise that?' she asked, worried.

'It will take everything I have and I'll have to borrow from the bank. I had been saving for a house even before I met Alva, but that doesn't matter now. I just want to get Alva and Roberto back.'

'We will help with the money,' Julie offered. 'We want to do that.'

'Thank you, Mum, I appreciate it.'

'When will you go on television? Julie asked.

'They're arranging a press conference and it will go out this evening during the news.'

'Let us pray that whoever has taken her will respond to it,' Julie said.

'I can't bear the pain of losing Alva and Roberto, my son.' Carlos lowered his head, defeated.

'It must be terrible for you. The loss of my own three children was desperately painful for me so I can understand how it must be for you. Although I've been re-united with my children in the last couple of years, I still feel the pain of all those empty years since the children were young. Now it's as if I've lost Alva all over again.' Tears drifted down her cheeks.

Carlos put his arms around her and held her close to him. It was the first time she had described to him her deepest feelings about the loss of her children. Alva had told him what her mother had told her, but to hear Julie describe it now herself meant a great deal to him and he really sympathised with her.

At the press conference, Carlos stepped forward and gathered his thoughts.

He was daunted by the crowd of journalists all standing there waiting for him to speak.

'As has already been explained to you by the Gardai, my wife Alva and my baby Roberto, are missing. We have searched for them but have not been able to find them. So now I am appealing to the public who are listening to me today to look at these photos here.' He turned to indicate the photos which could be seen on a screen behind him. 'And to phone the Gardai if you have seen either of them in the last few days. We are very upset about the disappearance of Alva and baby Roberto who was only born a few weeks ago. We have also offered a large reward to anyone who comes forward with information which leads to the finding of Alva and Roberto. It is €100,000.00. And I hope that someone will help us find my wife and baby.' He could feel tears moisten his eyes, and stood back. 'Thank you for listening to me.'

'Carlos, can you give us a few personal words?' A microphone was pushed into his face.

'As you can understand, this is a very emotional loss for me and all the family. We cannot believe that something like this has happened.'

'Do you love your wife?' A woman asked.

'Of course I do, she is everything to me, and my child.'

'When did you last see her?'

'I heard from her last Saturday.'

'What was she wearing?' Another shouted.

'A red coat, and dark trousers.'

There were more flashes.

The detective stood beside him.

'That's the end of the press conference,' he said. 'We appreciate your interest and hope that you can spread the word. We really want this woman and her baby back with her family as soon as possible.'

Carlos shook his hand. 'Thank you very much for presenting our story to the media. I appreciate your help very much. And to give us the opportunity to publicise the reward is great. I only hope that someone thinks it is worth their while to make contact with us.'

'They'll publicise it. Be sure of that,' the detective assured.

Chapter Forty-seven

Darren lay on the bed, stretched out in front of the television. He watched the news. It was as if life was going on without him and he needed to know what was happening. There was a Garda announcement, a press conference, and he sat up straight and watched. A woman and her baby had gone missing. Alva and Roberto. The Gardai were looking for her. And then the husband, Carlos, stepped forward. Darren stared in shock. He was offering a reward to anyone who had information. It was €100,000.00, a huge amount. But no one knew anything about her. He laughed to himself. It was unlikely that anyone would offer information. They hadn't any.

It angered him to have to watch Carlos talk about Alva and Roberto. How dare he. He wanted to beat the other man. Punch him. Tell him that he had no right to them. They were his. He possessed them. His soul grew very black as he thought about being discovered. All he wanted to do was to make contact with Carlos. Call him up on the phone, laugh at him and tell him that he was never getting Alva or Roberto back again.

There hadn't been a sound from the baby since he had brought him back to Alva, and now he wanted to have him in his arms again. He loved that child. Always feeling that he was his. When the brown eyes looked up at him and he thought he saw a response to him, his heart tumbled in his chest and he couldn't believe how amazing that baby was.

Should he call the Gardai and tell them where Alva and Roberto were and apply for the reward. But then reality hit, and he realised that he'd only give himself away. Alva would definitely tell them that he had taken her and the baby. No, that wouldn't work. Anyway, money wasn't important. If he said anything at all he wouldn't see Alva and the baby ever again. And that was the last thing he wanted. He turned off the television.

Fuck that bastard and his reward.

Now Darren had settled into a new world, no one else around to cause a problem, or knock on the door, the phone quiet unless he wanted to make a call on the new cheap phone he had bought. All he could do was to make calls and send texts. Before he destroyed his phone, the only person who rang him was Naomi which he had ignored. He felt guilty about her. Glad to know that she still loved him. But had no intention of ever seeing her again. She should have understood that she had been replaced by Alva once more. He loved Alva. The love he professed for Naomi was nothing compared to how he felt about Alva.

In this world there was only Alva, Roberto and himself. Three people who lived in this place. Surrounded by the obscurity of a house. The darkness of shadows. Separated from the outside by locked doors. And he was in charge of Alva and Roberto. In control of them. He liked that. And it was wonderful to talk with her now that she seemed to have an affinity for him once again. She had smiled at him when he went in earlier. And her eyes were warm. He was so sure that she wanted to kiss him. Her lips told him that. At least that was what he felt. But yet he hesitated making the first move in case she rejected him. He couldn't bear that. It would have been too hard.

He called her name. 'Alva?' Out loud. Then he slid off the bed, and went to the door of the room where he kept her. Silently leaning against it. Arms spread-eagled. He wanted her so badly but he couldn't utter a word. Only her name once again. Longing to hear her voice whisper his name too from inside. Would she respond? Did she hear him at all? Suddenly, he regretted having used the knife to threaten her and the baby. It was too violent. Far too aggressive. And he must have frightened her. But she wouldn't have come with him otherwise, he rationalised. It was the only way he could have persuaded her.

Now he had her where he wanted her. She was waiting inside for him. Lying on the bed. Her arms around her baby. And he wanted to be in there with them. He wanted her to hold him close. And kiss him. And tell him that she loved him. He felt she had changed. He was certain of that. She was coming around. He didn't know why. And couldn't understand either. But knew this change had to mean something. How long would it take before she would make a move and commit herself to him again? Desire for her dominated him. How would he know how she was feeling and when to make the first move?

He let his hands slide down the door. There seemed little point in staying there. His fingernails scraped along the wooden surface as they moved downwards. It was uncomfortable. And reminded him that he was probably wasting his time. His hands flopped loosely to his sides. He felt defeated and pessimism swept through him suddenly. He had been saving hard over the past year so that he could put a deposit down on a house. That was something he wanted to do with Alva. It had to be a joint choice between the two of them. Somewhere they would be really happy again.

He had called his office on Monday and said he was sick but he would have to go to work tomorrow. In his new job, he covered Dublin city and it gave him more flexibility in general. Although he had to go back to the office every evening and discuss the orders he had received that day.

There was another thing that he had to remember, even

though it was something he really wanted to put out of his head altogether. But every now and then it pushed its unwelcome way into his mind. One of these days he would be summoned to court to answer the charges. Before he left his apartment, he had received a letter from the solicitor informing him that the case had been adjourned and he hoped that it would be again, giving him enough time to persuade Alva to say to the court that he wasn't guilty of any of the crimes he had been accused by the Gardai so that he could forget about it altogether. Now that he was living in this new place, he knew that the solicitor didn't have his address, or knew where he worked, so perhaps the whole thing would go away altogether.

'How are you enjoying the dinner?' Darren asked.

'It's all right.' She picked at the mound of pasta.

'And our baby is fine.' He put his hand into the cot and patted Roberto's face.

She stared at him.

'You're a very good mother,' he said. 'And I want to be a good father.'

'No, I'm not, I'm a terrible mother,' she retorted. 'I've had enough.' She pushed the plate away from her.

'But I thought you always liked spaghetti?'

'I'm not hungry.'

'You must eat. I've said that to you before.'

'I can't eat if I'm not hungry.'

'You must if you're to have enough milk for the baby.'

'He's getting enough.'

'I'm going out to do the shopping, what would you like for tomorrow?'

'Whatever.' She seemed disinterested.

'Go on, give me an idea.'

'Please yourself.'

'Maybe I'll get some nice lamb chops, or fillet steak, we used to enjoy that when we were together. Or I could do meatballs, that was your favourite at one time.'

She shrugged.

'You're not in good form today.'

'I'm tired, Darren, I want to go home, can't you understand that?'

'This is home, for now anyway.'

She didn't answer. Tears ran down her cheeks.

That surprised him.

'Why are you crying?' he asked.

'I told you, I want to go home. This is like a prison.'

'I'm looking for somewhere better. If you promised not to run away on me, I could take you shopping some time. Will you promise?'

'Yes, it would be so nice to get out into the fresh air. And its nearly Christmas,' she said it just to please him, but knew it was an empty promise. Both his words and hers.

'We'll have a lovely celebration, just the three of us. I'm looking forward to it,' he said, smiling.

'If you would just let me go home for Christmas,' she whispered. Seeming beaten down, crushed almost as she said those words. 'Please?'

'You don't need to go back to that Spanish fellow.'

'He doesn't know where I am, or where Roberto is. That is so cruel.'

'Fuck him, he doesn't deserve you. Shut up about him.' He was suddenly angry and could not bear to listen to her talk about her life with that other man.

'I can't live like this. You're a tyrant, Darren,' she screamed at him.

The baby cried loudly in response and she felt guilty for upsetting him.

Chapter Forty-eight

Carlos was desperately lonely. As time passed, he began to come to the conclusion that Alva had left him. Her love for him had died and she needed to get away from him with their child. He had to admit that he hadn't loved her enough, or given her enough, and felt very guilty. He had allowed his work to take precedence and she had not been able to handle that, particularly when she had become pregnant, and especially since Roberto was born. He remembered situations which had occurred, and could see where he had made mistakes, said the wrong things, and so alienated Alva completely and drove her to leave him without giving him a word of explanation. He remembered she did try and explain how she was feeling and he had promised her that he would change. But obviously his promises were empty and meaningless, and he couldn't keep to them. He criticised himself and took all the blame for the situation he was in now. But then the fact that she hadn't used her credit card at all since she had gone couldn't be explained. But perhaps she had another source of money. She had sold her own apartment when she had moved in with him, and opened another investment account in both their names so he was able to verify that, but when he checked he found that there was no request to withdraw any part of it recently.

Feeling so bad, he even explained to Julie how his relationship with Alva had been in the last while and was so ashamed of himself.

'It has to be my fault,' he said despondently. 'You probably don't believe that I could have been so selfish.'

'If you think Alva has left you, then it must have been very hard for her to do such a thing. To leave you and take your son. You are his father and entitled to know him. But she is my daughter and I have lost her as well,' she said, tears in her eyes. Carlos put his arm around her. He couldn't bear the thought of bringing so much pain upon Julie. He was a disreputable person and didn't deserve to have such a wonderful family.

He went to see her brothers again. Both David and Cian had both been involved in all the searches which had been arranged when Alva and Roberto had gone missing at first, and they were still searching, refusing to give up.

'Carlos?' Cian opened the door of his apartment and looked surprised to see him.

'Sorry to call so late but I wanted to see you.'

'Sure, come in. Is there any news?'

He shook his head.

Natalie, Cian's partner, put her arms around him and hugged.

'We're still looking for her even around here if she didn't remember where home was, and might remember this place,' explained Cian. 'I'm still handing out flyers with her photograph to anyone I meet. Sometimes I even stop outside the supermarkets, or anywhere else I can think of. Not everyone watches RTE.'

'I was in Grafton Street yesterday handing them out, and a lot of people were very interested, although no one said they had seen them,' Natalie said.

'She wasn't in a good place after the birth of Roberto although she was improving, but now I'm thinking perhaps that she may have wanted to leave me and was afraid to say anything to me thinking that I might insist on having custody of Roberto,' Carlos

274

said.

'It's possible, I suppose. But I thought you were both very happy,' Cian said.

'We were. But I wasn't a good husband, my job is too demanding and she may not have wanted to stay with me particularly since she had Roberto.'

'But you've checked her bank accounts and there is no activity, so what is she living on?' Cian asked.

'I wondered if she had an account that I don't know about.'

'And I checked the company account but there was nothing withdrawn from it by Alva since she disappeared. And she put in no claim for expenses since either. But then she was on maternity leave so wouldn't have been using expenses anyway. The Gardai came around and did a search in her office on Monday. They took away her computer to examine it but they haven't come back to me about that.'

'They took away our computers as well, but apparently nothing was found,' Carlos said.

'It's all just a blank. Inexplicable.'

'I wondered if perhaps you or David might be helping her with money, but he told me that he hasn't heard anything at all from her.'

'The Gardai brought us in and asked those questions too. I didn't know whether I should bring my solicitor with me. But I felt that might seem as if I was guilty of something, so I didn't. David didn't either.'

'They've asked me in twice and questioned me as well. It's a bit nerve-wracking as I have to remember exactly what I said on the previous occasion and not change a word.' Carlos found it hard to hide his upset about that.

'There is always the fear that they are questioning us because they think we could be involved. That we did something to injure her in some way.' Cian was equally concerned. 'I hate the thought that something happened to her, could someone have attacked her and the baby?' he suggested. 'Or is that crazy.'

'Who would have any reason to do that,' Natalie murmured.

'There are always random attackers, or serial killers out there,' Cian said.

Carlos was silent. He couldn't answer. He had avoided thinking along those lines up to this, blaming himself for Alva's disappearance. But now Cian had put into stark words the situation that he had not wanted to face himself.

'What did David say?' Cian asked.

'He was very concerned and said that Alva's disappearance has destroyed the family's life, although they've tried to shield the children from it and don't talk about it in front of them.'

'Natalie and I are very upset too. We can't put it out of our minds. It's there all the time.'

Carlos left eventually, glad that he had called, and was quite certain that both David and Cian seemed to have no connection with the fact that Alva had gone missing, and grateful to them for continuing to search for her.

Carlos went to the Garda station again, praying there would be some news about Alva and Roberto, but there was nothing and he had to return home to Julie and let her know that her daughter was nowhere to be found.

'Have they looked at the CCTV?' she asked.

'Apparently, the nearest cameras weren't working so there was nothing to see near the apartment.'

'Are they still searching.'

'I don't know.'

'Why don't you get a private detective?'

'I've thought of that.'

'Have you made contact with someone?'

'Now that you mention it, I think it's something I will do.'

'You should. Don't delay.'

'I was hoping the Gardai would come up with something.'

'Get on with it, Carlos, a fresh eye will make all the difference,' Julie encouraged.

'Perhaps. The worst part of it is that the Gardai seem to have no leads. When they checked on Darren, they have no information on where he works or lives these days, so it's a dead end.' He was despondent.

'There's something I have to tell you,' Julie said.

He stared at her, astonishment written on his face. 'Is it something to do with Alva?' he stuttered.

'No, it's nothing to do with Alva, but Pedro was on to me and he told me that you are a beneficiary of Abuela's Will.'

'What do you mean?' he gasped.

'They had a family meeting with the notary.'

'I didn't know that was happening. There's so much going on.' He had to admit.

'You've been mentioned in the Will.'

'Have I?' he was surprised and certainly hadn't expected it.

'Yes, the notary will be writing to you about that.'

'It was very good of Abuela to remember me.'

'You were always her favourite,' Julie said.

'I'm glad she never knew about what's happening over here. To know that Alva and Roberto are missing would have been too much for her.'

'I'm thinking it might have been just as well she passed when she did.'

She would have been very worried and it wouldn't have done her any good.'

Carlos called Naomi.

'I was thinking of employing a private detective, well, it was Julie who suggested it.'

'I don't think that's a good idea. You'll only have this

person stepping on the toes of the Gardai and perhaps causing confusion. It's still a case which is at the top of the list for the Missing Persons Unit and they're working hard on it. I've been keeping an eye on progress, but you know I'm not involved. I'm too close. I wish I could help, but it would compromise it in the future.'

'You are certain that there is no news about them at all,' he said slowly. 'They told me they have checked all the hospitals. Would that include every hospital in the country?'

'Yes, and they just have to put in their dates of birth to search, as you probably know.'

'Private and public?'

'I'm sure.'

'Would there be any point in my doing the same?'

'You could if you wish. Although the Missing Persons Unit have a special channel.'

He had to accept what she said and he decided to leave it to the Gardai although he found that very frustrating.

He was called in for questioning again by the Gardai, and as he was away in Spain at the time Alva vanished he felt that he had a good alibi and that it was not necessary to bring his own solicitor with him. And that if he did, as Cian and David, it would only seem as if he was guilty of some crime.

Chapter Forty-nine

Alva was very hungry. It must be the next day. But she couldn't tell whether it was or not as Darren hadn't come near her. Yesterday, he had told her he was going back to work and left her there in the silent house, without any sound of radio or television which she could sometimes hear when he opened the door. Today he had gone to work as well, she assumed. There was a terrible emptiness about the place which frightened her. She hadn't wanted to eat anything he cooked for her and refused the spaghetti he made some time ago. But every now and then she had to accept whatever it was. Mostly it was bread with maybe an egg, or just marmalade, or cheese, with a cup of tea, and she would nibble at that and drink the tea. She was aware that she had to eat something for the sake of Roberto.

Her son seemed amazingly well, but she still worried all the time about him, and whether he might get sick. What would she do then?

Darren came in. It must be night now, she thought, as he had probably come home from work. But he brought her nothing to eat. And she refused to ask for anything, as this might be the reason he was getting his own back on her.

But she tackled him about the baby.

'I have to take Roberto back to the hospital for a check-up,' she said.

'We can't do that. Anyway, there's nothing wrong with him, I think he seems quite healthy, the little lad.' He glanced over at him.

'They check for various conditions, I think.'

'Looks all right to me.'

'It's a physical check-up and I don't know what they are looking for exactly. And I'm supposed to go back to the hospital as well.'

'Why do you have to go back?' he asked, puzzled.

'It's just a normal thing.'

'We'll have to leave it for now, we can't go.'

'But they could discover Roberto has something wrong with him and needs treatment.'

'Not at all. He's OK. Look at him.' He glanced into the cot.

'There are tests they have to carry out.'

'I can't bring you there.'

'I could go myself.'

'And never come back?' he laughed.

'How long do you want me to stay here anyway?' she asked gently, careful not to sound too demanding. She had decided to change her approach again. Maybe it would confuse him.

'I haven't decided. So there's no hurry. I give you everything you want. But you'll suffer if you try to get away or attack me like you did, you'll pay for it or he will.'

She had a sudden vision of the knife he had threatened her with in the beginning, and the thought of him hurting the baby was too much for her. 'I thought you loved him?'

'If you step out of line again, just wait and see what I can do,' he warned.

She was silenced.

The weather was very bad and Roberto was really upset, and crying continuously, obviously very frightened by the sound of the wind and rain which lashed on to the roof loudly all afternoon. Alva was nervous, frightened by the sound of thunder which rumbled overhead and crashed down on top of the house so loudly she was afraid the roof would collapse. While she was sure there had to be lightning as well, she couldn't see it, but could sense it. She pulled out the electric plugs just in case they attracted the lightning, and turned off the light too which left them sitting in pitch darkness. She tried to console Roberto but he refused to be comforted.

She shouted for Darren out through the crack in the door jamb, but he didn't come in. He must be still at work, she decided. Or maybe it was the middle of the night and he was asleep. If he was working, then surely he must realise they would be frightened because of the wind and rain and come home early. But he didn't come. The noise grew even louder. Things crashed and banged around the house. It must be the bins or something like that, she thought and decided to turn the light on for a few minutes. She couldn't bear to be in the dark any longer. And she needed to change Roberto and make him more comfortable. She quickly put him on the changing mat and gave him a fresh nappy. But he still cried, and she took him up in her arms again and comforted him. She gave him her breast but he didn't want it, and that upset her even more as she walked up and down holding him.

It was only then she noticed the water which seemed to be coming under the door from the hall. She was shocked and bent down to push one of the pillows into the gap under the door, but it was soaked in seconds and even more water spread across the wooden floor. She put another one underneath but it was soaked in seconds too. She tried not to panic but it was hard not to as she was locked in here and couldn't get out. If the water continued to come in and get deeper and deeper then where would she go with Roberto?

She stared around to see there was water dripping down from

the ceiling too in more than one place. With one hand she pushed Roberto's bath over to catch some of the drops, and looked around for any other receptacles which she might use. But couldn't find any. She left the light on and hoped the lightning wouldn't cause an electrical short and set the house on fire. The thought of that terrified her.

It was only then that she considered the possibility of Darren not coming back at all. What if he decided it wasn't worth it. And that he would be in more trouble if he had to admit to anyone that he had kidnapped her and Roberto.

The drip drip of the water from the ceiling was annoying. Like the sound of a ticking clock. And she watched the water coming under the door with a sense of fear. She covered Roberto with a towel so the water from the ceiling wouldn't fall on him. But couldn't judge where it was going to come from, bending over him and feeling it splash on her own shoulders, and dribble down her back, which was very uncomfortable. She went into the bathroom but found the water was coming down from the ceiling as well so couldn't stay there either. All the time she watched the progress of the water and was alarmed when she saw it begin to creep up even further on the skirting board.

Alva sat up on the bed and covered herself and the baby with the duvet.

She prayed then, Hail Mary, Our Father and Glory Be, over and over. She had to admit to herself that it wasn't often she prayed like this to God but now there was no one else to pray to.

Her mind took her then to a *what if* situation. If the water crept even higher and higher then she and Roberto would be drowned. The possibility of that was horrific. Not so much for herself, but for her baby who had only started out on his young life. Since he had been born, she had felt inadequate and wasn't a good mother. To have drawn him into this situation with Darren was something for which he would always blame her. If she had never fallen in love with Darren. If she had never known him at all, then this child would not have undergone this terrifying experience. Would it stay with him for his life? A ghastly trauma. Always wondering as he grew up why he over-reacted to certain events. If they survived would she spend her life looking for signs that indicated he had gone through the ordeal but that it left an indelible mark on him?

The sound of water dripping was becoming ever more frightening. There was a crash of waves. Normally she heard nothing from outside the room. Darren had mentioned he liked to walk on the beach so they must be very close to the sea. At that crash another rush of water flowed in under the door. It was the sea. She could see a white flurry of foam at the edges. The height of it was now almost two inches.

She thought she might push the duvet under the door, but then there was nothing to protect them from the water which dripped down from the ceiling. And the pillows had been of little help. They were both saturated and flat now, sodden, being pushed this way and that by the force of the water. She looked down at Roberto in her arms. He had stopped crying and slept now. But he felt cold, as she was herself, and she was afraid he would get hypothermia. She cuddled him close. Wrapping the duvet tighter around him for warmth. At her movement, he woke up. His dark eyes looked at her. She tried to latch him on to her breast and he caught on at last, suckling. She kissed his forehead. Holding his head in her hand. He still wore the white wool cap, and she held him even closer in a desperate effort to keep him warm.

Chapter Fifty

Naomi was on late shift and she parked close by Darren's office at around four-thirty as she knew he had to report back to the office for a meeting with his boss at the end of every day. There was heavy rain and wind from a storm which had hit the east of the country, thunder and lightning too. She was afraid of lightning and almost considered leaving a number of times but decided that under these circumstances she could follow Darren undetected as he would have to concentrate on his driving and it might be difficult to recognise her car behind him. This was her one opportunity to find out where he was living and she turned on the engine ready to move quickly.

Since she had begun to think that he might be holding Alva and Roberto somewhere, she became even more anxious to find out where that might be. Their welfare becoming even more important than her own feelings about his rejection, and pushed the crazy feeling of jealousy which dominated to the back of her mind.

Suddenly she recognised his new car stopped on the other side of the road, indicating that he was turning across to go into the carpark. She switched on the windscreen wipers and peered at the number plate of the car and just about managed to discern some of the numbers, before she had to turn the wipers off again almost immediately in case he recognised her. Yes, it seemed to be his. Thank God. She whispered. Now he was there and would have to leave later.

He didn't stay long and after about fifteen minutes his car came to the exit and stopped as he watched the traffic waiting for a chance to cut into the line of cars passing by. She prayed it was him. A car slowed down to let him out, and she was very relieved when another car made space for her. She drove after Darren, one car between them, which was perfect. The rain grew heavier and the windscreen wipers barely cleared the screen but she put them on fast and leaned forward in an effort to see properly. The thunder and lightning seemed to have moved off but the rain didn't cease its battering. Darren was driving on to the north side of the city towards the airport and she followed. At least there weren't too many sets of lights at which she had to stop, just a couple of roundabouts. The car in front of her exited on one of these and she was glad that Darren was just in front of her. She didn't drive too close and now was able to see the number plate and know it was definitely him. He took the next exit which led towards the coast and she followed. Her heart pounded. She was careful as the road narrowed, leading to Lusk, and Rush. She wasn't that familiar with the area and had to be very careful as there was a lot of water gathered on the road, creating large puddles which splayed water out on either side of the car. She could still see Darren's car, the lights red. He drove through Lusk, and continued on. There weren't too many cars on the road now and that helped with the amount of water being sprayed by oncoming vehicles.

Now he arrived in Rush, drove along the street, and then he indicated right. Naomi followed, holding back a little. The road was very narrow and as they turned a bend she saw flashing lights up ahead and a number of men in yellow hi-vis jackets. She slowed down, as did Darren, at a barrier that had been erected across the road which seemed to be flooded up ahead.

285

Darren talked to one of the men, and another came up to Naomi.

'The road is blocked,' he said. 'It's high tide shortly and we are evacuating people.'

'But I have to follow that car,' she explained.

'You can't go down there, it's too dangerous, there's only a couple of houses and they've all been flooded, the sea has come up because of the high tide. Try to swing around here and go back up.'

She took out her ID and waved it at him. Suddenly, he gave a shout as Darren's car broke through the barrier and drove on. When she followed, the men stood back and didn't stop her. She drove carefully, and she could see a house up ahead. Darren passed that house and continued on to the next one. In the dimness of a street light outside, it seemed to be completely surrounded by water.

Darren's car stopped as she did herself. He climbed out of the car, and struggled up to the house through the sea although it was almost up to his knees and dragged him this way and that. But he kept on and she realised then that Alva and the baby could be in there and that was why he was making such an effort to get in. Her engine cut out. Immediately, she called the Garda station and reported the situation, asking for assistance.

Chapter Fifty-one

Alva stood up on the table with Roberto in her arms. There was nowhere higher that she could stand. She tried to keep the duvet from trailing down into the water. She had taken off her jacket and wrapped the baby in it to keep him warm. She was in tears now. Screaming for help but aware that no one could possibly hear her.

Suddenly, she wondered if the wooden door might have become weakened with the water and if she was able to push it would the lock give way. She looked around and it struck her that if she put the baby on top of the wardrobe, then she could try and break down the door with the table. She moved along it and leaned against the closed doors of the wardrobe and did that, covering Roberto with the duvet.

'Stay there, my love. Don't move,' she whispered. And then holding the edge of the table she stepped off into the water. It was icy cold and slopped up above her knees. She was freezing. She dragged the table with her hands until it reached the door. Then she went to the other end and pushed it against the door which shuddered, but didn't open. It held fast. She looked back at where the baby lay. He hadn't moved. She tried a second time. Forcing the table against the door with her legs. Again and again. But had no success, only remembering then that it opened inwards and she was pushing in the opposite direction which probably made it even more difficult. And almost impossible.

She grabbed the handle of the door, and pulled it towards her with all her strength, but it didn't open. She looked at the baby again but he seemed all right and she was relieved that the bulb in the ceiling still glowed dimly.

Suddenly, the door moved and pushed against her. She lost her footing and fell in the water as Darren burst through. She screamed and grabbed hold of him trying to point towards the wardrobe and struggled to get to it herself. But as he was much taller than she was, he strode through the water and reached up to grab the baby and the two of them made their way out into the hall, he holding Roberto above his head.

To her surprise, Naomi was at the door. She pulled Alva towards her and they pushed their way through the water outside the house, trying to avoid the bushes that blew wildly in the wind. She didn't know which direction she was going in the darkness but Naomi kept hold of her hand and she held on tight as she struggled to keep her footing on the uneven surface of the ground below.

Suddenly she could see lights bobbing towards them and saw a boat draw close. There were men on board and hands leaned down to drag them in. Darren handed the baby to one of them, and within a few minutes they were all in the boat and it was crashing through the water back in the direction of the town.

They reached a group of men at a barrier and there was a Garda car and two ambulances parked nearby. The man holding Roberto got out, and handed the baby to the paramedics who took him to the ambulance first and as Alva wanted to be with the baby she sat in with him, desperately worried. As his clothes were not sodden completely, as she was herself, he was further wrapped in tinfoil by the paramedics and his vital signs were checked. They attached drips, and continued to attend to him. The ambulance drove off at speed, siren roaring and blue lights flashing. Alva sat there wrapped in a blanket, her teeth chattering from cold, her eyes on Roberto, praying that he would be all right.

They arrived at the Emergency quickly and the baby was taken into a cubicle by a doctor and two nurses, and Alva was in another cubicle. Her wet clothes were taken off, and she was wrapped in a gown and tinfoil, warm blankets and a drip attached.

'Is my baby going to be all right?' she asked them.

The nurse nodded. 'We're keeping him in a warm environment to bring up his temperature, I'll check how he is for you.'

'I want to see him,' tears moistened her eyes, and she began to shake.

'I'll come back, and bring you some tea.'

She was as good as her word and in a couple of minutes she brought the tea, and sweet biscuits. 'Your baby is doing well, he wasn't quite so cold so you'll be able to see him soon.'

'Thank you,' she was very grateful. 'Could I call my husband please, he doesn't know where we are.'

'Certainly, I'll get a phone.'

She brought it in. 'Can I call for you, I want you to stay warm. Just tell me the number.'

Alva did that, and the nurse left a message on his voicemail.

'What hospital is this?' Alva asked.

'Beaumont.'

'Oh my God, my husband works here.'

'Can you give me his name.'

'Carlos Rodrigues, he's a neurosurgeon.'

'I'll call the department and ask that they give him a message. And then, if you don't mind, I'll need to ask you to give me some details?'

'Could I ring my mother first?' Alva asked.

The nurse waited with the phone and pressed in Julie's number when Alva gave it to her.

'Mum?'

'Alva? Are you all right? Oh my God, I am so relieved. And how is Roberto? Where are you?'

Beaumont.'

Julie was in tears and could hardly speak.

'We're fine, Mum.'

At that moment, Carlos appeared, still dressed in his green scrubs. He stared at her, in tears, and knelt down beside her. The nurse went outside.

'Querida, donde has estado? Te he tanto de menes,' he whispered in Spanish. His arms curled around her and he held her close to him. Then he raised his head, and looked at her. 'I love you so much. Are you all right, my love?'

She nodded.

'How is Roberto?'

'He's just next door in the other cubicle. Will you go and have a look at him? I'm just on to Mum.'

The nurse came back in a few moments and Alva gave her their details as she had requested. After that, she lay there, so glad to see Carlos again and feeling relieved that she was going to be at home soon. She sipped the tea and began to feel a little better. But her mind took her back to the last few days. It had been so terrifying particularly the storm which tore the house almost to pieces today. But at least Darren had carried Roberto out and she was grateful to him for that.

Julie arrived then, and their reunion was very emotional. She had brought a change of clothes for Alva and Roberto, and all Alva wanted was to go home as quickly as she could with everyone she loved.

Chapter Fifty-two

Naomi and Darren were wrapped in blankets, and the second ambulance followed the first. The paramedics checked them both, blood pressure, heart, temperature. Naomi sat there. She felt numb. There was no conversation between herself and Darren. She didn't know what to say. Driving out here had been something she felt she had to do and find out if Darren had taken Alva and Roberto. Their own situation could wait.

Or had Alva actually left Carlos and gone to live with Darren again? Maybe Alva still loved him. Naomi thought that would explain why Darren no longer loved her. He had fooled her and she had been like a silly girl and fallen for his charm and sexual appeal. She should have known better, she reminded herself.

They arrived at the hospital and were quickly admitted. Naomi insisted she felt all right, although they suggested she remove her wet trousers and lie on a trolley until she warmed up to some extent. In the adjoining cubicle, she could hear Darren giving out to the staff that he didn't want to take his clothes off. It was only now she realised that she should have been on to her office to explain why she had not reported in for duty. Her phone was in her trousers pocket and she took it out now and discovered it had got wet and wasn't working. She asked to borrow a phone, called a colleague at the station and explained what had happened. Also asking that she get the key to her locker from her desk and then

291

bring over a change of clothes which she always stored there. She came around to the hospital almost immediately and Naomi was able to dress in dry clothes. She went into Alva, talked to her, Carlos and Julie. The baby was sleeping and the staff were confident he would be all right. Carlos seemed very happy to see Alva again, and that puzzled Naomi. She mustn't have told Carlos that she and Darren were together again if that happened to be the case. Still, this wasn't the place to explain why she was with Darren these last few days. Carlos was a really nice guy, and didn't deserve such treatment.

Naomi said goodbye to them, but didn't bother with Darren. She wouldn't have known what to say to him.

Then she went to see the baby who was in the next cubicle. But he wasn't there now. She went to the nurse's station.

'Have you moved the baby who was in one of the cubicles?'

The girl looked at her in a puzzled way.

'His mother is there as well, Alva Purtell.'

'No, we haven't moved him, he was there a few minutes ago, and his mother was feeding him earlier.' She came out from behind the counter, hurried to the cubicle, pulled back the curtains fully and went in but came out immediately. 'Maybe his mother has taken him in again with her,' she suggested.

The nurse went in to Alva, followed by Naomi, but she was asleep now. Julie was sitting beside her, and Carlos had gone back up to his department.

'Julie, did you see Roberto?' she asked.

'No, he is in the next cubicle.'

'He's not there now.'

Julie stood up, panic on her face.

'Did Carlos take him upstairs for some reason?' Naomi asked Julie.

'No, I don't think so. He has to be kept warm.'

Naomi waited impatiently, but then decided to check on

Darren. But he wasn't there. 'Where could the baby be?' she asked the nurse. 'Would any staff have taken him to check him out or maybe carry out some tests?'

'I don't know,' she seemed very concerned, and went to talk with the other staff at the station. They were in a huddle then, looking through their notes.

'I'll go up to see Carlos myself,' she said, and rushed to the lift, staring at a list of the departments and which floors they were on. She pressed the buttons and stepped in when the lift arrived. Hoping that Carlos had taken the baby up to show him to his staff or something like that. She stepped out of the lift and ran to the nurse's station.

'Is Dr. Rodrigues here?'

'He's operating at the moment.'

'Did he bring his baby up here?' she asked.

The woman shook her head, and frowned in confusion.

'Can you get a message to him?'

'We've already done that. Emergency were on to us trying to contact him.'

'His child has disappeared. We can't find him.'

The woman's eyes widened. 'I'll go in,' she said and hurried away.

Naomi went back down to Emergency and talked to the nurse again. 'Have you found him?' she asked urgently.

'We've put out a call to security and they are looking for him.'

'Does his mother know?'

'We told her.'

'Oh my God, she must be very upset.' Naomi rushed into the cubicle where Alva was sobbing incoherently in Julie's arms.

'Alva,' she hugged her. 'Don't worry, he'll be found.'

'Who has taken him?' she asked.

'Call the Gardai,' she said to the nurse.

'We've already done that,' she reassured. 'And everyone is

looking for him.'

'But who took him?' asked Alva again.

Carlos appeared.

'Someone has taken Roberto,' said Alva. 'It has to be Darren.'

'We'll find him querida, he couldn't have gone far.'

'Find him, Carlos, please?' she begged.

'I'll talk to security,' he went out. 'And get them to look at CCTV.'

'I'm going to search around here,' Naomi said to Alva, and left the cubicle. Then she ran along the nearest corridor. Going in and out of any doors which were ajar, but could see no sign of the baby. Then she went out of a door into the area outside. To be met by two Garda cars driving up to the entrance, sirens screaming. She talked with one of the Gardai and filled them in on what had happened. They drove to the entrances to the hospital and closed them off.

But Roberto couldn't be found.

Naomi went back into the hospital to comfort Alva and Carlos. She had been taken to a private room and Carlos sat beside her, his arm around her. She was still in tears and both of them were desperately upset. Naomi then went to see where the Gardai were examining the CCTV and she was astonished when they saw clear photos of Darren carrying baby Roberto out of the hospital.

There was a Garda with them when Naomi returned, and she was taking notes as Alva sobbed, and blurted out what had happened to her over the last few days when Darren had kidnapped her and the baby at knife point and kept them imprisoned in a house by the sea.

Naomi was shocked. Only now realising that Alva hadn't left Carlos for Darren, he had obviously wanted her back at all costs, and now he had taken the baby and left Alva and Carlos devastated.

Chapter Fifty-three

Roberto hadn't been found and no one knew where Darren was. As Naomi's car had to be towed to a garage from Rush, she had taken a taxi home. As she let herself into the foyer, she sensed someone behind, and felt something being pushed into her back. She knew immediately that it was Darren.

'Get into the lift,' he muttered.

'Darren?' she gasped.

'Go on in,' he said again, and pushed her.

She did as he ordered. 'Have you got the baby with you?' she demanded.

'Course I have, he's my child. Mine and Alva's.'

'Don't be ridiculous.' She took a chance, turned around, and stared into his face. Fully aware of the baby tucked underneath his jacket, and the knife which he held.

Suddenly, the baby began to cry.

'That baby is starving,' she said.

'He'll survive, I don't carry food around with me.'

'When are you going to return him to his parents?'

'When she comes back to me and leaves that Spaniard.'

'I don't think that's likely. You've treated her like shit by keeping her prisoner in that house. Are you mad?'

'Shut-up,' he snarled, and pointed the knife at her.

'You're going to kill me, are you. Am I next in line?' She wasn't afraid of him and wanted him to know that. 'What are you doing here anyway?'

'Phone Alva and get her to come over here.' He pressed the button for the lift and it came down. They stepped in and Naomi was sorry there was no one around to whom she could appeal for help.

'Carlos will come with her, you know that. Anyway, her phone isn't working, so I'll have to call him.'

'She must come on her own. And you're not to call any of your lot. I want to see Alva herself.'

They arrived at Naomi's floor, and he pushed her along the corridor, the knife still digging into her back.

She opened the door.

'I'll have to call on the landline in the bedroom, my phone is bunched as well. Sit down and rock the baby, he might stop crying.'

She went into the bedroom and picked up the phone.

'I've dialled his number,' she shouted to Darren, 'It's ringing out.' As she said that, quickly she went to the wardrobe, took her gun from a box at the bottom, loaded it, and slipped it into her pocket. 'I'll try it again,' she said, walking back into the lounge as she held the phone to her ear. 'Carlos, Naomi here, give me call as soon as you can please, it's urgent, this is my landline,' she said, and called out the number. Although she omitted to tell Darren that Carlos had actually answered the phone.

'Do you want a cup of coffee?' she offered Darren. Now that she had a weapon in her pocket she felt she could control him.

She made the coffee, and put a mug down in front of him. 'Drink up. It'll do you good.' She played it normal.

'Thanks.' He sipped it, but still held the knife in his other hand pointed at the baby's neck.

The phone rang. She picked it up. 'Yes?'

'It's Carlos.'

'I need you to ask Alva to come over to my apartment, Carlos.

But she must be on her own. Where are you now?'

'We're at home, but I don't think I can do that.'

'It would be better.'

'Is Roberto there, and Darren?'

'As quick as she can.' Naomi put the phone down.

She sipped her coffee. She didn't know whether she was putting Alva into more danger by asking Carlos to bring her over, but felt this was her only chance of getting the baby back to them. If Darren ran off somewhere else with him, then God knows what would happen.

Darren kept him under his jacket, but he still cried.

Time passed. Naomi knew it would take probably fifteen minutes for Alva and Carlos to get here from home.

She rinsed the coffee cup, and slowly dried it with a tea towel, putting it back up in the press. He hadn't finished his coffee yet.

They waited in silence.

The doorbell rang.

'It's me.' Alva said through the intercom.

Naomi pressed the button, and then went through the door into the hall, but Darren came behind and pushed her aside.

'Get out of my way,' he grunted. Waving the knife at her.

She let him pass.

He opened the door, and waited until the sound of the lift could be heard and then he walked down to the lift carrying the baby.

Alva stepped out.

'Is Carlos here?' he barked.

'No.'

'He'd better not be,' he held the knife at Roberto's throat.

'Please Darren, don't do that, what has the baby done? Please?' She begged, in tears.

'Get into the apartment,' he muttered and hunted her in. He stood back and she rushed at Naomi who stood in the hall and held on to her.

He banged the door.

'If you don't agree to come back to me, you will lose your child,' he yelled.

'What's that supposed to mean?' Alva snapped.

'What I said. I want you. You,' he glared at her.

'I'm not going back to you. You're a pig.'

'Bitch,' he yelled, holding Roberto up above his head by his babygrow in one hand, his little legs dangling. The baby screamed. 'All it takes is one slash. Look. Like this.' He held the knife to the baby's throat.

'Don't you dare.' She leapt towards him in a fury. 'Give him to me, Darren.'

'Or I could just drop him on the tiles.' He held him even higher above his head. The child kept screaming.

'Darren,' Naomi intervened. She had to wait for the right moment. 'Please don't.'

'Shut-up you.'

'Give him back to me,' Alva moved closer to Darren.

'Not until you agree to come with me.'

'When you give him to me I'll think about it,' she said defiantly.

'There's no time to think. Just say you'll come back to me.' Darren still held the knife to the baby's throat.

'Put down the knife.' She held out her arms. 'Don't hurt him.'

'Are you ready to catch him if I let him fall on the floor, his head will split open if I do that?' he laughed. His smile had a look of evil about it. 'Come with me now? Phone a taxi. And we'll go together.'

Alva's hands were visibly shaking. 'When you give him to me.'

He swung Roberto from side to side. The knife following.

The baby screamed again.

'Say you'll come back, I want to hear the words. Say them.'

'Give him to me first,' she demanded angrily.

Suddenly he let go of the babygrow and the baby began to fall towards the tiled floor.

Alva lunged. She caught Roberto in her arms but had difficulty keeping her balance, and staggered against the wall.

At the same time there was the sound of a gunshot.

Darren pressed his hand against his chest with a strangled shout, and fell backwards on to the floor.

'Get out Alva, go, go,' Naomi shouted and stood over Darren with her gun trained on him, as Alva rushed down the hall, opened the door and ran into the corridor, carrying Roberto to safety.

Chapter Fifty-four

Alva took the stairs down. She couldn't have waited until the lift came up. It would have taken too long. But she met Carlos leaping up two stairs at a time, and he threw his arms around them.

'Querida, my love, Alva, are you all right? And Roberto?' He held them both for a few minutes.

She was overcome with tears again, and really couldn't even speak.

There was rumble of footsteps above.

'This is the Gardai, drop your weapon,' someone shouted from upstairs.

Roberto still cried loudly.

'Would you like to sit down for a few minutes?' asked Carlos.

'No, I want to get out of this place now. Away from him.'

'Come on, then.' Carlos held her close, and she kept her arms around Roberto who wouldn't stop crying.

They took it step by step, slowly, and reached the foyer.

Outside were three Garda cars, and an ambulance. A paramedic came over.

'Are you all right?' he asked.

'Yes, I'm fine thanks,' Alva said.

They went outside.

'Sit into the jeep.' Carlos held the baby and helped Alva in. Then handed the baby to her.

'I'll call Mum and tell her we are all right, can I use your phone?' she asked him.

Carlos went back up to see how Naomi was doing.

When he reached the open door of the apartment he was met by two paramedics carrying a stretcher out into the corridor, and he could see that it was Darren who lay there. Then a Garda prevented him from going into the apartment although he could see Naomi talking with some of her colleagues.

When Naomi had called him, he had contacted the Gardai, and after Alva had gone up to the apartment, the Gardai arrived and had told him to wait in the foyer, while they went up in the lift. When he first heard the gunshot, he did not know what had happened, but decided to rush up the stairs immediately. When he saw Alva carrying Roberto he had been so relieved to see her with him he hadn't wanted to quiz her about what had happened as she was so upset.

Now he stood outside, aware that some of the residents talked together in a group at the end of the corridor. The detective he had spoken with earlier came out of the apartment and walked over to him.

'We will need to talk to your partner,' he said.

'She's very upset.'

'She was involved in this crime so it must be soon.'

'Is it possible for her to go home for the night and rest?' Carlos asked.

'I would rather talk to her now, when everything is fresh in her mind. Could you ask her please?'

'I will.'

He went down, and sat in beside Alva.

'How are you, querida?' he asked softly.

'A bit better. I'm so happy to have Roberto back in my arms. I thought I would lose him.'

'He seems very contented now.' He held his hand around the baby's cheek.

'He is, the poor thing was almost starving.' She cuddled him closer.

'I'm sorry to ask you this, but the detective I was talking with has asked if you would agree to be interviewed about what happened.'

'I was expecting that to happen,' she said.

'Do you feel up to it?' he asked.

'It has to be done I suppose. Although I hate to leave Roberto even for a few minutes.'

'I'm so happy I have both of you back with me at last. I thought that would never happen.' He kissed her, and Roberto.

'I thought I'd never get away from Darren.'

'You have escaped from him now.' He kissed her again.

'I found strength somewhere in those last few minutes.'

'We'll talk about it later.'

'Will I have to go to the Garda station?' she asked.

'I expect so.'

'Better get on with it, the sooner I talk to them, the sooner I'll be home, it's very late now.'

'Yes. I'll be there with Roberto. And you're not to worry about it. Just ask for a break at any time, I'm sure they'll allow that.'

'Let's go then.'

'I'll talk to the detective and be back soon.' Carlos climbed out of the jeep and went back into the foyer where the detective waited.

'She will talk with you but I hope it doesn't take very long,' Carlos said.

'We'll keep it as short as possible.'

Alva sat in a bare room. With four chairs, and a table, and not

302

much else. There were two detectives interviewing her, and they read her rights, offered tea or coffee, and she accepted a cup of tea which came with a couple of biscuits on the saucer. Gently they began to ask about what happened. Carlos had told them some of it when he talked with them after calling them when Alva had gone into Naomi's apartment, but they needed to hear it directly from Alva herself.

She described the time Darren had held her at that house by the sea. How her days were spent. Telling them about the fear of being confined in a room alone with her child. And having no chance to breathe in fresh air. Or see daylight. And how it was always night. Although the light in the bare bulb was on, she had no idea of time.

They took notes, and she knew her words were recorded as well. As they hadn't made any accusations against her, she had decided against calling John, her solicitor, and hoped she wouldn't need him. They went back over her explanations a few times, and then they continued on to the events which occurred tonight in Naomi's apartment. In this case, she made a supreme effort to tell them how Darren had threatened her and the baby with a knife, and how violent he was with such a young child. And finally, to explain what happened at the end which forced Naomi to shoot him. That was very important, she knew. Her words might incriminate Naomi and she could be blamed for injuring Darren. Alva couldn't bear it if her dearest friend was caught up in this situation which was created by her ex-partner.

Alva was there for over an hour, and at the end she asked to see Naomi. But they said she was at a different station and it wasn't possible anyway. They let her go, and she was so happy to see Carlos and Roberto waiting for her outside. He handed Roberto to her and she held him close as they drove home.

Chapter Fifty-five

Carlos waited while Alva was being interviewed by the Gardai. First, he had called Julie, who had stayed in the apartment while he had driven Alva over to Naomi's. Then her brothers, and the family in Spain, and all the people who searched for Alva and Roberto. He ordered a take away for dinner as there was nothing much in the fridge as things had been so hectic recently.

Alva was so glad to be home at last after the interview with the Gardai, and she hoped that she had explained everything clearly. They put Roberto to bed in the Moses basket and he seemed content.

'I hope he doesn't ever remember what happened. I was thinking it would be like a trauma and affect him in the future,' she said, worriedly.

'He's very young, that won't happen.' Carlos put his arm around her.

'I hope not.'

'He will be fine,' Julie reassured her. 'We'll all make certain of that.'

He served up the Thai meal, and she was surprised to find that she was actually hungry and enjoyed it. Inevitably, they talked in detail about what had happened for the first time.

'I can't understand how Naomi arrived at the house. And just in time to help me out. Do you think she knew I was there?' Alva asked Carlos, as they sat on the couch with the baby between them.

'She couldn't possibly. If so, why didn't she admit earlier that she knew where you were?' he responded.

'She came out to search for you every night,' added Julie.

'So, it was a complete coincidence you are suggesting?'

'It may have been. She's always been very genuine.'

'Naomi never mentioned she knew anything about Darren or what he was doing, I'm surprised about that.' Alva was doubtful.

'Well, she knows him, has known him as long as you were his partner. Maybe they kept up the friendship?' Julie suggested.

'It seems strange she wouldn't tell me that.' Alva felt disappointed.

'I hope you're not interested in him anymore?' Carlos asked with a grin, covering her hand with his own.

'No, of course not, I hate his guts,' she said vehemently.

'I'm glad to hear that. While you were missing, I certainly didn't think you had run off with another man, although I was afraid you had left me because you were tired of me. Isn't that right, Mum?' He looked to Julie for confirmation.

'I didn't think that,' she responded. 'And I told you not to think along those lines either.'

'I'll never tire of you, my love,' Alva murmured.

'While Darren had you, I think I was in some weird dark place. Nothing made any sense and I knew my life would be over if I lost you and Roberto. Maybe I have no confidence and I thought that was the worst thing that could have happened to me.'

'I'm sorry to have given you so much grief because of Darren.'

'Alva, querida, you and Roberto are the most important people in my life. Let's not talk about it now. I shouldn't have mentioned how I was feeling. Now I know what happened and that's it. And every time I met Darren before, I wanted to smash his face in,' he groaned. 'Now I think I would kill him if I see

him again for doing what he did to you and Roberto. They were the actions of a mad man. Someone who is completely crazy.'
'He is crazy,' Julie said.

'Let's go to bed now. You must be exhausted.' Carlos stood up and brought the baby in the basket into the bedroom.

They didn't talk about it again that night. Carlos had to go into the hospital in the morning for a couple of hours, although he didn't want to go he was glad that Julie was with her. One of the first people who called was Naomi.

'How are you?' Naomi put her arms around Alva when she arrived, and they hugged tight.

'I'm all right, thank you.'

'And Roberto?'

'He's fine. Come and look.' They went into the bedroom.

'Thank God he's all right,' Naomi whispered as she bent over the basket.

They stayed there for a couple of minutes.

'You've no idea how good it is to be home,' Alva said. 'I'm so grateful to you for helping me out of that house. I think I might have lost my way in the water.'

'Thank you, Naomi, for saving Alva, I couldn't have borne it if anything had happened to her.' Julie put her arms around her and hugged.

'Yet I was grateful to Darren for carrying Roberto out of the house. I know that sounds a bit strange.'

'Both Carlos and I feel he's crazy,' Julie said.

'He's one of those control freaks,' added Alva. 'As you know, when I threw him out he couldn't accept it. And that's the reason he tried so hard to get me back. I wonder if you could tell me if he's out on bail, Naomi?'

'No, he's in custody.'

'That's such a relief.'

'Although when he appears in court he could get bail. It depends on the judge. And there are many aspects to the case, especially the letters he sent to Carlos.'

'What letters?' Alva was surprised.

'He's been sending threatening letters to Carlos for months now, though he denies it and it's hard to prove.'

'And Carlos thought it was connected with a patient who died,' explained Julie. 'Although he talked to the family of the young man, but they didn't give the impression that they were angry with him, in fact, they were the opposite and appreciated his call when he rang.'

Alva's heart almost stopped when she heard that. 'He never told me.' She was surprised.

'He wasn't going to worry you about it.'

'He didn't tell anyone,' Naomi said. 'But he should have gone to us, we'd have looked into it.'

'I could have told him who it was,' said Alva grimly. 'It's obvious that it was Darren. Remember all those letters I received from him.'

'When Carlos told me about the letters, that's when I got suspicious.'

'It's just the sort of thing Darren might do,' Alva said.

'Carlos has been very worried over the past few months and I didn't know why, so that's it.' Alva was concerned.

'And there's something else I want to tell you,' Naomi said slowly. 'And you may as well both know.' She was silent for a moment.

Alva and Julie listened.

'I fell in love with Darren,' she said.

They stared at her, astonished.

'When?' Alva spluttered.

'I can't say exactly, but it was after you had split up with him and married Carlos.'

'Why didn't you tell me?' Alva asked her.

'I felt it would have been a betrayal. We had been friends for so long how could I tell you that I was in love with your ex-partner. You would have thought it was going on for much longer and that would have given you a lot of grief.'

'I may have, I suppose.'

'He came into my life when I was at a very low point. You know how I always hoped to meet someone. The guy for me,' she laughed. 'And there were too many men who didn't fit into my life for various reasons, and you know all about that. You've been there all that time and helped me to deal with the ups and downs. And I really appreciated it. I felt very guilty about betraying you.'

Alva didn't know what to say for a moment.

'Can you forgive me?' Naomi begged.

'Of course I can. And you didn't betray me really. It wasn't as if I was still in love with Darren.'

'That's such a relief,' Naomi said with a broad smile, stood up and hugged her. 'Thank you.'

'You are very honest, Naomi,' said Julie with a smile.

'So did you know he had me imprisoned in the house by the sea?' asked Alva.

'No … well, not at first.'

'What brought you there?'

Naomi went on to explain how Darren had ghosted her and she couldn't make contact with him over the time he had Alva imprisoned, and that she had gone to his office to follow him to his new home.

'That was very hard on you.'

'I was very frustrated, but didn't make the connection between his treatment of me and your disappearance. If I had known then I would have done something of course. It must have been terrible to be locked in that house. He wasn't violent towards you, was he?' Naomi asked.

'He did threaten me with that knife he had.'

'I was sorry I had to shoot him, but glad that I didn't kill him in one way.'

'What will happen in work?'

'They're investigating the situation, and I've been suspended from duty.'

'I'm so sorry, I hope you won't be penalised.'

'When they take all the evidence into account, then it will be seen if I have to bear the brunt of it.'

'But you were trying to save Roberto from a crazy person? They can't blame you.'

'I hope they see it like that. Anyway, I don't care. The thought that he might have killed or injured the baby is too much. When he threatened to drop him on the tiled floor I nearly panicked altogether, but couldn't see how I was going to disarm him without injuring Roberto.'

'They told me I'll be interviewed again so I'm going to explain exactly what happened. I may have been a bit confused last night.'

'That's understandable. Don't worry.'

'You shouldn't be held responsible. You saved Roberto's life and I want to thank you so much for your heroism. You put your own life on the line and I'll never forget that.' Alva put her arms around Naomi and they held on to each other.

Chapter Fifty-six

Carlos, and Alva left the court. He held her hand in his.

'At last,' she sighed. 'I can't believe he's going to be imprisoned now for all of his crimes.'

'And with all those adjournments, I thought it was never going to happen at all,' Carlos said.

'He got ten years anyway.'

'And he'll be out on parole probably before that. Although in my opinion it's not enough. I'd have given him life,' Carlos said vehemently.

'I thought he'd get a longer sentence too.'

'He admitted his guilt. It makes all the difference in a court case. The judge is always lenient in such circumstances.'

'At least I didn't have to testify. That was such a relief.'

'You were lucky. We were lucky. I couldn't have borne it if I had to watch you being interrogated by the legal teams. They were lethal. God only knows what would have happened if he still pleaded not guilty and you had to endure questioning by the prosecution and the defence.'

'Most of all, I'm so glad Naomi was cleared of any responsibility,' she said.

'Do you think she'll go back to Darren when he is released from prison?'

'She was in love with him.'

'Will she wait until he completes his sentence. Many lovers

do?'

'If she wants him, she will.'

'She was prepared to kill him to protect you and Roberto.'

'That was surprising. And she put her career on the line.'

'She loves you.'

'And I love her.'

'You're very generous.'

Outside, there were journalists pushing towards them with their microphones, shouting questions. And photographers jostled for space as they took photos.

'Let's go quickly, keep your head down,' Carlos murmured, holding her hand tight.

One of the journalists stood in their way, and barked another question. But Alva didn't even look at him, and they made their way down the steps and managed to get to the jeep without any further interruptions, as the crowd had now turned its attention to the next person who came out of the court.

Carlos drove away quickly, and they went straight home.

'It's such a relief to find it's all over.' They walked in, and he kissed her. 'I'll go down and collect Roberto from the minder. I'll be back in a minute, you sit down and relax.'

Alva closed her eyes and took that few minutes to gather her thoughts. It was a marker, this day, and a time that she would never forget.

'I have a plan,' Carlos announced.

Alva smiled.

'We're going out this evening to celebrate.'

'It's lovely to think we can go out without looking over our shoulders to see if Darren is skulking around.' She was delighted.

'And Naomi is coming over to babysit Roberto.'

'Thanks for organising that. Where are we going?'

'Surprise.'

As Carlos drove over towards the south side of Dublin city, Alva was still unsure where they might be going, but eventually the penny dropped when he parked near a restaurant in Glasthule.

'Now I know where we are going,' Alva laughed.

'You haven't been here in a long time I suspect, so hopefully you will enjoy it.' He held her hand as they walked up the stairs which led to the Rasam Restaurant, to be met at reception by the owner who kissed Alva affectionately.

'It is so lovely to see you again, Alva.'

'It's been a while, Nisheeth, sorry about that. This is my husband, Carlos Rodrigues.'

'It is so good to meet you,' the two men shook hands.

'I have a special table for you, come along.' He led them through the restaurant. The atmosphere was inviting, the lighting golden hued, a warm ambience created by the buzz of voices from patrons already there. He pulled out a chair for Alva, and one of the waiters did the same for Carlos.

'I hope you will enjoy the evening,' Nisheeth smiled. 'And we are still enjoying your wines. I hope business is going well for you?'

'It is, and I must send you samples of some interesting new organic wines we have on our list. I'd be interested in your judgment.'

'Please do, I would like to try them. Now, have a glance through the menu and we'll be around to take your order in a few minutes.'

'It's lovely to be here again, I love their Indian food.' Alva opened it up and they spent a few minutes perusing the various dishes.

One waiter came to ask what they would like to drink, and another placed a bowl of pappadums and dips on the table.

'Have a glass of champagne,' suggested Carlos. 'We're

celebrating.'

'I will,' Alva giggled.

'And I'll have sparkling water,' he laughed.

'What would you like to eat?' asked Alva.

'There's so much on the menu it's hard to decide.'

'For starter you choose what you would like, and I'll suggest the main dish. It's called Mansahari Thali, a platter which is served in silver dishes and covers a selection from the menu, which are delicious.'

'That's what we will have.'

'And Peshwari Nan, that's lovely on the side.'

Eventually they placed their order, and clinked glasses in a toast. 'To our new future,' Carlos smiled, and leaned forward to kiss her.

They took their time eating, enjoying all the different appetising flavours of the dishes, and Nisheeth came along with little bite sized pieces a couple of times to add to their enjoyment.

They were in no hurry, knowing Naomi was staying over as she wasn't working the following day. It was a really pleasant evening, and Nisheeth came along to chat later as well, offering after dinner drinks which only Alva accepted.

'This is a wonderful restaurant, and this is the best Indian food I've ever had. We'll have to come here soon again.' Carlos was enthusiastic.

'We will.'

It was late when they said goodnight to Nisheeth and his staff.

'It has been lovely to see you again, Alva, and I hope to see you both soon.' He kissed her.

'I'll send the wines out for you to taste.'

'I look forward to receiving them.'

'Let me know if you like them.'

'I will, of course. Goodnight.'

'It was a lovely evening. Nisheeth is such a nice person,' Alva said.

'And so generous.'

'Yes, exceptional.'

When they arrived home, Naomi was waiting for them, although Roberto was asleep by now.

'I hope you had a nice evening, I'm so happy for you,' Naomi hugged Alva. 'I'm sure you're glad that today is all over.'

'Yes, thank God. At least Darren has gone out of our lives and we could relax completely,' Alva said slowly. 'How long do you think he will serve?' she asked.

'Possibly five or six years. He will get parole for good behaviour probably.'

'Thank God you didn't get into trouble for shooting him.'

'No, I was lucky. I had very good witnesses,' she smiled.

'Can I ask you something very personal?' Alva asked.

'Of course, anything,' Naomi agreed.

'Do you still love Darren?'

'That's a difficult one.'

'Would you keep in touch with him while he is in prison? Sorry, I feel I'm being very intrusive,' Alva murmured. 'It's just, I have to know if you would get together again when he is released?'

'To be really honest, I don't know.'

'Do you long to be with him every day?' Alva pressed her for an answer.

'There are times I do miss him I suppose,' she said.

'Are you hoping to continue your relationship?' Alva felt embarrassed even asking that.

'He probably hates me because I shot him. Although I'm glad he recovered from his injury. Anyway, I know he loved you more than me. I think he only used me to get to you,' Naomi admitted.

'I'm glad you shot him, it saved our lives. Otherwise Roberto and I could be dead, particularly Roberto.'

'I had to do that, there was no choice.'

'Thank you so much, I don't know if I have told you how much I appreciate what you did for all of us.' Alva looked at Carlos.

'Yes, Naomi, you were wonderful,' he said.

'There's no need to thank me. You know how I feel about you all,' Naomi smiled.

'We used to tell each other everything,' Alva giggled.

'We'll always be like that. I'm glad that you asked me about Darren and I'm sorry I'm not able to give you a definite answer.'

'I understand,' Alva murmured.

Naomi put her arms around Alva and they held each other close.

The question Alva had asked her friend was left unanswered. It was something only the future would reveal.

Chapter Fifty-seven

'Here we are,' Carlos smiled as the car turned into the driveway of Caballos Rodrigues in Seville, and drove up towards the house. As soon as José pulled in, they could see Julie, Pedro, Pacqui and Nuria hurrying out to meet them. Alva climbed out of the car and embraced her Mum. 'It's wonderful to see you.'

Carlos unstrapped Roberto from his car seat and lifted him out of the car.

'Let me see my little grandson, hello my pet,' Julie smiled at him. But he was shy, and clung on to Carlos. It was a while since Carlos and Alva had visited Spain and he had forgotten his grandmother which was understandable for a child who was just two years old.

'Bienvenido,' Pedro put his arms around Carlos, and father and son made their way up the steps of the veranda into the house. He carried Roberto, and Carlos's sisters hugged Alva. They had promised to come over to Seville for Christmas, and were all delighted to see each other.

Later, Carlos and Alva went to see the house of his great grandparents. This was the house which had been inherited by Carlos from Abuela. It was a lovely old country house built in the 1880s. A motley collection of buildings which had been the original horse farm his great-grandfather had built for his wife Valentina.

'This is our home now,' Carlos said with a smile.

'It's amazing.' Alva looked around.

They walked up the steps to the entrance door which Carlos unlocked and they made their way into a patio surrounded with archways supported by marble pillars in the Moorish style. Water sparkled as it sprayed out of the fountain into a pool. The sound atmospheric.

Carlos bent to take hold of Roberto's hand and they walked together in and out of the rooms off the patio and into the gardens.

'Does the house have everything you want now?' Carlos put his arm around Alva.

'Oh yes, Mum did an amazing job with the architects, I'm glad we asked her to oversee the whole renovation. And I think she really enjoyed it.'

'And both of you can enjoy doing the interiors together.'

'She has great ideas. It's going to be wonderful. Then we'll be able to come over whenever we feel like it.' Alva was delighted.

'I didn't mention this until we came out here to see the house properly, but I've been offered a position in a new facility here.'

Alva was surprised. 'When did that happen?'

'Just a few weeks ago.'

'You didn't tell me?'

'I thought you'd like to see the house before I asked you about living here.'

Alva wasn't sure what to think.

'Anyway, I didn't think you would ever consider it.'

'It would be a permanent move?'

'Yes.'

'I work in Dublin, and that might cause a problem.'

'Could you work remotely, and run the Spanish side of the business from here?' he asked her with a smile.

'I'm sure it's possible. I work from home as it is now anyway, and since our new baby is on the way.' She touched her stomach gently. 'That would make a difference. Are you interested in taking up this offer you've received?' she asked him.

'It's a new challenge,' Carlos smiled. 'And it shouldn't be quite as busy as my present position. It would be more managerial, and I would have an opportunity to do some research which I would like to do. But there are other aspects that appeal to me.'

'What are they?'

'We know that Darren is in prison now, but he will receive parole eventually and be released. And that's when I worry about him. Will he ever change? Will we have to look over our shoulders every day?'

'I had thought about him too. A lot of victims of crime have to live with it and are not even told when the perpetrator is released. He or she could even be living next door,' Alva murmured.

'But we have somewhere to go, and that makes all the difference.' Carlos pointed out softly.

'Maybe we might sell the apartment?'

'We could do that anyway or keep it for when we go to Dublin for various reasons, which would be bound to happen.'

'I hope Darren doesn't shadow our lives forever,' she said sadly.

'He won't,' Carlos said firmly.

They sat on a bench overlooking the gardens, watching Roberto play with his little toy cars in front of them.

'You know, the more I think about moving to our new home, the more it appeals to me. Mum is living here and that means everything to me. David and Cian can visit. And, as you say, we can go back and forth as we wish. And we couldn't live in a more beautiful place than this, Casa Valentina.' She looked around.

Carlos and Alva embraced and kissed each other lovingly. Looking into her eyes he murmured. 'Just remember, I love you and you love me, and we both adore Roberto and our new baby who is on the way. It's all that matters. No one, least of all Darren, can come between us ever again.'

TO MAKE A DONATION TO
LAURALYNN HOUSE

Children's Sunshine Home/LauraLynn Account
AIB Bank, Sandyford Business Centre,
Foxrock, Dublin 18.

Account No. 32130009
Sort Code: 93-35-70

www.lauralynnhospice.com

Acknowledgements

As always, our very special thanks to Jane and Brendan, knowing you both has changed our lives.

Many thanks to both my family and Arthur's family, our friends and clients, who continue to support our efforts to raise funds for LauraLynn House. And all those generous people who help in various ways but are too numerous to mention. You know who you are and that we appreciate everything you do.

Thanks to all at LauraLynn Children's Hospice.

Special thanks to our dear friend, Vivien Hughes, who proofed the manuscript. We really appreciate your generosity.

Special thanks to Martone Design & Print – Brian, Dave, and Kate. Couldn't do it without you.

Special thanks to Workspace Interiors.

Thanks to CPI Group.

Thanks to Power Home Products Ltd., for their generosity in supplying product for LauraLynn House.

Special thanks to Cyclone Couriers and Southside Storage.

Grateful thanks also to Permanent TSB. Supervalu.

Many thanks to Elephant Bean Bags – Furniture – Outdoor.

Special thanks to CarveOn Leather – Custom Engraved Leather Goods.

And in Nenagh, our grateful thanks to Tom Gleeson of Irish Computers who very generously service our website free of charge. Nick Long, Website Designer. Walsh Packaging, Nenagh Chamber of Commerce, McLoughlin's Hardware, Cinnamon Alley Restaurant, and Caseys in Toomevara.

Many thanks to Ree Ward Callan and Michael Feeney Callan.

Special thanks to Nisheeth, of Rasam Restaurant, Glasthule, Co. Dublin.

And much love to my darling husband, Arthur, without whose love and support this wouldn't be possible.

MARTONE DESIGN & PRINT

Martone Design & Print was established in 1983
and has become one of the country's most pre-eminent
printing and graphic arts companies.

The Martone team provide high-end design
and print work to some of the country's top companies.
They provide a wide range of services including
design creation/development, spec verification,
creative approval, project management, printing, logistics,
shipping, materials tracking and posting verification.

They are the leading innovative all-inclusive solutions
provider, bringing print excellence to every market.

The Martone sales team can be contacted at
(01) 628 1809 or sales@martonepress.com

CYCLONE COURIERS

Cyclone Couriers – who support LauraLynn Children's Hospice – are the leading supplier of local, national and international courier services in Dublin. Cyclone also supply confidential mobile on-site document shredding and recycling services and secure document storage & records management services through their Cyclone Shredding and Cyclone Archive Division.

Cyclone Couriers – The fleet of pushbikes, motorbikes, and vans, can cater for all your urgent local and national courier requirements.

Cyclone International – Overnight, next day, timed and weekend door-to-door deliveries to destinations within the thirty-two counties of Ireland.

Delivery options to the UK, mainland Europe, USA, and the rest of the world. A variety of services to all destinations across the globe.

Cyclone Shredding – On-site confidential document and product shredding & recycling service. Destruction and recycling of computers, hard drives, monitors and office electronic equipment.

Cyclone Archive – Secure document and data storage and records management. Hard copy document storage and tracking – data storage fireproof media safe – document scanning and upload of document images.

Cyclone Couriers operate from
Pleasants House, Pleasants Lane, Dublin 8.
Cyclone Archive, International and Shredding, operate from
11 North Park, Finglas, Dublin 11.
www.cyclone.ie. Email: sales@cyclone.ie Tel: 01-475 7000

SOUTHSIDE STORAGE
Murphystown Road, Sandyford, Dublin 18.

FACILITIES

Individually lit, self-contained, off-ground metal and concrete units that are fireproof and waterproof.

Sizes of units : 300 sq.ft. 150 sq.ft. 100 sq.ft. 70 sq.ft.

Flexible hours of access and 24 hour alarm monitored security.

Storage for home
Commercial storage
Documents and Archives
Packaging supplies and materials
Extra office space
Sports equipment
Musical instruments
And much much more ....

Contact us to discuss your requirements:

01 294 0517 - 087 640 7448
Email: info@southsidestorage.ie

Location: Southside Storage is located on
Murphystown Road, Sandyford, Dublin 18
close to Exit 13 on the M50

ELEPHANT BEAN BAGS

Designed with love in Co. Mayo, Ireland, Elephant products have been especially designed to provide optimum support and comfort without compromising on stylish, contemporary design.

Available in a variety of cool designs, models and sizes, our entire range has been designed to accommodate every member of your family, including your dog - adding a new lounging and seating dimension to your home.

Both versatile and practical, our forward thinking Elephant range of inviting bean bags and homewares are available in a wealth of vivid colours, muted tones and bold vibrant prints, that bring to life both indoor and outdoor spaces.

Perfect for sitting, lounging, lying and even sharing, sinking into an Elephant Bean Bag will not only open your eyes to superior comfort, but it will also allow you to experience a sense of unrivalled contentment that is completely unique to the Elephant range.

www.elephantliving.com

THE MARRIED WOMAN

Fran O'Brien

Marriage is for ever ...

In their busy lives, Kate and Dermot rush along on parallel
lines, seldom coming together to exchange a word or a kiss.
To rekindle the love they once knew, Kate struggles to lose
weight, has a make-over, buys new clothes, and arranges a
romantic trip to Spain with Dermot.

For the third time he cancels and she goes alone.

In Andalucia she meets the artist Jack Linley. He takes her with
him into a new world of emotion and for the first time in years
she feels like a desirable beautiful woman.

Will life ever be the same again?

Available now online
McGuinness Books
www.franobrien.net

THE LIBERATED WOMAN

Fran O'Brien

At last, Kate has made it!

She has ditched her obnoxious husband Dermot and is
reunited with her lover, Jack.

Her interior design business goes international and TV
appearances bring instant success.

But Dermot hasn't gone away and his problems encroach.

Her brother Pat and family come home from Boston
and move in on a supposedly temporary basis.

Her manipulative stepmother Irene is getting married
again and Kate is dragged into the extravaganza.

When a secret from the past is revealed Kate has
to review her choices ...

Available now online
McGuinness Books
www.franobrien.net

THE PASSIONATE WOMAN

Fran O'Brien

A chance meeting with ex-lover Jack throws Kate into a spin.
She cannot forgive him and concentrates all her passions on
her interior design business, and television work.

Jack still loves Kate and as time passes
without reconciliation he feels more and more frustrated.

Estranged husband Dermot has a
change of fortunes, and wants her back.

Stepmother, Irene, is as wacky as ever
and is being chased by the paparazzi.

Best friend, Carol, is searching for a man on the internet,
and persuades Kate to come along as chaperone on a date.

ARE THESE PATHS TO KATE'S NEW LIFE OR
ROUNDABOUTS TO HER OLD ONE?

Available now online
McGuinness Books
www.franobrien.net

ODDS ON LOVE

Fran O'Brien

Bel and Tom seem to be the perfect couple with successful careers, a beautiful home and all the trappings. But underneath the facade cracks appear and damage the basis of their marriage and the deep love they have shared since that first night they met.

Her longing to have a baby creates problems for Tom, who can't deal with the possibility that her failure to conceive may be his fault. His masculinity is questioned and in attempting to deal with his insecurities he is swept up into something far more insidious and dangerous than he could ever have imagined.

Then against all the odds, Bel is thrilled to find out she is pregnant. But she is unable to tell Tom the wonderful news as he doesn't come home that night and disappears mysteriously out of her life leaving her to deal with the fall out.

Available now online
McGuinness Books
www.franobrien.net

WHO IS FAYE?

Fran O'Brien

Can the past ever be buried?

Jenny should be fulfilled. She has a successful career,
and shares a comfortable life with her husband, Michael,
at Ballymoragh Stud.

But increasingly unwelcome memories
surface and keep her awake at night.

Is it too late to go back to the source
of those fears and confront them?

Available now online
McGuinness Books
www.franobrien.net

THE RED CARPET

Fran O'Brien

Lights, Camera, Action.

Amy is raised in the glitzy facade that is Hollywood.
Her mother, Maxine, is an Oscar winning actress, and
her father, John, a famous film producer. When
Amy is eight years old, Maxine is tragically killed.

A grown woman, Amy becomes the focus of John's
obsession for her to star in his movies and be as
successful as her mother. But Amy's insistence
on following her heart, and moving permanently to
Ireland, causes a rift between them.

As her daughter, Emma, approaches her eighth
birthday, Amy is haunted by the nightmare of
what happened on her own eighth birthday.

She determines to find answers to her questions.

Available now online
McGuinness Books
www.franobrien.net

FAIRFIELDS

1907 QUEENSTOWN CORK

Fran O'Brien

Set against the backdrop of a family feud and prejudice
Anna and Royal Naval Officer, Mike, fall in love.
They meet secretly at an old cottage
on the shores of the lake at Fairfields.

During that spring and summer their feelings for each
other deepen. Blissfully happy, Anna accepts Mike's
proposal of marriage, unaware that her family have a
different future arranged for her.

**Is their love strong enough to withstand
the turmoil that lies ahead?**

Available now online
McGuinness Books
www.franobrien.net

THE PACT

THE POINT OF THE KNIFE
PRESSES INTO SOFT SKIN ...

Fran O'Brien

Inspector Grace McKenzie investigates the
trafficking of women into Ireland and is
drawn under cover into that sinister world.

She is deeply affected by the suffering of one
particular woman and her quest for justice
re-awakens an unspeakable trauma in her own life.

CAN SHE EVER ESCAPE FROM ITS
INFLUENCE AND BE FREE TO LOVE?

Available now online
McGuinness Books
www.franobrien.net

1916

Fran O'Brien

On Easter Monday, 24th April, 1916, against the
backdrop of the First World War, a group of
Irishmen and Irishwomen rise up against Britain.
What follows has far-reaching consequences.

We witness the impact of the Rising on four families,
as passion, fear and love permeate a week of
insurrection which reduces the centre of Dublin to ashes.

This is a story of divided loyalties, friendships,
death, and a conflict between an Empire
and a people fighting for independence.

Available now online
McGuinness Books
www.franobrien.net

LOVE OF HER LIFE

Fran O'Brien

A man can look into a woman's eyes
and remind her of how it used to be
between them …once upon a time.

Photographer Liz is running a successful business.
Her family and career are all she cares about since
her husband died, until an unexpected encounter
brings Scott back into her life.

IS THIS SECOND CHANCE FOR LOVE DESTINED
TO BE OVERCOME BY THE WHIMS OF FATE?

Available now online
McGuinness Books
www.franobrien.net

ROSE COTTAGE YEARS

Fran O'Brien

The house in the stable yard is an empty shell
and Fanny's footsteps resound on her polished floors,
the rich gold of wood shining.

Three generations of women, each leaving the home they loved.
Their lives drift through the turmoil of the First World War,
the 1916 Rising, and the establishment of the Irish Free State,
knowing both happiness and heartache in those years.

Bina closes the door gently behind her.
The click of the lock has such finality about it.
At the gate she looks back through a mist of tears, just once.

Available now online
McGuinness Books
www.franobrien.net

BALLYSTRAND

Fran O'Brien

The future is bleak for Matt Sutherland when he is released
from prison after being convicted of murder. He faces life in a
changing world and rehabilitation begins in a homeless shelter.

His sisters, Zoe and Gail, anticipate his return with trepidation
and are worried that their father will react badly.
When Matt calls to see them on Christmas Eve, this visit
precipitates events which change their lives.

A letter is found. A secret is revealed. An unexpected meeting
causes Matt to reach the limit of his endurance.

**WILL IT TAKE ANOTHER DEATH TO
RIGHT THE WRONGS OF THE PAST?**

Available now online
McGuinness Books
www.franobrien.net

VORLANE HALL

Fran O'Brien

TWO WOMEN LIVE OVER
TWO HUNDRED YEARS APART.

STRANGELY THEIR LIVES SEEM
TO MIRROR EACH OTHER.

Beth Harwood, passionate about history, is invited by
Lord Vorlane to research his family archive at Vorlane Hall
in Kildare, where against her better judgment
she is attracted to his eldest son, Nick.

In 1795, Martha Emilie Vorlane lived with her husband
on his sugar plantation in the British Virgin Islands.
In her journal she described her love affair with an
army captain and the pain and loss she suffered.

Reading Martha Emilie's journal captures
Beth's imagination and leads her into a situation
which changes her life dramatically.

Available now online
McGuinness Books
www.franobrien.net

THE BIG RED VELVET COUCH

Fran O'Brien

Claire allows ex-husband, Alan, to take their son, Neil, to visit his Chinese grandparents in Beijing. Alan doesn't bring his son home after the holiday and tells him that his mother doesn't want him anymore. Neil blames himself for doing something to upset his Mum.

Claire is heartbroken and travels to Beijing, but Alan refuses to reveal where Neil is, only allowing her to speak to him on the phone. If she takes legal action, he threatens to disappear with Neil and she will never see him again.

Back at work in Dublin, Claire rents two rooms in her house to help pay the mortgage and finance her trips to Beijing. But the family still refuse to allow her see or talk to Neil. She meets Jim. They fall deeply in love. But until her son comes home, Claire cannot share her life with anyone.

In a twist of fate, a pandemic overwhelms the world. Will Claire and Neil ever find happiness together again?

Available now online
McGuinness Books
www.franobrien.net

CUIMHNÍ CINN

Memoirs of the Uprising

Liam Ó Briain

(Reprint in the Irish language originally published in 1951)

(English translation by Michael McMechan)

Liam Ó Briain was a member of the Volunteers of Ireland
from 1914 and he fought with the Citizen Army of Ireland
in the College of Surgeons during Easter Week.

This is a clear lively account of the events of that time.
An account in which there is truth, humanity and, more
than any other thing, humour. It will endure as literature.

When this book was first published in Irish in 1951,
it was hoped it would be read by the young people of Ireland.
To remember more often the hardships endured
by our forebears for the sake of our freedom
we might the better validate Pearse's vision.

Available now online
McGuinness Books
www.franobrien.net

A SPANISH FAMILY

Fran O'Brien

Alva's personal life disintegrates when she finds her partner
Darren in their bed with another woman. Trust is gone. She
throws him out. He becomes very dangerous.

The sadness of her father's unexpected death sends her days
spinning into despair.

In their family business she discovers financial fraud and vows
to identify the culprit.

This mix of emotions threatens to destroy her until she meets
her mother, Julie, for the first time in many years. Her mother
left home when her children were very young and their father
had never revealed to Alva and her brothers the reason why.

The two families are reunited in Cadiz in Spain, and when an
accident occurs, all their lives splinter like shards of glass.

Will this tragedy bring them together or divide them forever?

Available now online
McGuinness Books
www.franobrien.net